THIS
MONSTROUS
THING

THIS

MONSTROUS

THING

Mackenzi Lee

 KATHERINE TEGEN BOOKS
An Imprint of HarperCollins Publishers

Katherine Tegen Books is an imprint of HarperCollins Publishers.

This Monstrous Thing
Copyright © 2015 by Mackenzie Van Engelenhoven
For information address HarperCollins Children's Books,
a division of HarperCollins Publishers, 195 Broadway,
New York, NY 10007.
www.epicreads.com

Library of Congress Cataloging-in-Publication Data
Lee, Mackenzi.
    This monstrous thing / Mackenzi Lee. — First edition.
        pages cm
    Summary: "When a talented mechanic in 1818 Geneva brings his brother
back from the dead using clockwork parts, the citizens of Geneva think
they may have inspired the recently published novel *Frankenstein*"—
Provided by publisher.
    ISBN 978-0-06-238277-1 (hardcover)
    [1. Cyborgs—Fiction. 2. Dead—Fiction. 3. Supernatural—Fiction.
4. Shelley, Mary Wollstonecraft, 1797–1851. Frankenstein—Fiction.
5. Geneva, Lake (Switzerland and France)—History—19th century—
Fiction. 6. Switzerland—History—19th century—Fiction. 7. Science fiction.]
    I. Title.
PZ7.1.L42Thi 2015   2014041260
[Fic]—dc23   CIP
                                                                             AC

15 16 17 18 19   PC/RRDH   10 9 8 7 6 5 4 3 2 1
❖
First Edition

FOR MOLLY AND HER AUTOCLAVE HEART

Did I request thee, Maker, from my clay
To mould me Man, did I solicit thee
From darkness to promote me?

—John Milton, *Paradise Lost*, quoted in *Frankenstein,
or The Modern Prometheus* by Mary Shelley

 My brother's heart was heavy in my hands.

The screws along the soldered edges flashed as the candlelight flickered, and I checked one last time to be certain the mainspring was fastened tight. It was smaller than I had imagined a heart would be, all those cogs locked together into a knot barely the size of my fist, but when I laid it in its place between the exposed gears in Oliver's open chest, it fit precisely, the final piece of the puzzle of teeth and bolts I had been laboring over all night.

He wasn't broken anymore. But he was still dead.

I slid forward onto my knees and let go a breath so deep it made my lungs ache. Below me, the inner workings of the clock tower hung still and silent. The gears had been unmoving for years, though tonight the pendulums swayed in the wind funneling from the jagged hole in the clock face. When I looked through it, I could follow the path the Rhone River cut across Geneva, past the city walls, and all the way to the lake, where the starlight was fading into milky dawn along the horizon.

When we dug up Oliver's body, it had seemed fitting to bring him here, Dr. Geisler's secret workshop in the clock tower where the resurrection work had begun, but now the whole thing felt stupid. And dangerous. I kept waiting for the police to swarm in—they'd kept a close watch on this place since Geisler's arrest—or for someone to discover us, to walk in and spoil it all. I kept waiting for Oliver to sit up and open his eyes like nothing had happened. As though by simply being in this place I could reach out and pull his soul back from where it had landed when he'd crashed through the clock face and plunged.

"Alasdair."

I looked up. Mary was kneeling on the other side of Oliver's body, her face still spattered with cemetery dirt. We were a sight, the pair of us, Mary with her muddy dress and wild hair, me with the knees torn out of my trousers, braces unfastened, and my shirt smeared with blood. We looked mad, Mary and I, exactly the sort of people who would be digging up corpses and resurrecting them in a clock tower. I felt a bit mad in that moment.

Mary held out the pulse gloves and I took them, our fingers brushing for a heartbeat. She already had the plates charged, and when I pulled the laces tight around my wrists, I could feel their current thrumming inside me, fuzzy and electric like a second heartbeat that started in my hands.

"Alasdair." She said my name again, so softly it sounded like a prayer. "Are you going to do it?"

I took a breath and closed my eyes.

When I remembered my brother, it would always be with his face bright and his gaze sharp. I would remember the days of being wild-haired boys together, of running in his shadow, of the hundred different ways he'd taught me to be brave and loyal and kind. Of falling asleep on his shoulder, and holding on to his sleeve in every strange new city we landed in. Of hunting with him in Lapland, skating the canals together in Amsterdam, watching him sneak away to visit the forbidden corners of Paris, and the nights he let me come along.

It would not be watching him take his last breath two nights before, already more corpse than man as he lay collapsed and bleeding in the velvet darkness on the banks of the Rhone.

I wouldn't remember the night my brother died.

Instead, I would remember tonight, and what was about to happen, the moment hurtling toward me like a runaway carriage, when Oliver would open his eyes and

3
—◆—

look up at me. Alive, alive, alive again.

I knelt beside him and pressed my palms to either side of his shaved head, my fingers running along the track of stitches there. The metal plates beneath his skin were cold and tight. I closed my eyes as the shock of electricity leapt from my gloves, let it sing backward into my hands and all the way through me, and forward into Oliver, into his clockwork heart and his clockwork lungs and every piece of the clockwork that would bring him back.

There was a pulse, a flash, and the gears began to turn.

The clockwork arm jumped on the workbench as the pulse from my gloves hit it.

I stepped backward to Father's side, both of us watching the gears ease to life and intertwine. The ball joint in the wrist twitched, and Father's eyes narrowed behind his spectacles. His fingers tapped out a quick rhythm on the top of the workbench. It set my teeth on edge.

Finally, eyes still on the arm, he said, "You used the half-inch stock for the center wheel."

It wasn't a question, but I nodded.

"I told you to use the quarter."

I thought about showing him the four quarter-inch gears I'd snapped the teeth off of trying to follow his directions before I had gone with my gut and used the half-inch, but instead I simply said, "It didn't work."

"Half-inch is too wide. If it slides off the track—"

"It won't."

"If it slides off the track—" he repeated, louder this time, but I interrupted again.

"The ratio wheel's running fine on half. The problem is that the ratchet's catching on the—"

"If you don't do the work the way I ask, Alasdair, you can stand out front and mind the counter instead."

I shut my mouth and started putting my spanners back in their sling.

Father crossed his arms and glared at me over the workbench. He was tall and thin, with a boy's frame that he'd passed on to me. I kept hoping I'd bulk up a bit, grow lean and toned like Oliver had been, but so far I was just skinny. Father looked dead harmless, with his tiny spectacles and receding hairline. Not the sort of man you'd expect to be illegally forging clockwork pieces to human flesh in the back of his toy shop. Some of the other Shadow Boys we'd met looked the part, with scars and tattoos and that sort of shady, underground air about them, but not Father. He looked, more than anything, like a toy maker. "Morand's coming for this tomorrow before he leaves Geneva," he said, tapping one finger against the clockwork arm. The pulse had been so small that the gears were already starting to slow.

"There isn't time for trouble with it."

"There won't be." I dropped the sling of spanners into my bag, careful to avoid the stack of books nestled in the bottom, and turned to meet his frown. "Can I go now?"

"Where are you rushing off to?"

I swallowed hard to push back the dread that bubbled up inside me when I thought of it, but I had put it off for the last three days—longer than I should have. "Does it matter?"

"Your mother and I need you home tonight."

"Because of the Christmas market."

"No. We need you for . . ." He pushed his spectacles onto his forehead and pinched the bridge of his nose. "Because of what day it is."

My hand tightened on the strap of my bag. "You thought I forgot?"

"I didn't say that."

"How could I forget that today's—"

He cut me off with a sigh, the weary, heavy sort I'd heard him use so many times on Oliver but now belonged just to me. *I know*, I wanted to say, *your older son was a disappointment, and now your younger son is even worse.* But I kept my mouth shut. "Just be home on time tonight, please, Alasdair. And put your coat on before you go out into the shop, you've got grease all over your front."

"Thank you." I swept the rest of my tools and the set

7

of pulse gloves into my bag, then picked my way across the workshop toward the door. There were no windows, and the flickering shadows cast by the oil lamps made the room seem smaller and more cluttered than it was. My breakfast dishes from that morning were still stacked on the chair where clients usually sat, and my teacup had tipped over so the dregs soaked into the worn cushion. There were gears and bolts everywhere, and a layer of rusty shavings coated the floor like bloody snow.

"French in the shop," Father called to me as I pulled my coat on.

"I know."

"No English. You sound more Scottish than you think, especially when you and your mother get going. Someone could overhear you."

"Sorry. *Désolé.*" I paused in the doorway, waiting for the rest of the lecture, but he seemed finished. He was still staring at that damn center wheel with his hands folded, and I wondered if he'd switch it out while I was gone. He'd get a pinched finger if he tried, and it'd serve him right for doubting me. I turned and headed down the short corridor that led to the shop.

The workshop door couldn't be opened from inside—Father had rigged up that precaution after Oliver opened the hidden door in our shop in Amsterdam when there were nonmechanical customers out front. I gave a light tap and waited. There was a pause, then a *whoosh* of air as the door chugged open.

After all morning shut up in the workshop, the winter sunlight through the front windows nearly knocked me over, and I had to blink hard a few times before the toys lining the walls came into proper focus. "Come in quick," Mum said, and I stepped past her as she threw her shoulder against the door and it eased back into place with a piston hiss, leaving the wall behind the counter looking again like a shelf stacked with dollhouse furniture.

Mum wiped her hands off on her apron, leaving a smear of plaster dust from the door, then looked me up and down. She was dark haired, same as I was, and thin as my father, but I could remember a time when she hadn't been. The last few years had carved her out. "Goggles," she said, pointing to the magnifying lenses slung around my neck. As I shoved them under my shirt collar, she added, "And you've got grease on your face."

"Where?"

"Sort of"—she gestured in a circle with her hand—"everywhere."

I scrubbed my sleeve across my cheeks. "Better?"

"It'll do until you wash up properly. Did you get Morand's arm finished?"

"Yes." I decided not to mention the spat over the center wheel. "Don't let Father hear you speaking English."

"Is he in one of his moods about it?"

"Isn't he usually?" I did my best imitation of Father. *"Nous sommes Genevois. Nous parlons français."*

She picked up the interior of a gutted music box and the set of jeweler's pliers beside it. "Well, he can say it all he wants, doesn't change the fact we aren't Swiss, same as we weren't French when we lived in Paris."

"Or Dutch in Amsterdam," I added, adjusting the strap of my bag as I turned.

"Hold up, where are you going? I've got something for you."

I stopped halfway to the door. "Just an errand."

"This late? It's nearly supper."

"It's for the Christmas market," I lied, then added quickly, "What have you got for me?"

She fished a wrapped package from the mess strewn across the counter and held it up. "It came this morning."

I'd never gotten a letter in my life, let alone a package, and I took it curiously. There was a London port-of-origin stamp in one corner, and across the front was my name in thick, loopy handwriting that caught me under the chin and zapped me like an electric shock from the pulse gloves. "Bleeding hell."

Mum frowned. "Don't cuss."

"Sorry."

She poked hard at the pin drum with the tip of her pliers. "How'd I end up with two boys who cussed like sailors? We didn't teach you that."

I held up the package so she could see the front. "It's from Mary Godwin. Do you remember her?"

"That English girl who hung about you and Oliver the summer before—" She stopped very suddenly and our gazes broke apart. I looked down at the package, but that made my heart lurch, so I looked back up at Mum. She was staring at the music box, her fingers running a slow lap around its edges. "Everything happened that year, didn't it?" she said with a sad smile.

It was such an understatement I almost laughed. 1816 had been the year that cleaved my life into two jagged halves, the before and the after—before Mary had come and gone, before Geisler had been arrested and then escaped Geneva, before Oliver had died.

Mum twitched her pliers in the direction of Mary's package. "What do you think she wants?"

I didn't have a clue. I couldn't imagine Mary would stick any of the unsaid things between us in a letter and drop it in the post after a two-year silence. "Probably just a catch-up," I said lamely. "You know, how are you, I miss you, that sort of thing."

I miss you.

I checked my heart before it ran away with that one.

Streets over, the bells from Saint Pierre Cathedral started chiming four. I should have been long gone by now, I realized with a jolt. I dropped Mary's package into my bag, then started for the door again. "I've got to go,

I'll see you later."

"Be back for supper," Mum called.

"I will."

"You know what day it is."

The inverted shadow of our name painted on the glass—FINCH AND SONS, TOY MAKERS—fell at my feet as I turned the knob. "I'll be back," I said, and shoved my shoulder into the door.

A gasp of December air slapped hard enough that I pulled my coat collar up around my jaw. The sun was starting to sink into the foothills, and the light winking off the muddy snow and copper rooftops turned the street brass. A carriage clattered across the cobblestones, the clop of horses' hooves replaced by the mechanical chatter of the gears. I got a faceful of steam as it passed.

I didn't have money for an omnibus ticket, but I was running late and the books bouncing around in my bag made it heavier than I was used to. It was a good bet no one would be checking tickets today. When the police force had redoubled their efforts at exposing unregistered clockwork men in the autumn, things like free riders on the omnibus had slipped down their list of concerns.

I crossed the square and joined the crowds spilling toward the main streets that led to the financial district and the lake beyond it. On the stoop in front of Hôtel de Ville, a beggar was sitting with his head bowed and a tin cup extended. One of his sleeves hung empty, but the arm shaking his cup was made of tarnished clockwork, the leather gauntlet that covered the gears starting to feather with wear. Three boys in school uniforms sprinted by, and one spit at him as they passed. I looked away, but almost without meaning to, I started thinking about how I'd fix that rusted arm if he came into our shop. He needed thinner fingers with smaller gears, a hinge pin at the wrist—I would have added that to Morand's arm if I'd thought Father would let me get away with it.

The omnibus was already at the station when I arrived, and I found a spot to stand beside the door, close enough that I could bolt if a policeman got on to check tickets. As the omnibus pulled away from the curb with a pneumatic growl, I retrieved Mary's package from my bag and stared again at my name in her perfect handwriting across the front. Somehow it felt strange and familiar at the same time. I slid my finger under the seal and tore the wrapping off.

It was a book, green and slim, with the title printed in spindly gold leaf on the spine: *Frankenstein, or The Modern Prometheus.*

I didn't have a clue what a Frankenstein was, or a Prometheus. I thought for a moment it was some of the daft poetry she and Oliver had spent all summer obsessed with, but there wasn't an author's name on the binding— not Coleridge or Milton or any of the others they had gone mad over. I flipped through the first pages, then back to the spine to be certain I hadn't missed it, but there was only the odd title.

Curious now, I turned a few more pages and glanced at the first line:

My dear sister, you will rejoice to hear that no disaster has accompanied the commencement of an enterprise which you have regarded with such evil forebodings. I arrived here yesterday, and my first task is to assure my dear sister of my welfare and increasing confidence in the success of my undertaking.

The omnibus jerked to a sudden stop as a steamcycle cut into the street ahead of it. Someone bumped into me, and I lost my place on the page. I was a slow and stumbling reader on the best days, and the noise and swaying of the omnibus combined with all those massive words made it even harder. I tipped the cover shut. Mary knew I didn't like to read—that had always been what she and Oliver shared. They'd spent the whole summer trading books, though he didn't have many, and everything he gave to her she would return the next time we saw her, finished. When Oliver asked her how she read so quickly, she told him with a sly smile that she took books to bed like lovers. Perhaps she hadn't meant *Frankenstein* for me at all, but as a gift to pass on. The fact that it had arrived today of all days wasn't lost on me.

The omnibus sped forward out of Vieille Ville, the old town built around the cathedral, and along the Rhone toward the financial district. As the street opened into Place de l'Horloge, the clock tower loomed above us, the clock's black hands suspended at midnight and still as sentries. Built in celebration of Geneva joining the Swiss Confederation, it was the tallest tower in Europe, all industrial struts and iron beams, and boasted the largest clock as well—inside were gears wider than a grown man was tall, designed to operate on an electric charge. It was a spectacle, even though the clock wasn't running yet. The scaffolding had finally come down, the etched-glass face repaired and a sparkling reflection of the frozen lake beyond the city walls. I pulled my coat tighter and looked away from it.

A group got on at the clock tower station, and I had to slide into the corner to make room. I nearly dropped *Frankenstein* in the shuffle, and as the pages fanned, a thin envelope slid from between them. I snatched it from the air before it fell.

There was my name again on the front in Mary's looped handwriting. I stared at it for a long moment as the omnibus jerked forward, trying not to let all that stupid hope inside me fill in what it might say. As angry as I was at her after the way we had ended, it thrilled me to think that maybe, at long last, she wanted to make things right between us. All she needed was to say the word, and I would have been hers again in an instant.

I started to break the seal, but then a harsh voice from down the car growled, "Get up, you piece of machinery."

I froze. A police officer was standing at the other end of the aisle, navy greatcoat sweeping all the way to the floor like a shroud, and I'd been so busy mooning over Mary's letter I hadn't noticed him get on. I knew him at once—Inspector Jiroux, head of Geneva's police force—by the heavy gold cross he kept on a chain through the buttonhole of his waistcoat. It flashed as he folded his arms, glaring down at an old man with a shock of white hair and a brass button in the shape of a cog pinned to his coat collar. I shoved Mary's letter back between the pages of *Frankenstein* and started to shoulder my way to the door, my heart stuttering.

Jiroux kicked the old man's leg. There was a low metallic clang. "Get up," he said again. "Don't you see all these whole human men standing up around you?" He turned suddenly and pointed his baton at me. The old man and I both flinched. "Give this young man your seat."

"It's all right," I mumbled, eyes on my boots.

"No it isn't," Jiroux said. "It's not all right for men like you to be second to mechanicals like him."

"He's fine, really," I said.

"He's not fine, he's a machine." Jiroux seized the knee of the old man's trousers and tugged it up, revealing the metal skeleton and mess of gears sinking into scar tissue beneath. "Not even a man anymore," Jiroux said, and nudged the bars with the toe of his boot. They clattered softly.

The old man's shoulders slumped. "Please, I can't stand well. I lost it in the war."

"And so you chose to spit in the face of God by letting another man make you mechanical?"

"It is not disrespect for God, sir—" the old man began, but Jiroux interrupted him, voice carrying through the car like a priest from the pulpit.

"The form of man, as designed by God's hand, is perfect. If God had wanted men made from metal, we would have been born as such. With the decision to install a mechanical piece, you have made yourself an offense against Him and His divine creation, and you forfeit the God-given rights of a human man." He seized the old man by the collar and dragged him out of his seat. "Sit down," he barked at me. I didn't move. Everyone in the car was watching us. "Sit," Jiroux said again as the omnibus began to slow.

"I'm getting off," I said.

Jiroux glared at me, then shoved the old man, who

tripped, barely stopping his fall on the edge of a woman's seat. She jerked away from him like he had a catching disease. The doors to the omnibus flew open, and I stumbled down the stairs and out onto the pavement. It was two stops earlier than I'd meant to get off, but it still took the whole walk to the city's edge to convince my heart to slow again.

The French Revolution and the Napoleonic Wars that followed had left people across Europe with missing and damaged limbs and, in turn, more people than ever wanting clockwork parts to replace the ones they'd lost. Lots of the political expatriates from France had come down to Switzerland, and Geneva had become a haven for them, a city that boasted neutrality and sanctuary for war refugees. The veterans were a new set of clients for our shop, though we still saw the sorts of injuries we'd treated before we came to Geneva: limbs ripped up and ruined by factory work, arthritic joints, and club feet to be replaced with moving metal pieces, twisted spines swapped out with metal vertebrae. We'd grafted a set of steam-powered pistons to the hips of a man paralyzed from the waist down so he could walk again.

My father liked to say that prejudice didn't have to make sense, but I'd still never worked out how anyone could think what we did was wicked. People like Jiroux thought that as soon as metal was fused to bone and muscle it took something fundamental and human away, and that men and women with mechanical parts were machines, somehow less than the rest of us.

The clockwork men either lived broken, or hated. It was a shitty choice.

Through the checkpoint and beyond the city walls, the foothills stretched like open palms raised toward the sinking sun. I left the road and started upward along the vineyard roads that turned into narrow mountain paths, mud sucking at my boots as I climbed. Around me, the cliffs were silent, their stillness broken only by the somber wailing of the winter wind through the pines and the far-off industrial hum of the city, growing fainter with every step.

At the top of the final ridge, I stopped to catch my breath and look out. Far below, the surface of the iced lake sparkled like diamonds, with the villas of the magistrates and merchants that rimmed it peering out between the evergreens. On its banks, Geneva was outlined black against the sunset—the turreted roofs and spires of Vieille Ville divided from the factory district by the Rhone, with the clock tower standing in solitary silhouette above it all.

I counted backward from a hundred as I stared out at the view; then I turned. Across the craggy hilltop, a small dark-stone castle was perched, a feather of white smoke rising from one of its chimneys. Château de Sang, skeletal and dark, like a hole cut in the winter sky.

The cold was starting to get under my coat, but I didn't move. Part of me wanted to stand there and let the time run down until I had to return home. The gut-twisting mix of dread and necessity was rising like bile inside me, and I knew I couldn't swallow it. I'd just have to let it burn in my stomach until I could leave, but even then it never faded entirely.

I took a deep breath, braced myself, and started down the slope toward the gates.

I let myself into the castle through a service entrance in the back, the only way in that wasn't boarded. I had picked the lock the city installed and replaced it with my own that locked from both the inside and outside when it was closed, same as the one in our shop. I stuck a rock into the frame to keep the door propped.

Inside, everything was smoky with shadows. Dust motes wafted across the thin bars of sunlight that filtered through the high windows, all boarded up, and cobwebs decorated the walls like spun tapestries. The air was thick with the smell of age and mold, underscored by the sharp sulfur of the gunpowder and explosives the city kept stored in the cellars.

I took the familiar path across the kitchen, making only a quick stop to check that the pantry was stocked, then climbed a long set of winding stairs, listening hard to the silence and trying to decide where he would be.

When I reached the upstairs hall, I spotted the amber glow of firelight at the end and followed it.

The room looked like a heavy windstorm had swept through just before I arrived. Crumpled papers were scattered across the floor, and pens stuck out of the wall like darts in a pub board. A goose-down pillow I had stolen from my parents had been left lying in the center of the room, feathers blooming from a rip down its middle and carried by the wind slithering down the chimney. Plates festering with dried food were stacked in random spots, and most of the furniture left by the castle's previous owners, already spindly with age, was battered and abused. It looked like the remnants of a battlefield, somewhere looted and then left behind.

And in the center of it all, like a king on his throne, was Oliver.

Before his resurrection, Oliver had been a good-looking lad, the sort girls would stare at as he walked by on the street. He was trim and athletic, not skinny like me, and he had a swagger that I was beginning to doubt I would ever grow into. He hadn't lost the swagger in his second life, but it was different now, less confident and more menacing.

We shared most physical features—dark, curly hair and dark eyes, most notably—but we didn't look alike anymore, not the way we once had. Oliver's resurrection had added almost a foot to his height, and now he was made of sharp lines and strange angles. Clothes didn't fit him properly, and he wore a loose-fitting linen shirt with the sleeves rolled up, braces hanging down to his knees and trousers sagging in odd places. His dark hair had grown back as thick as before, but the strips of it atop his scars never would, leaving him with bald stretches amid the curls.

The resurrection had robbed him too of the bone structure that had given him sharp cheekbones and a square jaw before. Now one eyelid sagged, and the skin of his face, like the rest of his body, was rippled and perpetually bruised from the machinery that pressed against it from inside.

Two years later and it was still hard not to look away from him. I forced myself to meet his gaze and hold it steady as I stood in the doorway. When he didn't say anything, I dropped my bag on the floor beside the chaise and said, "Sorry I haven't been by." My chest was already feeling tight, and it was hard to get words out without sounding winded.

Oliver watched me from his perch atop the writing desk as I peeled off my coat and scarf, an unlit pipe jammed between his teeth. Smoking was hazardous now that his lungs were made of waxed paper and leather, but he still liked gnawing on his pipe as if it were lit. They were strange and unpredictable, the things like smoking that had carried over from before.

I kicked a balled-up bit of paper out from under the chaise. "What happened here?"

"I'm bored," he replied, sliding down off the desk so

that he was straddling the chair. His mechanical joints creaked when he moved. I had replaced one of his arms entirely with a clockwork one, and both knees as well, since that was easier than letting the splintered bones grow back wrong.

"So clean this place up, that'll keep you busy for a while. I mended your shirt," I added as I pulled it out of my bag and threw it to him. He caught it with his mechanical hand. "Anything else you need?"

"Tobacco."

"No." I pushed a ragged copy of *Paradise Lost* to the other end of the chaise and sank down onto the cushion. "Why'd you shred all the paper I brought?"

"Because writing's dull. Everything's dull. I'm so bored." Oliver tossed the shirt on top of the feather pillow. There was a metallic whine, shrill as a teakettle, and he winced.

I sat up. "Is it giving you problems?"

"Not the arm," he said, and rapped his knuckles against his chest. It rang hollowly.

"I brought my tools."

"I'm all right."

"Don't be daft, let me look." I pulled my work gloves out of my bag as Oliver raised the flame of the lamp balanced on the writing desk and pulled his shirt off over his head. The skin under it was so puckered and punctured that it hardly looked like skin at all. You could still see the stitches, the bolts, the blue patches where the needles had gone in. There were places in his side that bulged and rippled as the gears ticked beneath. My fingers stumbled as I wedged them under the seam in his chest and opened it.

Inside, Oliver was pure machine, all gears and pins like an engine. In a way that's all it was, an engine doing everything that his irreparably broken body no longer could. His rib cage on one side was gone, replaced by steel rods and a cluster of churning gears connected by leather tubes to a set of bellows that opened and closed with each breath. Where his heart should have been was a knot of cogs around the mainspring, pushing against each other as they ticked like a clock rather than beat like a heart.

The trouble was easy to spot. One of the bolts had come loose so that a gear was grinding against the oscillating weight as it turned. I tugged my magnifying goggles up from around my neck and fished in my bag for my needle-nose pliers.

"Can I ask you about something? It's been bothering me that I can't remember." Oliver held up his flesh-and-blood hand for me to see. A thin white scar ran across the knuckles. "What's this from? It's different than the others."

"Boxing, I think." I gripped the gear with my pliers and jammed it back into place. Oliver sucked in a sharp breath. "Sorry, should have warned you that might hurt."

He shrugged like it didn't matter, but his voice was tighter when he spoke again. "It doesn't look like a boxing scar. I thought I must have put my hand through a window or something."

"No, you told me someone threw a bottle in the ring and you sliced up your hand."

"Did I win the match?"

"God, Oliver, does it matter? You hurt yourself doing stupid things so many times. They all start to blur together."

"Were you there? Did you ever box?"

I slid the pliers from under the weight and swapped them for a spanner that fit around a loose bolt. "No, boxing is a bit wild for me."

"Wish I could box now."

I tightened the bolt harder than I needed to. Oliver yelped. "And then as soon as you took your shirt off in the ring, they'd see you're mostly metal and haul you away."

"God's wounds, Ally, it was a joke." He flexed his hand, watching the scar move with his skin. "It's strange, you know. Having scars and not knowing where they came from."

"Well, any others you can't remember?" I asked.

"All of them." He ran his fingertips along a seam in his skull. "I don't remember getting any of them."

I scrubbed at an oily spot on my spanner and said nothing.

Most of Oliver's memory had come back to him, slowly and with coaxing on my part. He'd returned to the world blank, but things like speech and reading and motor skills had come back quickly. The memories had been harder. I tried to supply him with what I could, but I had a sense that instead of genuinely remembering things, he mostly just took my word for what I said had happened. Sometimes he'd surprise me with a memory I hadn't fed him, though what came back was unpredictable—he remembered specific fights with Father but not a thing about Mum, the color of the walls in our shop in Paris though he had lost Bergen entirely, that he hated Geisler though I had to remind him why. It scared me a bit, the things he found without my help. Mostly because there was still a chance the truth of the night he died might return without warning, and it wouldn't line up with the story I'd given him.

I snapped the band of my goggles to keep them from sliding down my nose. "Well, lucky you've got me and I remember everything. Take a breath." Oliver obeyed, and I pressed two gloved fingers against the gear to test the placement. "That'll work for now. One of the bolts is stripped, so it won't stay in place for long. I'll bring a new one next time I come."

"And what am I meant to do until then?"

"You can hold on to my pliers in case you need to tighten it." I fished around in my bag until I found them, then tossed them on the desk. They skidded to the edge with a clatter. "They're not really meant for bolts, but Father will miss a spanner. How's everything else running?"

"My arm feels stiff."

"Probably needs to be cleaned. I haven't got oil today, but I can give it a pulse. It might help." Oliver pulled a face, and I almost made a smart remark about how he should be used to the pain by now, but changed my mind at the last second. I retrieved the pulse gloves from my bag and swapped them out for the leather work ones. Oliver slumped in the chair as I rubbed my hands together, both of us watching the pale energy gather between the plates. "Sorry, they take so bleeding long to get a charge going."

"Tell Father you need new ones."

"They're hard to get now. Every tool the Shadow Boys use is monitored dead close. Shopkeepers have to do an inventory of who buys them for the police. Some places you need a permit."

"Geneva's getting smarter."

I separated my palms with a grunt. A flicker of white-blue light ran along the edges. "Brace yourself."

I pressed the gloves to the conducting plates on clockwork shoulder. The metal connected with a faint flash, and Oliver's whole body jerked as the shock went through it. The gears in his arm sped up, electricity coiling through the mainspring. He bent his elbow a few times, and nodded. "Better."

"Next time give me some warning before it needs oiling."

Oliver swatted that away, then stood up and rotated his mechanical arm in its socket. "You think you'll stay in Geneva?" he asked.

"Father seems keen on it. You don't remember Morand, do you?" He shook his head. "He runs a boardinghouse over the border in France for clockworks who need a place to stay. He keeps trying to get us to come work for him there, but Father isn't interested. I think he and Mum are getting tired of moving around so much. I just wish they'd gotten tired somewhere friendlier."

"No, I mean you. Will *you* stay?" He scooped up a handful of paper scraps and tossed them into the fire. "Weren't you meant to apply to university this year?"

"I was."

"So what happened?"

I stripped off the pulse gloves and dropped them back into my bag. Thinking about university sent a heavy pang through me, like a taut wire plucked inside my chest. I'd planned on it for so long—going to university in Ingolstadt to study mechanics with Geisler, the way Oliver was going to before he died. Wanting it still stung deep, and it was worse with Oliver on the other end of the question. "I didn't."

"Why not?"

"Didn't fancy it. Father needs me. Money." I shrugged. "Why does it matter?"

He picked up a fire poker from beside the grate and jabbed the flames. "I just thought if you went to uni, maybe I could go somewhere too."

"Go where?"

"Somewhere not here. Away . . . and not with you." I didn't mean to, but I laughed. Oliver scowled, and I shut my mouth quick. "What's funny?"

"I couldn't leave you alone."

His scowl went deeper, and for a strange moment, I saw a shadow of Father in his face. "I could look after myself."

"Like hell you could. Oliver, all I've ever done our whole lives is look out for you when you did daft things. Even when we were lads. Who took the fall for stealing sweets so you wouldn't get thrown out of school? Who bailed you out of jail twice so Father wouldn't find out? Who fixed all those clocks so you wouldn't lose that shop job in Paris?"

"And don't forget, I'd be dead without you," he added, his voice suddenly closer to a snarl.

I pressed the heels of my hands into my eyes. "Please, Oliver, I don't want to talk about this anymore."

"You're not going to uni because of me. You didn't even apply because of me. Going to university used to be all you talked about, I remember *that*. I'm not an idiot, Ally."

A flare went off inside my chest, and I stood up so hard my chair wobbled. "Sod it, fine. You're right, is that what you want to hear? I didn't apply to Ingolstadt because I have to stay here and take care of you."

I didn't realize what I'd said for a moment. Then Oliver repeated, "Ingolstadt?" And my heart sank. "You want to go to university in Ingolstadt?"

"Oliver—"

"Because Geisler's on faculty there."

I could feel his anger—that feral creature barely controlled in his first life that now raged untamed in his second—rear its ugly head. I took a step toward him, one hand rising between us. "I didn't mean—"

He flung the fire poker, and it skittered across the floor. A few pieces of glowing charcoal separated from the tip and sparked against the stone. "Here I was touched by your sacrifice, and come to find out you're still obsessed with Ingolstadt and studying with the man who killed me."

A cold stone dropped in the pit of my stomach, but I kept my face blank.

When I had told Oliver the story of his own death, Dr. Geisler being responsible for it had seemed the best lie there was, and the easiest. It was the same story I'd told my parents, and the police, and Mary, and everyone since—there had been an accident in the clock tower while Geisler was escaping the city. It wasn't intentional, but it was Geisler who'd pushed Oliver, and he'd fallen through the clock face. It was too late to retreat from it now. I'd told Oliver the story too many times, burned it into him myself in an attempt to ward off the truth. But I wished desperately that I could go back and make up something else. Police, maybe, or too much wine, or loose floorboards. Something that wouldn't stand so firmly in the way of the things I wanted.

"It was an accident," I said. "I told you that."

"But I still ended up dead. Geisler's the reason I'm a monster!"

"You're not a monster," I said, though my voice rang hollow with the frequent reprise. If you say anything enough, even the truth, it starts to sound like a lie, and I wasn't certain what the truth was where Oliver was concerned.

"Then I suppose you lock me up for my own safety, is that it?" he said. "Because I'm fragile and you want to protect me, not because men would run screaming if they saw me."

"You're not a monster," I repeated.

"But Geisler is," Oliver said. "He killed me—he bleeding *killed me*, Alasdair—but you want to go to Ingolstadt and keep his mad research going."

"You're alive because of that mad research," I retorted.

"Well, I'd rather be dead!" He snatched up the copy

of *Paradise Lost* and flung it against the wall. It opened like wings and fell to the ground with a hollow thud. For a moment, we both stared at it. The silence between us felt thick and gasping, like a living presence.

"Don't say that," I said. "You don't mean that."

Oliver pressed his chin to his chest. "Some days I do." His voice still shook, but he'd gone quiet again. "Some days I want to tear myself apart."

"Don't," I said quickly. "Don't . . . do that. I'll come more. I'll come stay with you for a bit. I'll tell Mum and Father I'm going to see about a job with Morand—"

"Just because you don't scream out loud doesn't mean I can't still hear you screaming." He turned suddenly away from me and leaned forward, forehead to the wall. His silhouette against the firelight was so strange and twisted, like a too-sharp skeleton sewn into empty skin.

I sank backward into the chaise and blew a long breath out through my nose. The goggles around my neck fogged. "It doesn't matter," I said. "I'm not going to Ingolstadt, and I'm not letting you out. It's horrible out there for people like you."

"No one is like me," he replied.

"For clockwork men," I corrected. "Especially in Geneva. Oliver, people would rip you apart. They'd dissect you."

"I know." He jammed his pipe between his teeth and slumped down on the chaise beside me. We sat for a while without speaking. A log in the fireplace collapsed into embers, sending a spray of popping sparks up the chimney.

Then I remembered why I'd come today.

"I got you something." I retrieved my bag from under the desk and pulled out one of the books. "Happy birthday."

"Is that today?"

"December first, same as every year." I meant it as a joke, but Oliver didn't laugh. He took the book from me and stared at the cover like it was a portrait of someone he almost recognized. "Coleridge," I prompted. "You used to like him. You and . . ." I swallowed hard. I'd never mentioned Mary, mostly for the sake of my own broken heart, and I didn't know if Oliver remembered her.

He glanced sideways at me. "Me and who?"

"Just you," I said. "You liked Coleridge."

"What does he write?"

"Words."

He elbowed me sharply with his mechanical arm, and I yelped. It hurt more than I hoped he meant it to. "What sort of *things*, you ninny?"

"Poetry. He's a poet, I think. I don't really know." I reached for the next book on the stack.

"Like one, that on a lonesome road . . ."

I stopped. "What?"

"That's . . ." He screwed up his face, eyes closed in concentration. *"Like one, that on a lonesome road / Doth walk in fear and dread, / And having once turned round walks on, / And turns no more his head; / Because he knows, a frightful fiend / Doth close behind him tread."*

Behind us, another log snapped in the fireplace. "That's pretty grim," I said.

"I think that's Coleridge. I remember it."

"Oh." My stomach jolted at the word *remember* and I dumped the rest of the books onto the floor without looking at them. "Well, you can read it in your spare time, when you're not tearing the furniture apart."

Oliver looked up as I stood. "Are you going already?"

"I've got somewhere to be."

I didn't say *home*, but I knew Oliver heard it anyway. He tossed the Coleridge book onto the floor next to *Paradise Lost* and pulled his feet up onto the spot I'd just vacated. "Tell your parents I said hello."

It was a jab wrapped up as a joke, which aggravated me more than if he'd just been mean. "They're your parents too."

"I thought that was your honor now. Or do you prefer *creator*?"

"Hell's teeth, Oliver." I snatched up my bag and my coat—I didn't even bother to put it on, I just wanted away from him so badly. It felt like I was suffocating. "I won't be by much this week," I called as I headed for the door. "We've got the Christmas market and Father's going mental over it."

"Just like every year."

"Just like every year."

"I remember that."

I turned in the doorway and looked back. Oliver was cross-legged on the chaise with his shoulders slumped. He had picked up another book from my pile, and as he turned the pages, he reached up and ran his mechanical fingers over his bottom lip—an absent, deep-in-thought gesture I remembered from when we were boys.

I watched his fingers cross his lip, and thought, *I miss you.*

He was right there in front of me, close enough to touch. And all I could do was miss him.

I turned the knob behind my back and offered what I hoped was at least close to a smile. "I'll see you soon," I said, and retreated into the castle darkness, back toward the setting winter sun, before he could say good-bye.

I was six minutes late for supper.

When I let myself into our flat above the shop, both my parents were already at the table, Father staring at his pocket watch, Mum looking rather sheepishly at me as though apologizing for the whole show of waiting. I knew it hadn't been her idea. The table between them was laid with a roast goose, flanked by a dish of leek-and-potato *papet vaudois* and a whipped meringue. It was a far cry from most of our suppers, which were usually cold and stale and eaten standing up in the workshop between appointments.

Father snapped his pocket watch shut and glared at me over the top of his spectacles. "You're late, Alasdair."

Oliver had worn me out, and I was in no mood to joust with my father, so I sank into my place at the table without a word. Mum had put out embroidered napkins, and a bouquet of snowdrop flowers was nestled in a tea-cup between the candlesticks.

For a long moment, none of us said anything. Mum stared down at her empty plate, Father glared at the goose, and I looked between them, wondering which of us would speak first.

It was Father who finally raised his glass. I thought he would make a speech, because he was always one for lectures, but he simply said, "Happy birthday, Oliver." His features sat in their practiced scowl, but I saw the tremor in his jaw as he finished, "You are missed."

Mum nodded, her thumb pressed against her lips.

Father looked over at me, and I dropped my eyes to my own glass. "Would you like to say something about your brother, Alasdair?" he asked. "Something you remember."

There were so many things I remembered about Oliver, but the harder I tried to cling to them the faster they seemed to slip away. The images of our vagabond youth—children of the Shadow Boys, back when we were knotted so tight together—had been washed away by my latest memories of him in Château de Sang, raging and snarling and tearing apart the furniture. The fight in him that I had once admired had been transformed from glowing and bright into something you could fall and cut yourself on, and that was what was left of him—a man I didn't know who wore his ill-fitting skin and spoke in his voice. My brother, obliterated by himself.

All at once I thought I might cry, and I stared hard at my fingers around my glass to stop my eyes from burning. The scars on my hand from the loose gears and wires on resurrection night flickered from red to white. The flesh memories of the night I had killed my brother, and brought him back to life.

"To Oliver," I said, and I drained my glass.

Morand came by the shop the next afternoon to collect his arm.

He was a short, stocky fellow about my father's age with a head of thick graying hair that he wore long and loose. We saw him twice a year, consistent as clockwork, when he left his boardinghouse in Ornex for Geneva to pick up false identification papers for the clockwork men and women he harbored. The forgeries left mechanical parts unlisted, which made it easier to find work and travel.

Morand liked a good catch-up when he came, so it was usually Father who did the installation, but today he let me take Morand back into the workshop on my own. I thought that meant he was beginning to let out my lead, until he murmured, "We'll see about your half-inch stock" as I passed him behind the counter.

Inside the workshop, I did a quick lap around to light the lamps. Morand shifted my breakfast dishes off the chair and settled down, already rolling up his sleeve over the tarnished socket fused to his elbow.

"So how's Geneva treating the Finches?" he asked as I tugged my magnifying goggles over my eyes and hefted the clockwork arm up from the workbench.

"Good. Fine." I fit the arm into the socket, twisting until the bolts lined up, then started to tighten them. The gears settled with a soft groan.

Morand laughed. "I forgot, you aren't the chatty one, are you? Your brother used to—" He stopped and looked down at the floor.

I kept my eyes on my work. "You can talk about him. I don't mind."

He grunted, then rolled back his shoulder as I finished with the bolts. "He was always one for a good conversation, Oliver Finch. You look just like him, you know."

I mustered a smile and reached behind me for the pulse gloves. As I moved, the lamplight caught a bronze badge in the shape of a cog pinned to the lapel of Morand's coat, same as the old man on the omnibus had been wearing the day before.

Morand caught me staring at it and grinned. "Are

you admiring my Frankenstein badge?"

I nearly dropped the gloves. "What did you call it?" I asked, though I'd heard him clearly. I could see the word spelled out in gold leaf on the spine of the book Mary had sent.

"Frankenstein badge. Haven't you heard that? It's what my boarders coming out of Geneva call them. All the clockworks here have to wear them now."

"I know," I said quickly. "I just hadn't heard them called that before."

"Have you read it—*Frankenstein*?" he asked as I strapped on the pulse gloves and started to get a charge building between them. "Nobody knows who wrote it, not even the newspapers. I heard it's about Geisler, though. Your family doesn't speak to him anymore, do you?"

"No." The electric current gathering between my hands snapped like an affirmation. "Why would someone write a book about Geisler? He's still a wanted man in most places."

Morand shrugged. "It might not be about him, but it's a definitely about a Shadow Boy. I don't know, I haven't read it, I just hear about it from my boarders. Something about clockwork men and whether or not we're actually human. And then there's a doctor in it who makes a mechanical monster from a corpse and it turns on him."

"Hell's teeth."

"Sounds like Geisler's work, doesn't it? It's set here in Geneva as well. I thought the whole city would be in an uproar over it. It's quieter than I expected."

"Well, we've got to behave for Christmas."

He laughed as he stretched out his legs. "I had a man come from Geneva a few weeks ago called Emile Brien. Got his leg blown off at Waterloo and walks on cogs now. You know him?" I shook my head. "He said he was enlisted by a group of clockworks here who are trying to get some trouble started. Know anything about that?"

"No." I suddenly realized the plates on my hands were crackling with current—I'd been so intent on what he was saying I'd forgotten them. I touched my palms to the conducting plates on Morand's arm and a bolt tore from the gloves into the machinery.

I knew I was right about the half-inch stock, but I still held my breath as the gears leapt to life and inter-laced, smooth and soundless as the summer Rhone. No sparks or broken teeth. No sticky ratchet. And no strain on the center wheel. Morand bent his arm a few times, then worked the silver fingers in and out of a fist.

"Feel all right?" I asked.

"Outstanding," he replied. "Well done, Alasdair."

I nodded like it was all business, but I was pleased. Father would have to admit I'd been right about the half-inch stock. He was brilliant in matters of flesh and blood—back in Scotland, before he'd been recruited by

Geisler for his fleet of Shadow Boys, he'd been a navy surgeon—but only passable at machinery. He'd never admit that cogs and gears spoke to me in a way they never had to him. Father was a doctor, same way I was a mechanic. Some things you just are, deep and true inside your bones.

Morand retrieved his hat from where he'd hung it on the back of the chair. "Tell your father if he ever tires of Geneva, I have a job for him. My boarders could use a Shadow Boy. Or maybe you're interested. You've got quite the talent for it." He looked at me like he thought I would answer, but when I stayed silent, he added, "Or, God forbid, if you're ever in trouble, you can always find your way to Ornex. You know that. So do your parents."

"Thank you, sir."

He extended his metal hand and I shook it. "You're a good lad, Alasdair," he said. "Be certain you stay that way."

I hung back in the workshop when Morand went to say his good-byes to Father. As soon as the door hissed shut behind him, I reached for my bag and the copy of *Frankenstein* Mary had sent. I'd rather have my teeth pulled out than read most books, but I'd be damned if I didn't slog my way through one about Geisler and his work.

It wasn't there. I emptied the bag, ran my hands along the pocket, even held the whole thing upside down like an idiot, but the book was gone. I thought maybe I'd left it up in the flat, but I'd stowed my bag in the workshop before going upstairs to dinner. Perhaps I'd left it on the bus or dropped it on the way up to the castle. Perhaps I'd given it to Oliver by mistake with the other books.

I groaned aloud at that thought. If it was truly about Geisler, that was the last book in the world I wanted him reading. I'd have to go by later and see if I'd left it.

But it was already late. Father would have things for me to do, and wouldn't let me slip away as easily as he had the day before. I could go tomorrow, I thought, but then remembered we had the Christmas market. The next day, maybe, but I'd be exhausted. Perhaps after that. Wait until Sunday, when everything was settled.

A thousand reasons not to go.

I lamented less the loss of the book and more Mary's letter that had been tucked inside it. I cursed myself for not reading it as soon as I got it. Damn Jiroux and the clockwork veteran on the bus. Damn my stupidity for losing it. Damn the way Mary still had a hold of me, my heart as true as a compass.

I still couldn't fathom why she'd sent the book. Perhaps she'd heard it was about Geisler. She'd known we were familiar with him, and she'd left Geneva before he and Father had their proper falling-out over Oliver's death, so she wouldn't know we'd parted ways. Perhaps she'd seen it was about clockwork and thought of me. Or perhaps she meant it as a warning. I thought of that small brass badge blinking up from Morand's lapel.

I pulled my legs up on the bench and stretched out, lying flat on my back and staring up at the dark shadows that the lamplight carved on the pocked ceiling. Mary had been nineteen the last time I saw her. She'd be twenty-one now, same age as Oliver was. Would have been. I wasn't certain how I was meant to measure that anymore. We had that dreary summer together and the warm fall that followed it—Mary, Oliver, and I, thick as thieves, my mum had called us. Until Mary came along, I hadn't known what it was like to sit in the sunshine on the lakeshore and think about absolutely nothing except the pale triangle of freckles peering from the bunched neckline of her dress. Life had never been that simple before, and certainly hadn't been since.

Mary, the first girl I ever loved. First girl I ever kissed. The girl who'd dug up my brother's body with me. The sorts of things that stay with you.

The workshop door hissed, and I sat up as Mum appeared in the doorway. "You want some supper?"

"If you're offering."

"Come upstairs, then, it's hot. Your father's closing up early to get things in order for tomorrow. Were you sleeping?"

"No." I looped my arms around my knees. "Just thinking."

She came and sat beside me on the workbench. We

weren't a very familiar family—never had been—but she put her hand on top of my knee and her thumb worked in a slow circle. "It's a hard time of year, isn't it?" she said, and I knew she wasn't talking about the Christmas market. Then, like she'd overheard my thoughts, she asked, "What did Miss Godwin send you?"

"A book. And a letter."

"What did she have to say?"

I didn't want to admit I'd lost it, so I said, "Just a hello. Nothing important."

"Is that the first time she's written to you?" When I nodded, Mum made a soft humming noise with her lips pursed. "She was such a strange creature, wasn't she? Always running around with you two."

"Oliver and I weren't *that* strange."

Her mouth twitched. "I meant . . . well, there are rules about that sort of thing. About a young woman being out on her own with two lads. Though that never seemed to bother her. She was so contrary."

"Mistress Mary, quite contrary," I said without thinking, then laughed. It was what Oliver and I used to call her—I had forgotten until I heard myself say it. Mistress Mary, quite contrary, like the nursery rhyme, because Mary seemed not only to ignore the rules everyone else lived by—like ladies don't drink beer in pubs, they don't say exactly what they think about clockwork rights, they don't go gallivanting around Geneva with

Shadow Boys—but to make a display of how much she didn't care to follow them.

Maybe it was the book from Mary, or maybe it was seeing Oliver, or maybe it was both those things squashed together in one day, but all at once I remembered standing at the top of one of the grassy foothills with the pair of them, the sky above us gray and rumbling with a storm. Oliver was saying we were going to race down to the tumbled pine tree on the lakeshore where we launched our rowboat when we didn't have money to use the docks.

"Wait a moment," Mary interrupted, and bent down like she was going to take off her shoes, but suddenly she was hiking her skirts up around her waist, so high I could see her stockings up to her knees. All the blood left my head so fast I nearly fainted, and I turned away on reflex, though I would have been happy to keep staring. Next to me, Oliver was looking pointedly up at the sky, but when he caught my eye, we both started to laugh.

"What?" Mary demanded. "Running properly in skirts is a nightmare."

We looked at each other again, then chorused, "Mistress Mary, quite contrary."

"Oh, don't pretend like a lady's legs are the most shocking thing you've ever seen, Shadow Boys." She swatted at us, and we dodged in the same direction and smashed shoulders, which just made us laugh harder. Mary took advantage of our hysterics and shouted, "Ready, go!" Then she took off down the slope without looking back.

Oliver shoved me off him with a shout and started to run, and I took off after. The tall grass was still sparkling with that morning's rain, and it whacked sharp and wet against my shins. I was faster than Oliver—always had been—and I had passed him before the ground began to slope in earnest. He made a grab for the back of my shirt to slow me down, but I skated away. "Dammit, Alasdair," he shouted, and though he tried to sound cross that I was winning, a laugh shattered inside it.

I passed Mary as well and slammed into the tree ahead of both of them. Clutching at the stitch in my side, I turned back and watched them hurtle toward me, Mary with her skirts flapping around her knees and her hair coming loose as the wind grabbed at it, Oliver just behind her, his steps so high that each one seemed a leap.

And in that moment I remember a very clear and sudden certainty that there was no one in the whole world that I needed but them.

"How long has it been since Miss Godwin left Geneva?" Mum asked, and I had to blink hard to clear that overcast sunshine from my mind.

"Two years," I said. *Same as Oliver.*

We didn't say much over supper. Father was eating at top speed, and I swore I could feel him making mental lists of everything that needed to be in order before the morning. Then he put down his fork and looked across the table at me. "I spoke to Morand before he left today." When I didn't say anything, he added, "He said he offered you a job."

Mum looked up as well. "Alasdair?"

I tore a piece of bread in half and traced the rim of my plate with it. "Not really. He just said he could use a Shadow Boy in Ornex. I think he meant it more for you than me."

"He said he'd be pleased to have you, if I could spare you."

"Can you? I thought you needed my help here."

"We could manage. It would be good for you to get out of Geneva for a while." He was watching me with the same tight scrutiny he used on mechanical limbs, but I just shrugged. Father blew out a taut sigh and pushed his spectacles back onto the top of his head. "Well, what do you want, Alasdair? We can't seem to interest you in anything lately."

"Bronson," Mum said, his name a verbal step between us.

Father swiped the corner of his mouth with his thumb, eyes still on me. "You're nearly eighteen. Time to start making a life for yourself."

"Alasdair," Mum said from my other side, "why don't you want to go?"

I tossed my napkin on the table. "I just don't," I said, and my chair clattered against the floor as I stood. "I'm going to start packing things up for the market," I added, then headed for the door before either of them could protest.

Downstairs in the shop, I sat on the counter and shifted doll furniture from the back shelf into the straw-lined crates Father had prepared, and I thought about the offer from Morand. Father had seemed so keen on me taking it that I didn't dare tell him how suffocated I felt when I imagined working at a boardinghouse in a tiny French town. I didn't want to be a shop boy for-ever, not to him or to Morand. I thought of Ingolstadt again and the spot it held inside me, a spot hollowed out and smooth from running my fingers over it again and again. That stupid dream I just couldn't let go.

But any of that—even moving twelve miles up the road to France—was hopeless so long as Oliver was locked up in the foothills. There'd be nowhere to hide him in a town as small as Ornex, and there was no chance of letting him out on his own. The rest of my life seemed firmly shackled to Geneva and my resurrected brother, too wild and rough for the world.

With the strict regulations on clockwork men and the

Shadow Boys who made them, Geneva had always felt like a prison, even before Oliver kept me here. Geisler had encouraged my father to claim home in places where clockworks most needed allies—there was always more work for us there. We'd skipped from Edinburgh to Bergen when I was a child, then to Bruges, Utrecht, and Amsterdam in such quick procession that they started to blend together. All the timbered houses and canals, and the running and the fear and the never having enough to eat. It was hard to separate them anymore—everything was just seasons and years and the ages Oliver and I had been when we'd arrived and fled.

But it was always Oliver and me, together, everywhere we went. I did remember that.

I had better memories of Paris, where Father had started pressing Oliver harder and harder to start studying mechanics, and Oliver had pushed back with just as much strength. He horrified our parents by falling in with a group of boxers and coming home past dawn with his knuckles bleeding. Started smoking like a chimney. Never once showed up to the job Father had gotten him fixing clocks.

Then he'd taken up with a dancer and told her about our work. She'd threatened to turn us in to the police unless we paid her off. Father had been ready to throttle Oliver, but our only choices seemed to be complying and hoping she died soon of consumption, or fleeing. At the same time, Geisler had been commissioned to work on Geneva's new clock tower and he suggested we join him. He'd had his eye on Oliver for years, and when he offered an apprenticeship, Father had snatched it up in yet another hopeless attempt to mold Oliver into the Shadow Boy and older son that he so badly wanted.

And so we had left Paris for Geneva, and spent an uneventful year with Oliver and Father on the cusp of murdering each other, Oliver moaning to me about working with Geisler, and me pretending I wasn't sick with envy over it.

Then Geisler had been arrested, and Mary Godwin had arrived, and Oliver had died, and a piece of me had died with him, and unlike Oliver, it never came back.

The bell above the shop door jingled and Father entered. I slid off the counter, because he hated it when I sat up there—mostly, I knew, because Oliver used to. With his arms crossed, he gave the packing I had done a critical inspection. "Don't stack them too deep or the paint will chip," he said. Then he slid his spectacles down onto his nose and took his place on the other side of the counter, and I stood across from him, crammed in a shop, in a city, in a life that was far too small.

Father was up earlier than usual the next morning, mucking about in the kitchen and clattering the teakettle to rouse me. I'd been awake for a while but I stayed curled on my pallet with my head all the way under my quilt, delaying actually getting up as long as possible. Sunlight was worming its way through the stitching, but when I pressed my hand against the bare floorboards the cold snapped at me, and I retreated. It was too cold to be anywhere but under blankets, and I was about to spend all day standing outside.

By the time I dressed and dragged myself into the kitchen, the tea was lukewarm, but Father was putting his coat on and I knew I didn't have time to heat it. I choked down a cup as Mum, still in her dressing gown, watched from the table, with her hands wrapped around a mug. "Will you come down to the market?" I asked her as I laced my boots.

She shook her head. "It's always so crowded the first day. Next week, maybe." She smiled at me as she took a sip of tea. "Take a walk around for me and see if you can find the best-priced marzipan."

"There won't be any walking around, we'll be working," Father snapped from the doorway. He flipped his pocket watch open and frowned. "You've made us late, Alasdair."

I swooped in to kiss Mum on the cheek.

"Stay warm," she said.

"Not likely," I replied, and followed Father out of the flat.

We retrieved the crates from the shop and started up the road toward the Christmas market. With sunrise still blooming along the rooftops, Vieille Ville was closed and quiet, but as we approached Place de l'Horloge, the city began to wake around us. Clockwork carriages chugged past, expelling clouds of steam that sparkled in the sunlight, and merchants unlocking their doors shouted to each other across the walks. Some of the shops already had their Christmas decorations up, evergreen branches and strung cranberries draped between the icicles clinging to the window boxes. Bakeries were advertising Yule log cakes, and the metal mannequins in the dressmaker's window were wearing hats studded with mistletoe and candles. The air smelled like pine and steam.

Place de l'Horloge had been lined with market stalls built to look like miniature chalets, each with a dusting of snow on its beams, and holly garlands threaded the paths between them. There were already vendors setting up shop, laying out everything from meats and cheeses to fine glasswork to children's puzzles and marionettes. A giant mechanical Christmas *pyramide* had been erected near the center, the tiered wooden platforms lined with clockwork Nativity figures that rotated slowly. It was as tall as the buildings lining the square, but it looked small in the shadow of the clock tower. The whole market looked smaller beneath it—all the Christmas nonsense was usually held in Place de la Fusterie, nearer to the lakeshore and the financial district, but it had been moved this year in honor of the finished tower and the clock scheduled to strike on Christmas Eve.

I followed Father up one of the narrow paths between the chalets, trying to ignore his grumblings about being the last ones there, until we found our assigned stall. The wooden sign above the counter was still painted from the previous years—FINCH AND SONS, TOY MAKERS.

It took most of the day to lay out the toys in a manner that Father deemed acceptable. The market didn't open until sundown, and by midafternoon he was making minuscule adjustments to the lines of windup mice and jack-in-the-boxes. I watched him as I chewed idly on a piece of bread Mum had sent for our lunch, trying to ignore the smell of roasting chestnuts and gingerbread from down the row.

As twilight bled navy across the sky, clusters of candlelight began to appear around the square. The tree was lit and braziers smoldered orange against the night. Somewhere amid the stalls, a violin began to play "Un flambeau, Jeannette, Isabelle."

The shoppers arrived with the darkness, first in solitary groups of twos and threes, then in packs, until our time between customers shrank to nothing. A choir started singing just down the way, and I had to speak over them whenever I addressed someone. My voice went hoarse counting out change, listing prices, explaining how to wind the dancing dogs.

When I felt as though I was swallowing sand, I grabbed Father between customers. "I'm going to get a drink."

He readjusted his gloves, their tips cut off to better handle the toys. His fingers were red and chapped. "Don't linger."

"I won't. Do you want anything?"

"No," he said, like it was a daft question, then turned back to a woman weighing a windup mouse in her hand. I took that as permission, vaulted the counter, and set off in a snaking trail through the market.

I didn't linger, but I certainly wasn't direct about it either, and I kept a sharp eye out for marzipan.

I bought a mug of *glühwein* under the giant *pyramide* and stood at one of the tall tables while I drank it. Above the noise of the shoppers, I could hear the bells of Saint Pierre Cathedral up the hill chiming eight. It was going to be a long night. The market didn't close until eleven, and after that we'd have to clean up. I leaned over my mug and took a deep breath, letting the cinnamon steam from the *glühwein* dampen my face.

Then, from the other side of the square, I heard shouting. It might have been just a shopper with too much to drink, but then another voice joined, and another, and then a scream rose above the chatter of the market and the bells. I raised my face from my mug and stared in the direction of the noise. It was getting louder. The choir stopped with a squawk. All around me, people were turning to look.

An engine snarled from the street, and I turned to see two policemen on steamcycles plowing down the square. People had to leap into the snowbanks between the stalls to avoid being flattened. My first thought was of the trouble Morand had mentioned the day before, and a tight coil twisted in my chest. I abandoned my *glühwein* and jogged in the same direction the policemen had gone.

A crowd had gathered at the end of one of the rows.

People were jeering and shouting, and through the throng I picked out two more navy-blue-uniformed officers on foot. They had a man on the ground, his face pushed into the snow as they handcuffed him. The policemen on steamcycles were trying to hold back the crush of people, who seemed intent on getting to the man. I joined the edge of the crowd, trying to see over people's heads and avoid being knocked in the face. Something landed near my feet, and I looked down.

It was a windup mouse, gears in its belly exposed, head attached by a single spring.

Panic filled me suddenly, hotter than the *glühwein*. I shoved through the crowd, ignoring the shouts flung in my direction, until I could see into the center, where the two policemen were dragging my father to his feet. His nose was bleeding down the front of his coat, and patches of mud and snow clung to his hair. The lenses of his spectacles were shattered, the frames dangling off one ear. He didn't fight as the police forced the crowd apart and dragged him toward the wagon waiting at the edge of the square, but when he looked across the mob, he saw me. His eyes widened and he shook his head, sending his glasses skittering into the snow. Someone spit on him, and it landed, thick and yellow, just above his eye.

I turned and ran.

We had a plan for this. We always had a plan for this.

In every city we had ever lived in, we had mapped our escape routes, agreed where to pick up new identification papers, where to find money for a carriage ticket and who to ask if there wasn't any. I should go north, across the border into France, and we'd meet up in Ornex at Morand's.

But it had never been like this before, never me alone without Mum or Father or even Oliver. We had never been found out—we always fled together before they could catch up with us. And though I knew in my bones what I was meant to do, I found myself doing something else entirely and heading to the one place I knew I shouldn't: the flat.

I took side streets through the financial district and into Vieille Ville at a run, leaping over a pile of blacksmith's coal and skidding on bloody snow behind the butcher's. My lungs were burning by the time I reached our shop, but I still sprinted up the stairs and burst into the flat.

The room had been ransacked. Everything was turned over—our trunks, the bureau, drawers pulled from their places and the contents dumped on the floor. Most of the furniture had been smashed, mattresses cut open, and straw and feathers were strewn amid the wreckage like a fine snow. I took a few steps in, and a shard of my mother's teacup crunched under my boot. "Mum?" I called softly, though it was clear she wasn't there.

I did a quick lap around the flat, checking for any of the provisions we kept ready in case we had to bolt. The roll of bills in a kettle above the fire was gone, along with a gold medallion Father had been given in the Scottish navy. Whoever had been here, they had taken anything that would have made running easier. I checked what was left of my things and found that my papers were missing as well. It had been bleeding stupid not taking them with me that morning, but I hadn't thought I'd need them at the market. If the police had my name and description, it would be hard to get out of the city and into France undetected.

I slipped down the stairs and let myself into the shop, hoping for some money left in the cash box, but everything was smashed up and torn apart, same as upstairs. They had found the door to the workshop, forced it open and left it that way, like a gaping mouth stretched wide behind the counter. It bothered me almost more than the mess to see it like that, our secret so exposed, and I stood for a moment with one hand on the frame, looking down the passage.

Then, from deep in the darkness, I heard something move.

Hope flexed inside me, and I took a cautious step forward. "Mum?" I called. The shuffling movement stopped, followed by a cold silence. "Mum?" I called again, a little louder.

There was the scratch of a match, then a small flame appeared, illuminating the pale face I had seen on the omnibus the day before. Inspector Jiroux. The shadows intensified the contours of his face as our eyes met through the darkness. "Finch!" he bellowed.

I didn't know if it was me he was after or if he thought I was Father, but I didn't hang around to find out. I slammed the workshop door in his face. All the mechanisms that kept it from being opened from the inside had been gutted, but it would at least slow him down.

I scrambled out from behind the counter, stumbling on the ruins of windup toys that decorated the floor like spiked carpet, and burst out of the shop. The night air was sharp against my burning face as I turned down the first alley I came to and plunged deeper into the old town, not caring where I ran so long as I got away. The city here was a labyrinth, steep, decrepit passages without clockwork carriages or industrial torches. The moon was blotted out by icy laundry strung between windows, and most of the snow had been trampled into slick gray mud.

I sprinted past a rowdy pub where Oliver had once been arrested for brawling. Some men in the doorway shouted drunken nonsense at me, and one threw a glass of ale. I felt the spray on the back of my neck, but I didn't stop. As I reached the end of the street, I heard them shout again, this time with screechy catcalls. Was Jiroux still following me? I sped up, though my legs ached.

Two streets farther, I turned down a dead end. I whipped around to go back the way I had come, but a silhouetted figure appeared at the mouth of the alley, blocking my path. I snatched up the nearest weapon I could find—a cheap coal shovel with all the weight of a sheet of paper—and held it before me like a sword, bracing for a fight I knew I'd lose.

But it wasn't a policeman. It was a girl.

A young woman, I realized as she stepped into a chasm of moonlight, though it was only her long, plaited hair that made her look it. She was whip thin, her body a shapeless board like a boy's, and she was dressed in rough trousers and a heavy gray workman's coat, unbuttoned and lashed at the waist as though she had thrown on her father's coat from beside the door as she rushed out.

I lowered the shovel. Perhaps she hadn't been chasing me at all. It seemed more likely she had come out of one of the houses to see what the commotion was.

Then she called, "Alasdair Finch."

The shovel shot back up. "What do you want?" I said, and in my panic, the words fell out in English. She took another step toward me, and I shouted, "Stay back!" and whipped the shovel around a few times for good measure.

She raised her hands, palms forward. "Consider me threatened." She spoke English too, but with swallowed Parisian vowels that didn't match her tattered clothes.

"Are you with the police?" Even as I asked it, the question felt stupid. I could tell she wasn't just by looking at her.

She took another step forward, icy snow crunching under her boots. "I've come from Geisler."

I almost dropped the shovel. "Dr. Geisler? Is he here?"

"No, but he asked me to find you. I'm to take you to Ingolstadt to see him. You are Alasdair, aren't you?"

"Yes." My panic retreated just long enough to allow me a moment of reckless hope. Geisler was a name I could trust, and I needed to trust someone if I was on my own. I didn't lower the shovel, but I edged toward her. "How do we get there?"

"I have a wagon waiting outside the city."

"I won't get through the checkpoints." They didn't usually check papers on the way out, but I knew the police would be looking for me.

"We can go along the river. I know a way." A shout peaked from the men at the pub down the road, and the girl glanced over her shoulder, then back at me. "If we go, we go now."

Father was in prison. Mum was gone. But Geisler could help us, and I wouldn't have to run alone.

"All right," I said. "I'll go."

"Hurry, then." The girl turned back to the street, and I abandoned my shovel and followed her. We'd only gone a few steps when she stopped so suddenly that I nearly smashed into her. A light was bobbing toward us from the end of the lane, moving fast and accompanied by heavy footfalls.

"Damn." She seized me by the collar and dragged me after her back down the alley. Just before the dead end, she turned, wrenched open a door to one of the decrepit stone houses, and plunged us both inside.

It wasn't a house, I realized as my eyes adjusted to the darkness, but an abandoned shop with squatters and factory workers huddled together on the floor and against the walls. Glass display cases had been smashed out and small children slept inside them, curled around each other for warmth. A mist seemed to rise from the ground as everyone breathed, slow and steady in sleep. Somewhere amid the sleepers, I could hear clockwork ticking.

The girl picked her way across the floor toward a small window that opened onto the opposite alley. I followed, trying not to step on too many people as I went. Someone moaned, and someone else swore at me, but I reached her side as she jimmied open the window and climbed out. She was half my size and fit easily, but it was tight for me. I had one leg through when behind me, the door flew open with a bang. "Wake up! Police!" a voice shouted from the doorway.

I crammed myself the rest of the way, in spite of the imprint the frame left in my side, and lurched onto the cobblestones. "Police," I gasped as I steadied myself against the wall.

"We're close," she replied, and I followed her down the street at a run.

We weren't as close as I hoped. She led me all the way out of Vieille Ville and back into the financial district, until we finally stopped at a bridge, the Pont du la Machine. A few rough-looking shipmen were there, smoking with their backs against the industrial torches, but none of them looked twice at us as the girl led me to the edge of the bridge. A stone stairway ran down to the riverbank trail people used in the summer, but the Rhone had flooded to its winter height and the path was submerged. The stairs dropped into the waves.

She stopped on the step above the waterline and turned back to me. "How well do you swim?" she called over the rushing water.

I laughed, partly from astonishment but mostly refusal. I'd throw myself at the police's mercy before the Rhone's. "Are you mad? There's not a chance in bleeding hell I'm—"

"God's wounds, only joking." She smirked. I glowered. "Come on, follow me."

She jumped nimbly from the steps onto a rim of chain that the winter boats used for mooring. It hung in drapes between fat iron pegs, with the lowest links just above the waterline so that it formed a slick track against the stone retaining wall. I followed her, my work boots heavy and clumsy, forcing myself to keep my eyes on the back of her head and not look down at the rusted chain and the Rhone beneath. I could feel the spray on my face.

We followed the river until the chain began to go taut. I looked up from my feet just in time to see the girl hoist herself up over the edge and disappear from view. I followed, less gracefully. My limbs had gone shaky during our balancing act, and it took three tries before I managed to haul myself back onto solid ground. When I finally got sorted, I realized we were near the base of the foothills, surrounded by the bare vineyards that climbed up from the lakeshore. Behind us, I could see the city walls, Geneva's slate rooftops peeking over it. We were out.

The girl only gave me a moment to catch my breath before she started off again, down along a footpath cutting through the vineyard trellises, and I followed, my feet sliding on the frozen mud.

There were no industrial torches outside the city, and the only light came from the moon and a smattering of starlight spread like salt across the sky. I looked out, down the hill and across the smooth top of the lake, then up to the pinpricks of firelight that dotted the hillside from cottage windows. I thought of Château de Sang, black windows somewhere against the black sky, and I stopped.

Oliver.

It was like waking from a dream. I had been so panicked about getting out of the city I hadn't even thought about what I was leaving behind, and it all caught up with me as suddenly as if someone had grabbed me by the throat. "I can't go with you," I said, louder than I meant to.

The girl stopped too and turned. "What?"

"I can't leave," I repeated, but the words rang empty. This city had caged me for so long, and here I was on its edge, past the checkpoints and close to free, but I couldn't leave Oliver alone. His death was my fault, and now his life was too.

The girl crossed her arms over her chest. "I haven't got time for this. We need to go."

"I can't."

"What does that mean, you can't?"

"I just can't!" I said again. "There's someone who needs me here. So thank you for helping me get out but I can't . . . I can't go to Geisler." I turned and started in the opposite direction, back into the foothills and toward Château de Sang, but her hand clamped down on my elbow and jerked me back around. She was stronger than she looked.

"Where are you planning on going?" she demanded.

"I've got somewhere."

"Well, you can't go back to Geneva, not with the whole police force looking for you. Your only choice is to run, and I can help you. Geisler can help you." I tried to pull my sleeve out of her grip, but she clung on tighter. "I'll knock you over the head if I have to but I can't go back to Ingolstadt without you."

I yanked my arm free and took a few steps back. She looked too scrappy to throw a good punch, but I didn't think that would stop her from trying. For a moment we glared at each other, the silence interrupted by the bare grapevines clattering against their trellises as the wind rocked them.

I took a deep breath. I could go to Ornex. I *should* go to Ornex—that had always been the plan, and if Mum had gotten out, she would be there. Morand himself had said to come if I needed somewhere safe. But there would be nowhere to hide Oliver there, and I hadn't left him on his own for more than a few days since his resurrection. If I didn't show up, perhaps he'd figure we'd been run out of the city, though knowing Oliver and his flair for the dramatic, he'd probably assume I had abandoned him by choice.

But if I stayed with Oliver, there wasn't a thing I

could do for him. I had no money to go on the run, nowhere to go if we did. We'd sit together in that castle and starve slowly, if we didn't murder each other first.

And it was Geisler calling me. Geisler in Ingolstadt. This wasn't the way I had wanted it to happen, but here it was being handed to me. Wanting it felt sharp and glittering, like broken glass under my skin, but, bleeding hell, did I want it. I wanted to go to Ingolstadt. And I needed someone who could help me and my family better than I could help myself. Geisler could help me. That's why I would go, I told myself. To help my parents. And Oliver.

"Fine," I said, and fought the urge to look backward again. "Let's go."

At the end of the path, a stout wagon was waiting along the lakeshore; it was the old-fashioned sort with a horse hitched to the front instead of a steam pipe. "This is us," the girl called to me. As we drew level with it, I glanced over the lip and saw that the back was lined with coffins. It was an undertaker's wagon.

"Are we riding to Ingolstadt in coffins?" I asked as I hoisted myself up.

"Not all the way," she replied. "Just at the checkpoints."

I hoped this was more black humor, like her joke about swimming the Rhone, as I sank down into the narrow gap between coffins. The girl climbed up onto the seat and tapped the driver on the top of his bald head. He started. "Are you feeling quite awake, Monsieur Depace?" she asked him in French.

"Awake enough, Mademoiselle Le Brey," he replied. His voice wheezed like bellows. "I had a good nap while I waited for you."

"Well then, we're ready."

"You've got him?" Depace twisted backward in his seat for a look at me. His face was so wrinkled that it seemed to be collapsing in on itself. "That?" he said. "That's him? He's very small. I thought he would be older."

I felt a flush start in my neck, and it deepened when the girl, a smirk playing along her lips, said, "Well, I thought he would be better looking, so we're both disappointed."

"As long as you're certain he's the right one."

"Fairly certain."

"Well then, we're off." Depace flicked his reins and the wagon shuddered forward.

The girl slid down from the seat and settled across from me with her knees drawn up to her chest. I could feel her gaze through the darkness. "You should sleep," she said. "I'll wake you if there's trouble."

"I'm not going to sleep," I said, and my voice came out hoarse. Everything that had happened was starting to catch up with me, and it left me sounding haunted.

"I don't think I could if I tried."

"Certainly not with that defeatist attitude."

"What's your name?" I asked.

"Clémence Le Brey." The full flourish of her Parisian accent emerged, and I realized we were still speaking in English.

"French is fine," I said. *"Je parle français."*

"That's good," she replied, switching casually, "because I don't care for English."

"Where are you taking me?"

"I told you, to Ingolstadt. To Geisler."

"Did he know the police were coming for my family?" It seemed so strange she had arrived the same night they were arrested.

She tugged at her cap, and her blond hair flashed like moonlight through the darkness. "If he did, he didn't share with me."

"Then why does he want *me*?" That, more than anything, felt like a mistake. We hadn't heard from Geisler since he'd left Geneva, and before that I'd never had a real conversation with him without my father or Oliver present. For a time, I wasn't even certain he knew my name.

She shrugged. "All I was told was to collect you. When I went to your flat, your mother said you'd be home later, but the police came before you did. I was hoping you'd be stupid enough to turn up as well." Then, after a moment, she added, "You look very familiar to me."

"You don't to me."

"Did you work in Geisler's laboratory?"

"No, but I had a brother who did."

"The tall boy with the dark hair who was always scowling?"

I almost laughed. "Yes, that was him."

"That must be it, then. You look very similar." The wind rising off the lake struck the cart, and it wobbled. Clémence pulled her coat tighter around her shoulders. "I never saw him again after Geisler went to Ingolstadt. I thought he was meant to join us. Did he leave?"

"He didn't leave," I said shortly. "He died."

She blinked. "I didn't know."

"Are you from Paris?" I asked quickly, hoping to avoid the subject of Oliver.

"Yes," she replied. "But I work for Geisler now."

"Are you his . . . ?" I didn't have a clue what she was to him. I considered saying *mistress*, but that would be so dead embarrassing if I was wrong that I let her finish instead.

"Assistant."

"Assistant? You're his assistant?"

"That's right." She crossed her arms. "Is there a problem with that?"

"That was . . . ," I started, without knowing how I was going to finish. I thought of Oliver and it hit me again—I wasn't just leaving him, I was *abandoning* him. I tried to swallow the thought, but it pushed back, rising molten inside of me. *I'll come back*, I vowed. This wasn't for forever—just until things calmed down. *I'll come back*, I thought again—a silent, steady promise to shoulder some of the guilt. *I'll come back for you.*

"That was what my brother did," I finished. "That's all." Then I buried my mouth in my scarf and pushed a heavy breath into the wool so that it rebounded, warm and damp, against my dry lips.

"Is it a girl?" she asked.

"Is what a girl?"

"Whoever it is that needs you in Geneva. Is it your sweetheart?"

"No. It's not a girl."

Her mouth twisted into a sly smile. "How disappointing. A pretty girl's about the only thing that would keep *me* in a shithole like Geneva."

I barely had time to register what she'd said—or be properly shocked over hearing a girl cuss—when Depace's whistling voice carried back to us on the wind. "Patrol ahead. Could be trouble."

Clémence sprang into a crouch, head beneath the driver's seat, and cracked the lid of one of the coffins. "Get in," she hissed at me.

"You mean it?"

"What—are you afraid of the dark?" She knocked

the side of the coffin with her foot. "Get in."

"Not the dark," I said. The last coffin I'd seen was the one we'd buried Oliver in, and the memory was so sharp that for a moment I couldn't convince myself to move. *Go away*, I thought as Oliver prodded at me. *Leave me be.*

Clémence nudged the side again, and I could hear the horses down the road. They were getting close. I took a steadying breath, then wormed myself through the narrow gap into the coffin. Clémence shut the lid without another word, and I was left drowning in darkness.

I don't know how long I lay in the dark, trying not to think about where exactly it was I was lying, or about the day we buried Oliver, or the riders I could hear on the other side of the wooden walls that suddenly felt impossibly thin. The wagon stopped and started a few times, and I heard Depace's wheezy voice joined by others, though I couldn't make out individual words. My heart was beating so loudly I was sure it would give me away. After a few long minutes, the wagon started moving at a steady pace, but it was still a while before the coffin lid was flung open.

I flinched, but it was only Clémence, her round white face floating above me. "You can come out," she said. "Unless you're cozy."

I heaved myself out and collapsed across from her again, the coffins on either side scraping against my hip bones. The cold was sharper now, and the sweat from our sprint across the city was starting to dry and leave me shivering. I tucked my hands into my sleeves.

Across from me, Clémence huddled down against one of the coffins and pulled her scarf up over her face. "Get comfortable," she said. "It's a long way."

Our journey to Ingolstadt continued in much the same way as in those early hours, with Clémence and me hunched between the coffins until we approached a checkpoint, and then we climbed inside. Rather than risk being caught trying to sneak over the border, we went through Basel, a port city on the Rhine, and crossed from there into Germany. The border checkpoint took hours to get through, and when the patrol finally reached our wagon, there was enough banging and knocking about to make me stop breathing. "If they open the coffin, just lie very still," Clémence had advised me. "Most men won't bother the dead."

But we made it through without incident, and passed into the German Confederation. Clockwork regulations weren't as strict here, but I was still a wanted man without papers, and I kept a sharp eye out for trouble. Every cart or pedestrian we passed had me ducking out of sight and wishing for some better defense than hiding.

As we trudged along the snowy country roads, Depace sang tuneless Christmas carols that the wind carried back to us. Clémence and I spoke very little. The morning after we left Geneva, I got my first good look at her in the light. She was dead thin and pale, made paler by her brilliant blond hair, which I realized was properly white now that I saw it in the sunshine. Her eyes were as blue as Lake Geneva, and her best smile was no more than a smirk, so it felt as though she was always sneering at me. It reminded me a bit of Oliver, and I had to swallow that hot guilt back yet again.

All the traveling in silence left me little to do but fret over whether I'd done the right thing in leaving him, until I thought I might go mad with it. I hated myself for abandoning him, and hated myself more for that small piece of me that was relieved for having an excuse to go. I hadn't been away from Oliver for two years. Leaving still had its hooks in, but a part of me—a dark and wretched part—felt free.

Bavaria was all gray rolling hills and ghostly forests, with black pines that dropped snow on us from above and bare cedars wrapped in thorny mistletoe. We plodded across it for two days beyond the border before

Ingolstadt appeared on the road signs. I was shattered from all the travel and the constant worry about being caught, but my exhaustion faded as the houses spotting the hills began to multiply and the white spire of the university approached on the horizon.

There were no guards at the city limits—something that I once would have given no thought to, but after three years in Geneva it seemed a wonder. Clémence climbed onto the driver's seat to talk with Depace, leaving me to stare out the back of the wagon at the copper-capped buildings passing by.

Ingolstadt was a small town, and the mechanization that had shaped Geneva had hardly touched it. There were no factories or clockwork carriages or cogged omnibuses. No looming clock tower or industrial torches to illuminate the night. No prowling policemen either, and I spotted a few men with mechanical arms and legs walking unveiled. No one crossed to the other side of the street to avoid them or spit on them as they passed. Perhaps not a paradise, and not full equality—I didn't think the world would ever reach that point—but Ingolstadt could be close. It felt for the first time since we'd left Geneva like the danger had truly passed, and I could breathe again.

The university sat in the town's center—a monument to which every other building seemed to bow. Clémence directed Depace to stop at the gate; then she hopped down and I clambered after her, my spine cracking loudly as I stretched. We stuck out sorely among the students crossing campus, wrapped up in velvet cloaks and amber furs, but if we got curious looks, I didn't notice. I was too busy staring openmouthed at the stonework, the stained glass, the tapestries that lined the walls of the colonnades. I felt the pull again—the want I'd nursed since childhood, to study here with Geisler—so strong it hurt. I tried to imagine myself as a student, swapping test scores with mates as we crossed the snowy courtyard to the next lecture, but as hard as I squinted, I couldn't do it. Perhaps because whenever I tried to picture anything ahead of me, it was with the nagging notion that Oliver would always be nearby, holding me back.

Clémence led me into a gray stone building and up three flights of stairs before she stopped in front of a wooden door and knocked.

"Enter," called a voice.

Geisler's office was neat to the point of manic tidiness, with books on the shelves sorted by color and subject before they were finally alphabetized, and quill pens laid out by size, in descending order. The weak sunlight rippled through the green glass windows, casting a sickly shadow over the whole room that made me feel as though I were standing in the emerald cover of *Frankenstein*. A single beam fell through a clear pane at the top, illuminating the man himself, bent over a stack of parchment at his desk.

I had known Geisler since I was a boy, and in all that time I swear he'd never aged. I had watched Father go gray around the temples, then the eyebrows, then start wearing his spectacles permanently, but Geisler was just as I remembered, redheaded, with a thick beard bearing a single swatch of white down its center.

He looked up as we entered, and his eyes bugged at me through the fickle light. He whipped his spectacles from his face and stood up, as though he couldn't believe what he was seeing.

"Dr. Geisler," I said, when Clémence didn't make a sound.

As soon as I spoke, his face lost its glow and his eyes returned to their usual size. "Alasdair Finch," he said, his French edged by German vowels I assumed Ingolstadt had given him. "It's been some time."

"Some time," I repeated stupidly. With Geisler staring at me, I felt like a boy again.

"It is . . ." He polished his spectacles on the tail of his jacket, then placed them back on his nose and squinted at me. "Quite extraordinary, I must say, to see you standing here before me." He inched closer, still examining me with tight scrutiny, as though making sure I was truly who he thought I was. "You have grown," he said at last.

Clémence snorted, quietly enough that only I heard. I swallowed a terse remark in favor of a cordial "Yes, sir." If I was going to be enjoying Geisler's hospitality in Ingolstadt, I had to keep a civil tongue, though that had never been the struggle for me that it was for Oliver.

"You look . . ." He stared at me for a moment longer, then removed his spectacles again and tucked them in his pocket. At last he looked me in the eye in a manner that suggested conversation rather than inspection. "Remarkably like your brother." His smile lines creased.

I swallowed hard. "So I'm told."

"I thought for a moment you were he. It startled me." He clapped me on the shoulder, hard enough that my knees buckled. "Alasdair, I'm very pleased you're here! We have so much to discuss. So much." He bustled back to his desk and rooted through a drawer for a moment before producing a copper kettle. "Tea, perhaps? Or something stronger?"

"We should go home," Clémence interrupted. She was standing soldier straight, hands behind her back. "We've had a journey."

Geisler frowned at her. "Are you speaking for our guest?"

"I was thinking of him," she replied, her chin dipping to her chest. "He must be tired."

"Alasdair, what do you think?" Geisler glanced in my direction as though hoping I would disagree, but all I could think about was sleep.

"I'd like to get some rest," I replied.

"Ah. Well, that's understandable." He looked a bit disappointed, but he replaced the teapot and slid the drawer closed with his knee. "I'll take you to my home, then. We can have some supper, and you can rest, and we'll leave the business for later."

I still didn't have a guess at what that business was, but I nodded. Geisler retrieved his coat from the door and the three of us started back the way Clémence and I had come, across the courtyard, toward the university gates. I had the sense that he wanted to ask me something— many things, perhaps—but he kept his gaze forward, only tossing a few furtive glances in my direction. Beside me, Clémence stared up at the sky with her hands deep in her pockets. I looked up too, and noticed fat clouds, gray and thick with the promise of snow, shuffling in front of the sun. "Bad weather coming," she murmured.

"Thank you, mademoiselle," Geisler replied tersely. "Now we all have a firm grasp of the obvious."

Clémence buried her mouth in the collar of her coat and fell silent.

"Ingolstadt is lovely in spring," Geisler said to me as we crossed the snow-spangled courtyard, Clémence a few steps behind. "The winters can be bleak, but when the flowers bloom in April, it's a sight."

"How . . . nice," I said, unsure what response he was chasing.

"We should talk about your application while you're here." He looked sideways at me. "Your father told me once you wanted to study at the university. Is that still true?"

I nodded. "Yes, sir."

"Medicine or mechanics?"

"Both, if I could."

"Ingolstadt's one of the only schools in Europe where you can. You'd do well here, I think. I should introduce you to the head of my department. Make sure he knows your name. Lectures are nearly finished for the term or I'd find some for you to sit in on. And when your application comes in, I'll be sure to put in a good word."

"That's . . ." I had one moment of delirious happiness before I remembered the whole reason I hadn't applied to begin with. "That'd be brilliant, sir, thank you," I finished, trying gallantly to infuse my voice with some of the excitement I'd felt before I thought, yet again, of Oliver.

Geisler nodded at a pair of students passing in the opposite direction. "And what's the news out of Geneva these days? I heard the clock tower is finished."

"Yes, sir. The clock will strike on Christmas Eve."

"I'll bet it's a sight. I wish I could see it."

I glanced sideways at him, trying to work out whether he meant it in earnest. The reason Geisler had gone to

Geneva was that the city hired him to oversee constructing the clock, then had him arrested when they found out he was using their money and the room behind the face as a front for his own research. I couldn't imagine he harbored much fondness for the clock tower after that, but perhaps we were alike in thinking that all mechanical things—even the ones with jagged memories attached— were magnificent.

"And how are your parents?" Geisler asked as we left the campus and turned onto the cobbled street.

Clémence coughed in what I assumed was a too-late attempt to sidestep the topic. My stomach clenched.

"They were arrested," I said, "the night your assistant came to collect me."

"God's wounds." Geisler stopped walking. Clémence smashed into him, and he cuffed her on the ear before turning to face me dead on. "I didn't know. Alasdair, I'm so sorry." He rolled his lips into his mouth for a moment and released a heavy breath through his nose, sending steamy clouds rising above his beard that reminded me of a dragon. "I never thought they'd get your father, he was so sharp about staying hidden. And your mother, did they arrest her as well?"

I stamped my feet, less to keep warm and more for an excuse to stare at the ground. "I don't know."

"What about your brother?"

I gave him a moment to realize his mistake, but he

didn't, and when I met his gaze, he looked so unapologetic and earnest that it frightened me.

"Oliver's dead," I said.

"Yes. Of course. How foolish of me." He pivoted sharply and started again up the sloping road, Clémence and I following as the clouds sank across the rooftops, draping the street in shadows.

Geisler's home was outside the city limits and shielded from the road by a grove of towering black pines. It was larger than most of the slender town houses along the main streets, with a yard behind it outlined by a trim fence. We stopped on the doorstep, and Geisler fumbled through his bag for a while before swearing under his breath. "Must have left my keys in the office," he mumbled. "Never mind." He knocked on the door, and I heard the sound echo through the house. I thought it strange he hadn't asked Clémence for her set, but one look at her tight jaw told me she had yet to be trusted with her own.

There was a shuffling creak from the other side; then, a moment later, the door was flung open. I gasped aloud before I could stop myself. On the threshold stood a man made entirely of gears and bars and metal plates, but walking, upright and of its own accord. Its eyes were glassy and its mouth a rigid, lipless rectangle that I couldn't have fit a finger through. It stepped back from the door to let us in, each step stiff-kneed and ticking.

Geisler walked past it as he stripped off his coat, and Clémence followed. I edged in after them, keeping my eyes on the clockwork *thing*, not certain exactly what it was or what it was about to do.

The mechanical man pushed the door closed, then made a sharp turn and held out its arm. Geisler draped his fur-trimmed cloak over it. "Give it your coat," he instructed me, nodding at something over my shoulder. I jumped as another metal man, identical to the first, rattled out of a doorway off the entrance hall carrying a dressing gown.

Clémence smirked as I dodged it. "Don't fret, they don't bite." She pushed me forward into its path. "It's just an automaton."

I looked from her to Geisler. "An automaton?" I repeated. "But it's . . ."

"Sentient?" Geisler offered. "Not to the capacity I would like." He fed his arms through the sleeves of the dressing gown the automaton extended for him. "They have the mental faculties of a dull dog, and the ocular function as well. Only basic sight and auditory cues, but, like a dog, they can be trained, and they do learn over time. Not as fast as I'd like, but they do learn. By now they seem to know what I'm asking, though it took a hell of a long time to get them to this level."

"You made them?" I asked as the first automaton

shuffled toward me, its arms outstretched. I thrust my coat forward, which satisfied the metal man into retreat.

"Of course," Geisler replied. "Though they are hardly the masterpiece I envisioned when I first considered giving life to clockwork. They have no capacity for original or independent thought, no personality, and they couldn't function without specific direction. Nothing compared to my original designs for the resurrected man." He looked over at me, so quickly I almost thought I imagined it. When I didn't say anything, he smiled. "Well then. Let me show you the house."

Geisler gave me a brief tour, poking his head into each room just long enough to allow me a glimpse. Somewhere on the first floor we lost Clémence, and I assumed she had chosen sleep over seeing a home she already knew. The rooms were as tidy as his office had been, and everything was lit with Carcel burners—lamps with clockwork pumps in the base to circulate the oil and keep the flames burning longer, far too expensive for my family to afford. There were clocks everywhere—each room had at least one. Between the clocks, the mechanical lamps, and the automatons, which seemed reluctant to let Geisler out of sight, the whole house buzzed like a hive.

At the end of the second-floor corridor, Geisler led me into a small room with an iron-framed bed and a writing desk wedged into one corner beside a leaping fire. There were three clocks on the mantelpiece, pendulums swinging out of sync with each other and clicking loudly. "This can be yours," he said, stepping back to let me in. "I had fresh linens put down, but it hasn't been used in a while, so it may be dusty."

"That's all right." I crossed the room to the window. The first flakes of snow were starting to brush ghostlike against the rippled glass. The room looked out across the back garden, where fingers of sharp brown grass stabbed upward through the snow. I could see a coach house and a squat stone building nearly as wide as the main house, though single storied and with a thatched roof. "What's that?" I asked Geisler, and he stepped to my side.

"My workshop. Though I hardly use it now. I do most of my work at the university."

"Do you think you could show it to me?" I asked. "I'd love to see—"

Geisler cut me off with a laugh. "You certainly are eager. I'll show you if you like, but there's hardly anything out there." He put a firm hand on my elbow and turned me away from the window. One of the automatons had come in behind us and was standing so close that I started. "I've left some spare uniforms from the university in the dresser—why don't you change, we'll take a quick look at the workshop, then have some supper and a good talk?"

"Oh, I didn't mean I wanted to see the workshop now," I said, prying my arm from his grip. "Just . . . while I'm here."

"Supper, then?"

"I'd rather go to bed. If that's all right."

He squinted at me over the top of his spectacles, and for a moment he looked like he was going to argue. Then he nodded. "Of course it's all right. Completely sensible. I don't know what I was thinking, of course it can all wait until tomorrow, of course. Out!" he barked at the automaton that had followed us. It took several arthritic steps into the hallway. Geisler followed, but turned back to me in the doorway. "If you need anything at all, call out and one of them"—he nodded toward the automaton—"will come."

"All right," I said, though there wasn't a chance in hell I'd be calling the metal men into my bedroom.

"I've instructed them to make you comfortable. I do hope you're comfortable here." He smiled at me with such a sincere affection it felt foreign.

"Thank you, sir."

"Sleep well, then," he said, his face golden and warm in the firelight. Then he shut the door with a soft snap.

As soon as Geisler was gone, I stripped down to almost nothing and fell on top of the bed, which, I discovered with a stab of delight, was stuffed with feathers—I hadn't had a feather mattress since we'd lived in Scotland.

The house around me was quiet but not silent, with the three clocks ticking out of sync on my mantelpiece and drumming into my thoughts like dissonant heartbeats, joining the clamor already ringing around my head when I wondered again what I was doing here instead of back in Geneva with Oliver and my parents. I pressed the heels of my hands against my eyes and took a deep breath, trying to quiet my brain enough to sleep, but everything inside me felt riotous.

I stood, crossed the room in two strides, and ripped open the face of the first clock. I tugged a handful of gears from inside, pinching my finger hard in the process, and the clock froze, pendulum halting as suddenly as if I had seized it. I could have stopped the clock by removing a single piece, but I wasn't looking to be delicate or kind, I just wanted it quiet.

I silenced the other two clocks, then dropped the gears on the desk. It was quieter than before, but I was still left thinking about Oliver. No chance of ripping him out of me.

I wondered what he would say if he were here with me. Not the Oliver I had now, but the Oliver from before, the one who sought out strange adventures because they'd make a good story. Being brought to a solitary house on the cusp of a snowstorm by a girl with white hair—he'd go wild for that. It could be the start of a horror novel, he'd say, the sort Mary claimed she'd someday write. When I closed my eyes, I could picture him as he had been before he died: dark hair tousled, eyes alive with excitement, his fingers scratching at his bottom lip, always thinking. "It's never simple, Ally," he would say to me. "Nothing's ever the way it looks straight on."

He'd said that to me in Amsterdam. The first time he'd been arrested. I remembered it suddenly, like a door opening inside me, and heard his voice in my head. My memory shifted into an image of him standing in the police station while they took the irons off him, grinning at me like it was all a stupid joke.

I'd been the only one home when an officer came to inform us my brother had been arrested for punching out a man's teeth, and instead of waiting for my parents, I'd taken one of the bill rolls we kept stashed around our flat and gone to fetch him myself so Father wouldn't find out. I'd stood in the waiting room at the station, lamps bright as noon though outside everything was frosty and black, and watched as the cuffs came off. The officer handed him back his coat, and I didn't even wait for him to put it on. I turned and left the station without a word.

I didn't say a thing to him as we walked along the frozen canals. The only way I knew he was following was the sound of his footsteps in the snow. We were halfway home before he said, "You're walking so fast."

My temper flared against his voice like a struck match. "I want to get home."

"Can we stop?"

"No."

"Just for a moment."

"No."

"Ally, stop." He caught my arm, and I whirled around so fast he took a step back. "What's the matter?"

"Are you insane, or are you really as stupid as you act sometimes?" I cried, and I surprised myself with how loud and angry the words came out—I was usually so good at keeping my temper.

Oliver looked startled too. "What are you talking about?"

"I like it here! But if you go and do idiotic things like brawling in the street, we're going to get caught and have to leave. Or worse. And it will be your fault." The corners of my eyes were starting to pinch, and I scrubbed the back of my hand hard against them.

When I looked up, Oliver was watching me, his face tight. "I didn't mean to get into trouble."

"Well, somehow you always do." The words came out more teary than I meant them to.

We stood for a minute on opposite sides of the street, our shadows made skeletal by the lamplight. I was so angry at him. The angriest I'd ever been. Angry that he could be so careless and selfish, like I didn't matter to him at all.

Oliver turned away from me suddenly and took a few steps to the edge of the street until his toes were hanging over the short ledge above the frozen canal. He stood there for a moment, balanced, then eased himself down so that he was standing on the ice. His arms rose like a puppet on strings.

"What are you doing?" I called.

He grinned back at me, his smile a streak through the darkness—as bright as the frozen canal. "Come here."

"I haven't got skates."

"Neither have I."

"You're mental."

"Come on!" I didn't move. Oliver pushed himself off with his feet flat and slid straight ahead. He wobbled, but stayed upright. "This is brilliant," he called over his shoulder. "Can't believe you're missing it."

I hesitated, watching him glide away from me, then made an abrupt decision. I sat down on the lip of the canal and lowered myself onto the ice after him. I tried to stand like he had but lost my nerve at the last minute and sat down hard instead.

Oliver laughed. "Get up!"

"No!" I pulled myself after him on my backside, fingers sticking to the ice through the holes in my gloves.

Oliver laughed again, spinning in a half circle to face me. "Come on, Ally, get up!"

"I'm going to fall!"

"You won't fall! I'll help you." He held out a hand.

I pushed myself from my knees to my feet but stayed bent at the waist with my palms flat on the ice. When I did straighten, it was slowly, inch by inch, arms out at my sides and every muscle clenched. Oliver whooped encouragement.

I reached out for his hand, but as soon as I moved, my feet went in opposite directions. I tried to catch myself with a step but it turned to a stumble, and somehow I was sliding and running and falling all at the same time. I missed Oliver's hand and instead smashed straight into him. He grabbed me under the elbows so when I fell, we fell together, all the way down to the ice.

The landing smarted, but it didn't truly hurt, and it was so foolish that I laughed. Oliver laughed too, but then he winced, and my smile faded. "You all right?"

He held up his hand. In the splash of the streetlight, I could see that the skin of his palm was torn up and bloody, and there was a raw scrape running up his wrist and into his sleeve.

"Did that happen just now?" I asked, alarmed.

"No, it was . . . from earlier."

For a moment, I'd forgotten why we'd been out here to begin with, but it came back suddenly. Somewhere between the street and the canal, my anger had left me, floated away like snow on the wind, but I could still feel the weight of it between us. "The policeman said . . . He told me you punched a man. Is that how you hurt your hand?"

"No, that idiot shoved me and I fell on it. Then I punched him." Oliver blew a foggy breath into the air, then leaned backward until he was lying flat on the ice. I was already shivering, but I stretched out beside him, our heads together, staring up at the splash of stars above us. We didn't speak for a while. Then Oliver said, "There was this beggar on the street. He had a clockwork leg, but it was run-down and rusted, and his skin was infected. Bloody mess. I tried to help him and some bastard grabbed me and started calling me names and knocked me down. I didn't attack him, I just fought back. The police didn't arrest him, though. Just me, because I was helping the clockwork chap." He pressed his tight fist against the ice. The scrape on his wrist left a smear of pale crimson. "Nothing's ever that simple, Ally," he said then. "It's never just 'I hit him' or 'he hit me' or he was right and I was wrong. Everything's always got sides and angles and all sorts of bits you can't see. Nothing's ever the way it looks straight on."

I fell asleep remembering that—lying beside Oliver on the iced canal, our breath frosty and warm as it drifted up and away from us into that black, black night.

I woke suddenly, like an impact from a high fall. The fire had died to pulsing coals, and the sky outside was black. I climbed out of bed, flinching as my bare feet connected with the cold floorboards, and cupped my hands against the window to look out. The snow had swelled into a blizzard, and thick white flakes obscured the yard. I could hardly make out Geisler's workshop through it.

I dressed in the dark, not certain why I was up so early, or whether it was actually early or simply dark from the storm. The gutted clocks on the mantelpiece were still stuck at the same time they had been the day before. So, dressed in one of the large university uniforms Geisler had left, I abandoned my room to see if anyone else was awake.

The house was dark and silent but for the syncopated clicking of dozens of clocks. At the bottom of the stairs, I spotted a light and followed it to the kitchen, where a fire was burning in the grate. A loaf of bread was laid out on the table, a knife stuck into the cutting board next to it. My stomach growled audibly.

I wiggled the knife out of the board and started to saw off a slice of bread when something knocked into me from behind. I whipped around, knife held in front of me. It was one of the automatons, its arm outstretched, coming forward. I tried to dodge out of its way, but it knocked into me again so hard that I fell into the table. The legs screeched against the stone floor. The automaton took another shuffling step closer, and I considered burying the knife in it and hoping that jammed up its works, but stabbing servants—mechanical or not—didn't seem like the appropriate way to repay Geisler for taking me in.

The automaton's head twisted slowly until its glassy eyes were fixed on the knife in my hand. My grip on the handle tightened. "Like hell," I said, though I wasn't certain it understood. "You may not have this."

The automaton reached out. I tried to duck out of its way, but its hand fastened around my fist holding the knife and squeezed. I yelped in pain as my fingers buckled beneath its iron grip.

There was a *whoosh* as a door on the other side of

the room opened, blowing in a handful of snowflakes and Clémence, dressed in the same trousers and gray coat from the day before. Her white hair was fuzzy with snow. She stared across the room at me, bent backward over the table by the advancing automaton that I was certain was about to rip me to pieces with the knife it was trying to break out of my hand.

And she *laughed*. "You've got to let it slice the bread."

"What?" The automaton took another step forward, knees cracking against mine, and I flinched.

"It wants to serve you—that's what it's made for. It won't back off until you let it cut the bread."

"Are you certain that's all it's keen on cutting?" I asked.

Clémence flopped down beside the fire and raised her hands to the flames. "Never mind. Let it snap your fingers if you want."

I glared at the back of her head, then loosened my grip on the bread knife so that it slid from my fingers to the automaton's. The mechanical man straightened immediately, and I wiggled out from between it and the table as it took a lurching step toward the bread and began to saw at it. When it had a slice, the automaton pivoted sharply and extended it to me.

I took it. "Er, thank you."

Its spine snapped straight, then it turned and headed out of the room, each step ticking.

Clémence was watching me with her mouth twisted up in that stupid smirk. I glowered at her, then sank down in front of the fire and started to eat. The automaton had scared the hunger straight out of me, but I had gone to too much trouble to get the bread not to eat it.

"Sleep well?" Clémence asked.

"Yeah, good enough." I glanced over at her and realized she was shivering, arms wrapped around herself and cheeks pinched scarlet. "Are you all right?"

"Yes."

"You're freezing. Here." I cast around for something to warm her, but she cut me off.

"I said I'm all right. Let me save you the trouble of stripping off your shirt in an attempt to be gallant."

"Can I make you tea?" My eyes darted to the hallway. "Will they come after me if I try?"

"Not if you're sneaky about it," she replied.

I stood up and retrieved the kettle from the counter. It was already full. "What were you doing out so early?" I asked as I hung it over the fire.

"What are you doing up so early?" she returned.

"All the traveling mucked me up," I replied. "And my father always has me up early. It's habit. What time is it anyways?"

"I'm not sure." Clémence stood up for a better view of the clock on the mantelpiece, which, I realized after a silent moment, wasn't running. "Damn, it's stopped."

"Probably just needs to be wound."

"No, they're not made to be wound. Geisler started them with the pulse gloves." She flipped open the lid of the clock and stared at it as though unsure what she was looking for. Then she shut it and slumped back down onto her stool. "Never mind, he can fix it when he gets up."

"Here, let me." Clémence passed me the clock and I opened the face. I saw the problem right away—the gears were still moving, but the balance wheel was out of place. As soon as I tugged it forward on its axel, the clock sprang to life, and I replaced it on the mantelpiece.

"Well done," Clémence murmured.

"Couldn't you fix it?"

She frowned. "What's that supposed to mean?"

"You're Geisler's assistant. How'd you come about that job if you don't know how to fix a clock?"

Clémence stared into the fire, and I wasn't sure if it was the reflection of the flame on her face or if she was actually blushing. Then she looked back at me, pale as ever, and I guessed I had imagined it. "I could have fixed it," she said. "I just wanted to see if you are as clever as Geisler seems to think you are."

When two of the automatons took over the kitchen to fix breakfast, I carried my tea into the sitting room and settled in a chair beside the fire. Clémence followed, for reasons I couldn't fathom, and took a spot on the chaise across from me. "Are you afraid of them?" she asked.

"Of the automatons?" I shrugged. "They're a bit unnerving, aren't they?"

"More than living men who are half mechanical?"

"At least with clockwork men, there's some bit of them that's human."

"That's not a common opinion. Most people think you surrender your humanity if you adopt clockwork parts."

"I grew up a Shadow Boy—I'm not *most people*." I took a sip of tea and winced. It needed sugar, but there was no chance I'd brave the kitchen now that it was full of metal men.

A gust of wind blew down the chimney, and the flames in the grate parted for a moment. Clémence turned her gaze out the window. "We're lucky we beat the storm," she said. "It's not usually this bad."

"It used to snow like this all the time in Bergen."

"You lived in Bergen?"

"When I was young." I took another sip of tea, stupidly hoping it would taste better. It did not. "My family was thrown out of Edinburgh when my father started working with Geisler, so we went there."

"I've heard Norway is cold and dark all year."

"No, not at all. At least Bergen isn't. It looks out on this bay and across the fjords, and they're mostly green and lovely." I remembered something suddenly, and almost laughed before I'd told the story. "There was this poem Oliver—my brother—was really keen on when we were younger. It's about a pond or a lake or something. Some sort of body of water. And Oliver read somewhere that the pond—the real one, the one the poem is about—is outside of Bergen. So one day he took me out into the country, up into the fjords, and we walked for hours looking for that stupid pond. . . ."

I trailed off. I hadn't spoken about Oliver like this—stories from before—to anyone since he died, not even to my parents, and suddenly I could see him so clearly from that day, the sun on his face and the wind running its fingers through his curly hair as he darted up the path ahead of me, then turned back to wait until I caught up. Oliver, the way he used to be. The memory snarled something up inside me.

I watched the flames stretch up into the chimney, hoping Clémence wouldn't say anything more about it, but after a moment she asked, "Is there an ending to that story?"

"It wasn't really a story," I replied. "Just something I thought of."

"Did you find the pond?"

"No, turns out it *was* fictional." I picked up my teacup and drained it in two swallows. "Not a real place at all."

An automaton came in with its arms full of kindling,

and we fell silent. I didn't want to talk about Oliver anymore. I didn't want to talk at all, but Clémence was watching me like she had more to say. I searched around for something to show I was done with her, and my gaze caught on a book on the end table. I recognized the green binding, and knew what it was before I picked it up— *Frankenstein, or The Modern Prometheus.* The same book Mary had sent, with that strange title and no author, and I remembered that Morand had told me it was about Geisler.

I flipped through it, scanning the pages without really reading, wondering if I'd see his name somewhere. A block of text stood out, centered and lonely, and I stopped.

Like one, that on a lonesome road
Doth walk in fear and dread,
And having once turned round walks on,
And turns no more his head;
Because he knows, a frightful fiend
Doth close behind him tread.

I had to read it twice before I realized why it sounded familiar. It was the Coleridge poem Oliver had recited last time I'd gone to see him. It felt like such an impossible coincidence that I scanned the rest of the page. The last sentence jumped out.

*"Of my creation and creator I was absolutely
ignorant, but I knew that I possessed no money,
no friends, no kind of property. I was, besides,
endued with a figure hideously deformed by the
infernal engine that made me; being formed of
metal, I was not even of the same nature as man."*

My stomach lurched. The words felt familiar—not
because I'd read them before, but because they sounded
like Oliver. I flipped a few pages further, so fast I sliced
my finger on the edge.

*"'Hateful day when I received life!' I exclaimed
in agony. 'Accursed creator! Why did you form
a mechanical monster so hideous that even you
turned from me in disgust?'"*

I slammed the book shut hard enough that Clémence
glanced up from her tea. "You all right?"

"Fine," I said, but the words were beating in my
brain like blows from a hammer, a hollow echo of every
conversation I had had with my brother over the past
two years.

This book wasn't about Geisler. It was about resurrection.

"Oh, you're awake."

I jumped and almost dropped the book. Geisler was standing in the sitting room doorway, wrapped in a maroon dressing gown with his spectacles perched on his forehead. I jammed *Frankenstein* between the cushions and stood up. "Good morning, Doctor."

"Hardly morning yet." He brushed past me and sat down in the chair I had just vacated. Clémence had sat up straighter and was watching him warily from across the room. Geisler returned her stare. "You have work elsewhere, mademoiselle," he said. She stood without a word and glided from the room like a ghost. I tried to catch her eye as she left, but she kept her head down. Geisler gestured at her empty place on the chaise. "Please, Alasdair, sit down."

I perched on the edge of the stiff cushion as one of the automatons came in with a tray. "Would you like some tea?" Geisler asked me as the automaton poured him a cup.

"I've already had some."

"I'll have it left if you want more." Geisler frowned and reached between the armchair's cushions, emerging a moment later with *Frankenstein*. He smiled at the cover, then held it up for me to see. "Have you read it?"

"No, sir," I replied, though the words *accursed creator* were still ringing around my head like church bells.

"Really?" He set the book on the table and took up his teacup. "As a piece of fiction, it's sloppy and inept at best." He glanced at me over the rim, then, just before he touched it to his lips, said, "But it has its merits in other areas."

I nodded, though books—even ones about clockwork and resurrection—were the last thing I wanted to talk about. I was burning to ask why he'd called me here, but I kept my mouth shut. He went on sipping his tea and staring at me with that same keen intensity he'd had when I first arrived. I felt dissected. Finally he set down his cup and steepled his fingers before his lips. His spectacles slipped off his forehead and settled on the tip of his nose. "How very like your brother you look," he said softly. "In this poor light, I could almost swear you were Oliver sitting across from me two years ago."

I didn't say anything. Behind me, the windows rattled as the snow struck them.

"I'm sure the comparisons are endless," Geisler continued, "but you aren't like him at all, aside from the physical resemblance. After knowing Oliver so well, I find your stoicism startling. Nothing on your face, whereas with your brother—as soon as he felt something, you knew it. It was written all over him."

"I know," I said.

Geisler picked up *Frankenstein* again and turned it over. "Your father, he was never very clever," he said after a moment. "A good man, yes, but not particularly clever. When I met him, you were just a boy. Do you remember?"

"I remember," I said. I had been small, but not too small to recognize when life changed. Near my sixth birthday, Father had started taking apart clocks, skipping supper, carrying spanners and hammers in his bag alongside his surgical instruments. Our Edinburgh town house had been overrun by a new and unfamiliar group of men with limps and twisted arms, and it had all been prefaced by the first visit of the red-bearded man that Father called Geisler. I hadn't been certain what it all meant then, but I understood well enough that some irrevocable shift had occurred.

"We need good men for our cause," Geisler continued. "But I'd rather have clever men, and I find that most are one or the other. You're either good, or you're clever." He smiled as he took another sip of tea. "Now, your brother, he was clever. Not with machinery—he was never interested in that—but certainly clever. He wrote well, thought deeply. When I heard that he'd died . . ." He trailed off and ran a hand over his beard.

It had never occurred to me what I'd say if Geisler asked for the details of Oliver's death. I couldn't use my rehearsed story about the accident in the clock tower— the only living person who could say otherwise was sitting across from me.

But he didn't ask. Instead he finished, "I was devastated. I was very fond of him."

I almost laughed. Oliver hated Geisler, even before

he thought him responsible for his death, and from what he'd told me, they'd never gotten on. The only reason Oliver hadn't been at the workshop the night Geisler was arrested was that they'd had a row and Oliver had come storming home early. But I didn't correct Geisler. I just let him sigh for a minute until he said, "I still wonder if I could have done anything to prevent it."

"Nothing," I said. "You couldn't have done anything."

"If I hadn't asked you to go back for those damn journals."

"You couldn't have done anything," I repeated. My insides were in hard knots.

"But you found them—my journals?" I nodded. "What happened to them?"

"I don't know, sir. I think the police got them when they cleaned out the workshop."

I thought he'd be angry about this—perhaps he'd called me here hoping I could reunite him with his research, but I'd abandoned them in the clock tower once we took Oliver to the castle and never gone back— but instead he smiled. "But not before you put them to good use."

My heart made a sudden hurtle into my throat. "Sir?"

"Did you read them?"

I tugged at a stray thread on my trousers and focused on keeping my face blank. "A little."

"So you saw the problems. The holes. The gaps where

my work fell short. I've never been able to surpass the research I conducted in Geneva, or even duplicate it. And even then, at its best it was flawed. There were too many problems I could never puzzle out." He looked up at me, firelight glinting off his spectacle lenses and turning them to brimstone. "But you did."

My heart kept up its frantic rhythm, but I said nothing. I wasn't certain I'd have been able to get words out if I had tried.

"It was you, wasn't it?" Geisler continued, still watching me. "Your father isn't clever enough, but you are." He sat up a little straighter, bringing his eyes back into focus. "Oliver is alive," he said, and it was hardly a question, "because you brought him back from the dead."

It seemed pointless to deny what he had already guessed, pointless to continue carrying this heavy load on my own any longer. My heart sank back to my chest; muscles I hadn't realized I'd kept clenched for two years loosened as I handed the weight of Oliver over to him. "Yes," I said.

Geisler sprang up out of his chair—he seemed to be resisting doing some sort of jig or pulling me into a hug. "And he's all right, is he? Still alive, clockwork heart still ticking two years later?"

"Yes," I said. "He's hiding in Geneva."

"You are a wonder, Alasdair Finch, an absolute wonder!" he cried as he sank back into his chair. I wasn't sure what I was meant to say to that. I expected him to press me for more details of the process itself—the exact weight of the copper I had used, the circumference of the gears and the placement of the mainspring. But instead he said, "How difficult that must be for you, keeping your brother's life a secret."

"It is," I said, and admitting it felt like taking a deep breath after being underwater. "I think I did something wrong when I brought him back. He lost parts of himself."

"Speech? Memory? I thought that might happen."

"It's more than that. He's not the same as he was. He's wild. Impulsive."

"He was like that when he was younger."

"But it's sharper now, it's different. He's . . . wrong. I must have done something that ruined him."

"And your parents know nothing?"

"No," I said. "I never told them."

"Then perhaps I can offer you some assistance that you so clearly need." He leaned forward, elbows on his knees. "What if you were to begin at the university in January? If I were to give my department head a recommendation on your behalf, you'd be allowed to start classes in the new term without having to bother with an application."

"What about Oliver?" I asked.

"Bring him with you," Geisler replied. "The German

Confederation is far kinder to clockwork men than France or Switzerland or any of the cities where your family has worked. And in a town like Ingolstadt, a progressive university town that values research . . . well, he may not be wholly accepted, but he will not have to hide. He could attend some classes at the university himself. He was fond of poetry, wasn't he?"

"Once," I said, and I could hear Oliver's voice reciting Coleridge in my head. *Because he knows, a frightful fiend / Doth close behind him tread.* "I'm not sure he still is."

"Well, perhaps we can rekindle that. And if not, we can find him a job, something to keep him occupied. But the main point is that he will not be your burden alone, Alasdair. I can help you care for him. You don't have to think of him constantly, as I'm sure you do now. You can go to lectures. Meet young people your age. You don't have to be the only one taking care of your brother any longer."

It was like I had been sitting at the bottom of a river for two years, weighed down by Oliver, and with every word Geisler removed a stone from my pocket and I felt myself begin to rise, the surface in sight and sunlight rippling off the water. I felt light, lighter than I had in maybe my whole life.

I thought I could rise no higher, but Geisler continued. "You will work alongside me, of course. Not as my assistant, but my partner. You'll show me the process you used to resurrect Oliver, and we can see that the psychological defects he suffered won't happen again."

A stone sank back into my chest. "I'm not sure it should be done again."

"Nonsense. Do you have any idea what people will pay for it? And think of the notoriety! You are a pioneer of one of the greatest achievements of all time! Alasdair, you will be canonized in the bible of science."

I could have lived and died in those words, but then I thought of what I had put Oliver through when I brought him back—his waking in agony with no memory, the way he suffered every day at the mercy of his clockwork body, the gears that pinched his skin and tore what was left of him to shreds. I wasn't sure I was ready to inflict that on anyone else, nor the pain of being an outcast. But perhaps with Geisler beside me we could rid the outcome of the less desirable side effects. And with more people like him, Oliver wouldn't be so alone.

"Of course, if you are to work with me, our research would have to be kept secret until we were ready to reveal it," Geisler said as he picked up his teacup. He chuckled as the rim touched his lips. "No more embarrassing little slipups."

That tugged me from my thoughts. "Sorry, what?"

"Alasdair." He held my name with a long, lean smile. "Did you think it was so opaque that I wouldn't see your signature all over it? Surely all this was meant to attract my attention. And you wanted to brag. It's natural."

"I'm sorry, sir, but I don't know what you're talking about."

"I'm talking about this." He held up *Frankenstein*, spine toward me so I could see the title. The gold-leaf letters smoldered in the firelight.

"You think *I* wrote that?" I laughed out loud before I could stop myself. Oliver told me once I was border-line illiterate, and though he'd said it to be mean, it was barely an exaggeration. The thought of sitting down and writing an entire book, slim as it was, was daft. "Hell's teeth, what makes you think that?"

Geisler cocked his head like a bird. "Have you truly not read it?"

"I only heard about it for the first time last week. I know it's about clockwork. That's all."

"God's wounds, Alasdair." His face went pale, and when he spoke again, his voice wavered. "It's about bringing back the dead."

I'd already guessed it, but hearing him say it made everything inside me hush—a quiet so absolute it was several long seconds before I could drag words from it. "Using clockwork?"

"A resurrected mechanical man," Geisler replied. "The story is fictionalized, of course, but the premise is a damn ringer for what you've told me. And it's quite clear that the two leading characters are you and your brother."

"You . . . you think that book is about Oliver and me?"

"I have no doubt. How else did you think I guessed what you'd done? As soon as I read it . . ." He leaned forward and seized my shoulder. "Alasdair, you can be honest with me. I have people—friends—who can help us. We can still turn this in our favor."

"I didn't write it."

"If you're lying—"

"I'm not lying, sir, I swear it!"

"Then someone already knows." He stood up and took several halting steps across the hearth rug. "Who have you told about this?"

"No one. Not even my parents."

"You're certain no one knows? No friends, no one could have overheard you?"

I thought briefly of Mary, but I didn't want to have to explain her to Geisler. He was finally starting to see me as something other than Oliver's younger brother, and I wasn't going to spoil that by looking like a lovesick puppy. "No, sir."

"Oliver doesn't have contact with anyone?"

"Oliver could have written it," I said.

Geisler stared at me for a moment, then waved that away like stray smoke. "No."

"He used to write," I said, "before he died. He wanted to write poetry, why not this?"

"Because the portrayal of the resurrected man is less than favorable. Oliver would never paint himself such a way if he wanted any sort of recognition for it."

"He doesn't think he's a hero," I said. "He thinks he's a monster."

Geisler frowned. "I'll take that into account." He tossed the book to me, and it landed with a *flump* on the chaise. "You should acquaint yourself with it, Alasdair. This may prove more trouble than I'd care to deal with."

"How could a book be that much trouble?" I asked, though even as I said it I thought of the Frankenstein badges in Geneva.

"Because the whole continent is reading it," Geisler replied. "The account of a man turned monster. No one on God's green earth would want to come back if it meant coming back like this." He drained his teacup and set it back in its saucer so hard I was surprised it didn't shatter. "I recommend you spend the day reading," he said, glancing out the window at the sky turning from black to gray as the day surfaced. "I can't imagine you have anything else to occupy yourself."

He started for the doorway, but I called after him, "What happens . . . ?" and he stopped. I swallowed. "What happens if I say yes? If I agree to study with you?"

"Then we'd go to Geneva immediately," he replied.

"We'd fetch Oliver and bring him here, where you both will be safe."

"What about my parents?"

"If you're certain they've been arrested, then our time may be running out. With enough evidence, a conviction could happen before the end of the year."

I tallied the days in my head and realized that left us just shy of three weeks. "Could you help them?"

"I could try. I promise I will try."

I stared hard into the fireplace for a moment, my teeth working on my bottom lip. It seemed too far away to touch, too unreal to imagine that in a few weeks my whole world could be different. I could be free of my parents, free from Geneva and running and being so bleeding afraid all the time. I could be doing real, important work, work I'd dreamed about doing most of my life. And I'd have Geisler to help me take care of Oliver—I'd be free of him too.

"We can't leave until the snow clears," Geisler said. I could feel him watching me. "If you need to think about it."

"I don't," I said, and I looked up at him. "I'll go with you. And I'll show you where Oliver is."

His face relaxed into almost a smile. "I'm glad to hear it. It's the only sensible option, you do realize that, don't you?" I nodded. Geisler took a few steps back into the room and placed his hand on my shoulder—a gesture more fatherly than anything I could ever remember from my own father. "You'll be safe this way," he said. "You both will."

"And what about *Frankenstein*?"

His eyes narrowed, mouth tightening to a thin razor in the firelight. "I suggest you take some time to read it," he replied. "Perhaps you can figure out who wrote your story."

7

Talking with Geisler left me empty and exhausted, and I went straight up to my room and collapsed onto the bed. My ears were ringing and I felt so thick with what he'd told me that I couldn't think clearly. As the sun rose behind the storm, I tried to sleep for a few more hours, but my eyes kept snapping open—like they were attached to springs—and finding their way to the writing desk where *Frankenstein* lay. The green binding looked more acidic than emerald now.

I didn't last long against it. After a few minutes of giving it a good stare, I threw back the bedcovers and snatched the book off the desk, then slid down in front of the fire, my back against the headboard, and cracked the spine.

It only took a few pages before my stomach started to roll.

The story starts on a steamship expedition in the north, when a group of explorers pull a man called Victor Frankenstein, half-starved and frozen, from the ice. And as he dies, Frankenstein tells the captain the story of his life and the work that led his to dying in the Arctic.

Reading Victor's narration was like listening to myself speak, as though I'd been hurled years into the future and was reading the diary of an older version of myself. It wasn't my exact history, but the parallels were clear. We both began our lives as children of privilege and science, fascinated by clockwork and mechanics and the men made from it.

And Ingolstadt!—God's wounds, Frankenstein left Geneva when he turned eighteen for Ingolstadt, same as I wanted to, to study clockwork and medicine and making metal limbs that move at the body's command. He even had a professor to guide him, and I kept picturing the man red-bearded like Geisler. But Victor took things further than his professors thought he could. He wanted to use clockwork to reanimate dead tissue and restore life. He was cleverer than everyone else, and he knew he could do better work than anyone before him.

And then—there it was.

It was on a dreary night of November that I beheld the accomplishment of my toils.

The resurrection: it stared up at me from the pages like a ghost.

I lingered over that scene for a long time, read it three times and tried to wed it with my memories of my own dreary night in November and map how they differed. It was bleeding strange to see what felt like the climactic moment of my life boiled down to a single page of short sentences that bellowed true inside me.

How can I describe my emotions at this catastrophe, or how delineate the mechanical wretch whom with such infinite pains and care I had endeavored to form from cogs and gears? I had desired it with an ardor that far exceeded moderation; but now that I had finished, the beauty vanished, and breathless horror and disgust filled my heart.

That was how it had felt—missing Oliver so badly, knowing I could bring him back, and then as soon as I had, wishing I could undo it. Mary had told me once that we saw ourselves in books because humans, being creatures of vanity, look for their own reflection everywhere, but I didn't think even she could have disputed that this was a thinly veiled version of my life.

I knew it deep in my bones, in a way I couldn't explain.

It was Oliver, and it was me.

It took everything in me not to hurl the book into the fire. The story deviated from mine and Oliver's after the resurrection—Victor fled Ingolstadt with his friend Henry and left his mechanical creation to navigate the world alone, which seemed to me the most cowardly thing he could have done until I thought of Oliver, locked up in Château de Sang. Had I run from him in just the same way?

I couldn't stomach it any longer. I set the book spine-up on the floor and flung myself into bed, hoping desperately for sleep. But I lay awake for a long time, the memories of Oliver's resurrection night flitting like moths through my mind.

After Oliver died, my father had wanted everything taken care of quick and clean, like it might somehow hurt less that way. There was no church funeral, no flowers or mourning clothes. Just four of us at the graveside—Father, Mother, and me with a priest—two days after Oliver's fall. The sky was salt gray, the ground soft and black after a night of rain. It was the first week of November. The first proper cold day we'd had since spring.

My parents stayed to make arrangements for the headstone, so I went back to the flat alone and lay on my pallet in the colorless afternoon light. Oliver's mattress was still unrolled beside mine, and I reached out and rested my hand on the bare ticking. It felt like keeping his memory in place, like there was still some shadow of him in the room and it was my responsibility to hold on to it. I didn't move, even when I heard my parents come in. I just lay there, thinking, with the sharp corners of Geisler's journals digging into my back from where I'd hidden them under my mattress.

Mary came that evening and threw stones at my window until I met her on the stairs to the flat. She was wearing a white cotton gown, too summery for the cold, and she looked so pale and bright against the overcast sunset. I stopped a few steps above her and looked down.

"I'm sorry I didn't come to the cemetery," she said.

"I didn't want you to." I'd hardly spoken in two days, and my voice came out coarser than I expected.

She nodded, looked down for a moment, then back at me, her eyes squinting up against the reflection of the sun on the shop windows. "Are you all right?"

"No." The question was so daft, I didn't even try to make my tone cordial. "Of course I'm not all right."

She licked her lips. "What can I do?"

Nothing, I thought. *You can't do a bleeding thing. You can't make me love you less. You can't change what I did or loosen the knots inside me or fill the hole that Oliver left. You can't bring my brother back.*

But I could.

I'd read the journals. I'd gone to the trial, heard all the details the police had scrounged up about the work Geisler was doing in the clock tower. And I knew what was wrong with it. On the first day Oliver and I sat up in the gallery, the barrister was describing the dissection Geisler had been caught in the middle of, an attempt to bond clockwork parts to the inside of a corpse, and I knew instinctively why it had gone wrong. Without ever seeing his laboratory or watching him work—I just knew.

The possibility of trying it for myself had seemed mad when I'd first considered it, but the last two days without Oliver—of living with myself and knowing what I'd done—had been so painful that when held up against them, the idea seemed strangely sane. The memory of Oliver falling from the top of the clock tower was clawing at my insides, begging to be written over, and even if everything went wrong, it couldn't be worse than what I'd done already.

"You can come with me," I said. "There's something I need to do."

Mary followed me all the way to the cemetery without a question. She must have thought I wanted to go to the graveside, show her where we'd buried him, and have my own funerary rites, but instead I led her along the fence to the shed where the gravediggers kept their spades and handcart. I had my hand around the lock and was fishing a needle file out my pocket before she finally asked, "What are you doing?"

My fist closed around the file, so tight I felt it break my skin. "I need . . . ," I started, but my throat closed up around the words and instead I tried, "I want . . ." When I looked up at her, she had taken a few steps backward, away from me. "I know I can do it," I said.

"Do what?"

"Geisler's journals. I've got them. I know . . . I can do something. I can fix this."

Her eyes widened with understanding, and she shook her head so hard a strand of her hair tumbled from its pins. "No, Alasdair, stop. You can't use Geisler's research. It's just theories—it's fiction!"

"I can do it, I know I can, I can do it better than Geisler. I can do it."

"Oliver's dead—that isn't something you can fix."

She reached out, and all at once something inside me broke like a snapped wishbone. The world tipped, the file slid out of my hand, and I had to crouch down so I didn't fall over. That raw, bleeding mess inside me that had been curled up for days had detonated suddenly, and the pieces embedded in me were so sharp that for a moment I couldn't breathe. I had never felt worse than I did right then, crouched in the graveyard dark, with everything building on my back, bile rising in my throat and my insides twisted up and pulled tight. I thought I

124

might be sick, but I wasn't. I just crouched there, head in my hands, and let myself shake until Mary's fingers slid along the back of my neck.

When I raised my face to hers, she looked so concerned that it made me want to scream. I didn't deserve compassion or pity from her—from anyone—when it was my fault my brother was dead. I felt like screaming. I felt like swearing and shouting and ripping something apart.

I felt monstrous.

I shook Mary off and retrieved my file from where it had fallen. Three sharp clicks with it and the lock snapped open. Mary watched with her arms wrapped around herself, and I knew from the way she was looking at me that there was something wrong with what I was doing. I didn't care.

I retrieved a spade from the shed, but Mary stepped in front of the doorway, blocking my way out. "Alasdair, don't do this. You need to go home."

I swallowed back the urge to scream again and instead said as calmly as I could, "I shouldn't have asked you to come. That was too much. You can go. You don't have to help me."

"I'm not leaving you alone," she replied stoutly. "You're out of your mind and you're going to do something you'll regret. You need to go home—"

I held out a spade. "If you won't leave, then help me."

I didn't need her help, but the thought of being alone—truly alone for the first time in my life now that Oliver was gone—was so bleeding terrifying, and she must have seen that fear in my face, for after a long, still moment of staring, she reached out and wrapped her fingers around the handle, on top of mine.

It took us hours to dig up Oliver's coffin. The ground was soft and heavy after the rain, and we were both covered in it before long, mud and grime running in tracks down our skin. It was cold but I was sweating, and I kept stripping off layers until I was in just my undershirt and trousers. Mary had cast aside her bonnet and jacket, and her hair had fallen out of its arrangement and into a single plait that whipped about her face. We didn't say a word to each other all the while we dug.

And then my spade hit wood with an empty *thunk*. The guilt sank its teeth in again, but I held myself together this time. The deeper we had dug, the more focused I had felt, and with the solid planks of the coffin under my feet, all the helplessness left me in a rush, and into its place funneled a cold and frightening calm.

Above me, I heard Mary murmur, "This is mad, Alasdair, this is absolutely mad." She lowered herself from the lip of the trench into the grave so she was standing beside me. She was so spattered with mud I could hardly see her apart from the night. "No more secrets," she said. "You have to tell me exactly what we're doing."

I didn't quite know myself. But I had Geisler's journals, and I had read them, and I knew what had ruined his resurrections. I had Geisler's journals and Oliver's body and a snarled mess of grief and anger and guilt inside me, and I was going to do something about it.

"We're going to the clock tower," I said. "We're going to bring Oliver back."

The snow fell hard and heavy for three days. I hadn't seen the sun since I arrived, and gusty winds made the windows clatter like something outside was trying to claw its way in. Everything was wet and cold, and though the automatons kept the fires blazing, I never felt properly warm.

Geisler was adamant in his refusal to leave for Geneva until the snow settled and we had the promise of a safe journey. Waiting became a study in torture for me. I paced around the house, unable to sit still without my mind shuffling from images of my parents in prison, waiting to be executed, to my brother locked up in Château de Sang, probably ripping it apart brick by brick in an attempt to get out. I could already be too late, my new life tossed away before it had begun, yet here we sat, holed up in the ticking house, waiting for the snowstorm to pass.

And the only thing to do was read *Frankenstein*.

I pressed on with it, but it never got easier or better. Even when the story ceased to be ours, reading about Victor Frankenstein and knowing he was me stung. He made me think of what Geisler had said—you were either good or clever, and Victor was clever. He'd made his clockwork monster because once he knew that it was possible, he had to try it for himself. He didn't consider what he would do if it worked until the corpse was sitting up on his laboratory table. That wasn't me, I told myself. I'd brought Oliver back because it was *Oliver*, and I'd missed him, and felt so damn guilty for what had happened that I had to do something about it. I hadn't done it to be clever.

But I'd spent two years lying to everyone about what had happened. Maybe this lie had snuck in too, and I'd spent all this time thinking that I'd brought Oliver back because I didn't know how to live without him when really it was because I had to test myself, see if I truly could fill the holes Geisler had left in his journals and do the thing no one else had.

Maybe it had been about me and my own cleverness all along. Maybe I was just the same as Victor. And the Oliver I'd meant to bring back felt so far away that sometimes I forgot he'd ever existed to begin with. Maybe this book was precisely who we were: Frankenstein and his monster, neither of us as good as we once had been.

Like Geisler, I began keeping my own list of possibilities for who had written the novel, but mine was significant only for how short it was. There had occurred to me one true possibility: Oliver. He was the only person with any reason to tell this story. But even that was unlikely. I didn't know how Oliver would have communicated with a printer and publisher without me knowing.

The other possibility was that Geisler himself had written it or somehow been involved. How he had captured some of the details, I didn't know—maybe he'd pieced together stories he'd heard, stories from Father or Oliver, or perhaps he had puzzled it out and gotten lucky. After all, it was us, but it wasn't our story, not exactly. But he knew the research. The novel could have been his invitation to me to come find him, but as I had not come quickly enough, he had sought me out. Perhaps he meant it as advertising for the work he wished to undertake. But that theory had more holes than my idea that it was Oliver.

And more than that, there were the small things in the book, the uncanny things that no one outside my life should know. Those few lines of Coleridge Oliver had recited. An epigraph from *Paradise Lost*. A mention of a hot springs near Geneva we'd visited with Mary, and a story about a lightning-struck tree that I could have told from my own memory of a night in Amsterdam. Phrases I couldn't read without hearing them in my brother's voice. It was these fragments more than anything else that made me certain it was a story about me by the only person with reason to tell it: Oliver.

There was one other person who knew what had happened: Mary. She knew nearly all of it, about Oliver and the resurrection and selected scenes from our strange lives before Geneva. Mary, the girl who lived in a lakeside villa with a gang of poets and novelists and loved scary stories and hauntings and tales about monsters. I thought of the letter she'd sent, sealed and lost somewhere in Geneva, and wished with a hollow pang that I'd had a chance to read it.

But it couldn't be Mary who wrote the book. I was so sure of it. It couldn't be Mary because I couldn't believe that the only person I'd ever chosen to put my trust in could turn on me.

All the while I'd known her, she had been my most valiant secret keeper. Oliver and I had both fed her secret after secret—what our father did, Oliver's work with Geisler, how much I wished it was me in his place—and she'd kept them all for us, stored away inside her as though they were her own. It couldn't be Mary because the whole reason we met her—the whole reason we all became more than just a forgettable moment in each other's lives—was that we had given her the secret of what our family did entirely by accident and had to put our trust in her before we knew her.

It happened the second week of May, the start of that summer in Geneva, with a storm beating in the season. I was alone in the shop—Mum and Father were at Geisler's trial, and Oliver had gone to meet Morand—when the door opened and the bell sang and a young woman with dark auburn hair came in, shaking the rain off her cloak.

"Bonjour," she called to me brightly. "May I wait here until the rain stops? I forgot my umbrella and I'm all the way in Cologny."

She was so pretty, and she spoke such fast, polished French that my brain got tangled up. All I managed to stammer was "Uh," which she seemed to take as permission to stay.

"Thank you so much, the weather's just frightful." She swept off her bonnet and flashed a brilliant smile in my direction. "It's been so wet lately, hasn't it? Even for spring. *Water, water, everywhere, / Nor any drop to drink*."

"That's Coleridge," I said without thinking. I was proud I recognized it, even though she said it in French.

She beamed. "Yes! Do you like Coleridge?"

"No, I've got a brother who does. But he's good," I added when she looked disappointed. "Coleridge, I mean. So I suppose I do, I like him. I don't know, I don't really read."

"Oh, he's marvelous. When I was young, my father used to do recitations of the 'Ancient Mariner'—"

She was interrupted by the bell over the door, and in came Oliver, wet to the skin, with Morand behind him. Oliver looked in good spirits, but he stopped dead when he saw the girl standing across the counter from me. Morand turned away quick and tucked his clock-work hand in his pocket, eyes on a shelf of windup frogs.

Oliver crossed his arms over his chest and fixed the girl with a frosty stare. "Can we help you find something, mademoiselle?"

"Oh, no thank you," she replied. "I'm just seeking shelter from the storm. You must be the brother who likes Coleridge."

Oliver looked so startled that I almost laughed, but he shot me a scowl nasty enough to shut me up and stalked to my side behind the counter. "You need to get her out of here," he hissed at me in English. This had been our favorite trick for years—using one of our acquired languages so we could talk about clockwork business in the shop when there were nonmechanical customers about. English suited Geneva best. We hadn't met another soul in Switzerland who spoke it. "Morand got his arm smashed up by some men at the trial who were trying to make trouble for clockworks."

"Is it bad? I could fix it for him, if you don't want to."

"I'll manage. The framework's bent, but most of the

gears are all right. But I need to get him into the work-shop *now*." He cast a meaningful look at the girl, who was studying a shelf of windup horses.

"What am I supposed to do about her?" I replied, still in English.

"Find her a cab. Stick her on the omnibus. Bleeding hell, Ally, you knew we were coming, why'd you let her camp out? You can't go falling over your feet every time a pretty girl looks your way."

"Shut it," I snapped.

"Get her out of here," he replied.

I glared at him, even though he had already turned away, then went around the counter to where the girl was still standing. "Would you like me to find a cab?" I asked her in French. "I don't think the rain is going to let up for a while."

"That would be good, thank you," she replied, and her voice was more clipped around the edges than it had been before. Perhaps Oliver had put her off.

She waited under the shop awning while I got drenched hailing a cab on the street. When one finally stopped, I held the door so the driver wouldn't have to climb out. The girl lifted her skirts, hopped a puddle that was collecting between the uneven cobbles, and took my outstretched hand, her glove smooth as water against my skin.

"Sorry for the trouble," I said as she hoisted herself onto the step.

She glanced over her shoulder at me, and the corners of her mouth turned up in a pointed smile. "It wasn't any trouble," she said in bright, clear, Britain-born English.

My heart jumped, and before she could climb the rest of the way inside, I grabbed her arm and yanked her back down onto the street. She raised her chin, and a stream of rainwater cascaded off the brim of her bonnet.

"Kindly release me."

"You speak English?"

"I'm from London. I thought someone ought to teach you and your brother to be more careful."

"You can't—" I started, then changed course and tried, instead, "Please don't—" They'd hang us, all of us. Oliver and I were old enough, and we were both Shadow Boys in our own right. They'd string us up right alongside our parents. We'd known Geneva was dangerous, more than anywhere else we'd lived, but I hadn't truly felt it until that moment, with my life and my family in the hands of this stranger, whether she knew it or not.

Perhaps she did understand, or perhaps I just looked so panicked she took pity on me, for her face went soft again. "I'm so sorry, I shouldn't have frightened you like that. You won't have any trouble from me, I promise."

"You can't—" I tried again, but I was interrupted by the cab driver shouting at us over the rain, "What's going on? Are you in or not?"

"Just a moment!" she called, then turned back to me. "Why don't you come see me tomorrow and we can chat? I'm in Cologny, at Villa Diodati." She said that name like it should have meant something, but I shook my head. "Oh, do you not know . . . ?" Her words trailed into silence, and she looked away. "I'm staying with some friends there. Come see me. Ask for Mary Godwin. Now, please, I need to go." She pried my fingers off her arm, then climbed into the cab and shut the door. The clockwork kicked to life with a crackling hiss, and a jet of steam exhaust dissolved against the rain as the cab pulled away.

I waited until Morand had left and it was just Oliver and me in the shop before I rounded on him. "You bleeding idiot."

He hoisted himself onto the counter, grinning in an unconcerned way that made me want to slug him. "Are you still sore because I made you get that girl a cab?"

"That girl was from London. She spoke English, she understood everything you said."

He froze. "Shit."

"Right."

"Shit," he said again, louder this time. "God's wounds, I'm sorry, Ally, I didn't think . . ." He pushed a hand through his hair, leaving a track of dark curls standing straight. "Shit."

"She told me to come see her tomorrow. She wants to talk to us."

"Probably wants money to keep her mouth shut."

"We have to tell Father."

"No, don't tell Father," he said quickly. "We'll go talk to her, figure out what she knows, and then come up with some clever story that will explain what I said. We can do it. Everything will be all right."

I don't remember what clever story Oliver came up with, or how long it took before Mary saw straight through it. I do remember going to see her that next day. She caught us before we were shown into the grand house and took us to a hillside overlooking the lake, just the three of us for the first time. Oliver and I were both dead certain she was going to ask for money to keep silent or else call the police on us, but instead she wanted to talk about Coleridge. Then Wordsworth. Then Paris, then the best places for pastries in Paris, then the pneumatic lift that had just been installed in the opera house there. Then somewhere along the way we started talking about castles and ghosts, and Mary told us she'd heard about a haunted château in the foothills, and then we weren't standing any longer, we were sitting on the damp grass, then sprawled across it with our shoes off, and I told a story about Oliver thinking our shop in Amsterdam was haunted when really it was a squirrel living in the rafters, and Mary laughed so loud I swore the boaters across the lake must have heard her.

When we finally got around to talking about clock-work, I was already certain: Mary Godwin wouldn't tell a soul we were Shadow Boys.

So it seemed to me that *Frankenstein* had three possible authors, and though each of them felt impossible for their own reason, I kept them ranked in my head: Mary, the least likely; then Geisler; then Oliver.

As the storm outside continued to swell, I kept mostly to my small room, sick with the mystery of it all and growing sicker with every page I got further into *Frankenstein*. Victor returned to Geneva, where he and his creation were reunited. Then it was the monster's story. He told Victor how he'd survived in the world he didn't understand and that didn't want him, having no memories or language or understanding of himself or anything around him. How he suffered at the mercy of his clockwork body, the gears that shredded him from the inside, the scars and sutures that twisted his skin; how no other man he met could bear the sight of him and he was thrown out of every place he went. But he was strong and fast, with the power of both metal and man, same as Oliver. I kept hearing the words in his voice: *When I looked around I saw and heard of none like me. Was I, then, a monster, a blot upon the earth from which all men fled and whom all men disowned?*

And when the world had turned away from the monster, he turned his back on it. Burned a house to the ground. Murdered Victor's friend Henry. Victor's bride, Elizabeth. And his brother.

I had turned loose into the world a depraved wretch, Victor said. *Had he not murdered my brother?*

I shut the book hard around those words, tossed it onto the floor, and stood up. I had done nothing but read since we arrived, and I was starting to feel restless. My hands were itching after days without clockwork, and I was certain if I went a page further in *Frankenstein*, I'd throw up.

I searched the house for Geisler to ask if he had any projects I could muck about with, but I found his bedroom door closed and got no reply when I knocked. I was too impatient to wait for an answer, so I rescued several of the antique clocks from around the house, including the ones in my room I had gutted, and took them out to the workshop in search of tools. The wind was gusting, and even the short walk across the yard was a fight. Fresh tracks stretched between the house and the workshop, and I tried to step into them to keep the snow from falling down my boots. I was ready to pick the lock if I needed to, but it was unlatched, and I let myself in. The wind slammed the door shut behind me.

The workshop was built like a coffin, long and narrow with bare walls and a wood floor. The fireplace was empty, and the room was cold enough that my breath clouded before my face. I had hoped for some half-assembled project of Geisler's that I could study, but Geisler had spoken in earnest when he said he hardly used the place. It looked abandoned. There was a neat worktable with an unlit Carcel burner resting on one corner and a few tools arranged in a straight line across the wall. When I picked one up, it left an imprint in the dust. There were drawers full of gears rusted together, and a few steel rods propped in one corner, but it was altogether disappointingly empty.

I set my clocks on the workbench, selected tools from the slim lineup, and started in. It was dull work—once you've fused cogs to skin and bone, pure mechanics is hardly a challenge. I had the clocks reassembled in under an hour, then started taking them apart and putting them back together again just for something to do. I worked until my fingers were clumsy with cold and I decided to start the clocks again and go back inside the house.

I found an old pair of pulse gloves in a drawer, their metal plates rusted red around the edges. It took a long time rubbing them together before I got a charge built and pressed them against the exposed mainspring of the first clock. There was a snap of blue light like the center of a gas flame, then the gears began to turn. The clock hands did a full rotation, and a small cuckoo jutted out, shrieking. I watched it for a moment, letting it run its paces before I reached for the next one.

A hand fastened suddenly around my wrist, and I yelped in surprise. I twisted around to see who had me prisoner, but all I needed was a glimpse of the silver cogs to know it was one of Geisler's automatons, head rotating slowly so its glassy eyes were fixed on me. Its fingers felt strong enough to snap bone. "Let go of me!" I cried, but it didn't make a damn difference. The automaton held firm. As it dragged me to my feet, I clamped my free hand around its forearm, trying helplessly to pry it off.

Blue light leapt from my pulse gloves and into the automaton. A bright shock traveled through its whole body, then its grip loosened and it stilled, head nodding forward against its silver-plated chest.

I stared, waiting for it to spring back to life, but it didn't move. Either the pulse had overwhelmed the clockwork and the automaton was out of commission for good, or it had tripped an automatic shutdown before something blew and another pulse would restart it—Father and I had built systems like that into some of the more complicated limbs we'd made to prevent the circuit from burning up. Curiosity started to creep through me as my heartbeat slowed. As creepy as the metal men were, the mechanic in me was dead keen to know how Geisler had designed them to handle a burst of current.

I reached out experimentally and pressed my palm flat against the conducting plate on the automaton's shoulder. There was another flash and it sprang back to its feet, system restarted and hand shooting out toward me again before I could properly dodge it. I stumbled backward and tripped on the edge of the workbench, but the automaton seized my collar before I fell and I was hauled back to my feet. I cursed aloud, though there was no one to hear, and tried to zap it again, but the charge had gone from the pulse gloves. Before I could get them going, the stiff clockwork hands closed around my wrists, wrenching them apart and jerking me toward the door. I dug my heels into the floor, but they slid like I was on ice.

The automaton dragged me from the workshop and across the yard, metal fingers carving grooves into my skin. My arms were burning by the time we reached the house. I tried to bolt again in the kitchen, but the automaton adjusted its grip so its arms crisscrossed my chest, pinning my arms to my sides and making it hard to breathe, let alone escape.

I was tossed into my room so roughly that I stumbled, caught my foot on the edge of the rug, and crashed to the floor. The automaton stood at the threshold, eyes fixed on me, then slammed the door. A moment later I heard the shudder of a lock.

I tried the handle, but it wouldn't give. There wasn't a keyhole to pick, just the slick iron handle. I started pounding on the door first with my fist and then with my whole arm, shouting, though I was certain neither Geisler nor Clémence was about, and the house's only other inhabitants would likely side with their fellow who had locked me in. When that got me nowhere, I tried knocking off the handle with the fire poker, though I only half expected that to work, and giving it a shock from the pulse gloves, but that did even less.

When throwing myself into the door only left me with a bruised shoulder, I tried the window instead, but I could barely get my fingers wedged into the narrow gap between the latch and the ledge. When I finally did, I found the window had been frozen shut by the storm, and no amount of tugging freed it.

After a good quarter of an hour spent trying to crack the ice, I gave up and sank down with my back against the door, still halfheartedly hammering as I tried to work out what to do. I picked up *Frankenstein* from where I had left it on the hearth rug and stared at the neat type without reading, until my eyes crossed.

I don't know how long I was trapped in my bedroom—my newly repaired clocks had been abandoned in the workshop. But *Frankenstein* was still in my lap when a key scraped in the lock above my head. I tried to stand but wasn't fast enough, so when the door opened, I fell backward onto the hearth rug.

Geisler looked down at me from the doorway, Clémence peering over his shoulder. "God's wounds, Alasdair, what's the matter?"

"Your automatons," I said, scrambling to my feet. "One of them locked me in."

Geisler scowled. "Stupid things," he murmured. "I'm so sorry. Please understand, they are imperfect creations, and they always seem to take things a bit too far when dealing with strangers."

"It's all right," I said. "I thought . . ."

Geisler raised an eyebrow. "Thought what?"

I glanced at Clémence. She was scrubbing at a spot on her hand. "I don't know," I finished.

"Well, you're all right." Geisler smiled, then clapped me sharply on the shoulder. My arms were still sore from the automaton's grip, and I felt the throb all the way to my fingertips. "Were you out in the workshop, by chance?"

The question felt like a trick, but I knew I'd left enough evidence there that I couldn't get around the truth for long. "I was working on some clocks," I replied. "It helps me think."

"That must have been it, then. My automatons work on strict instructions to keep intruders from the workshop. There's always the danger of thieves, you know."

I nodded, though I couldn't think of a thing there worth stealing.

"If you stay away, I expect they'll leave you alone." He smiled again, but it felt a bit like a warning. "Apologies, Alasdair, my deepest apologies."

Geisler trooped down the hallway and disappeared into his bedroom, but Clémence stayed behind, watching me with no hint of a smirk on her face. "Are you all right?" she asked once Geisler was out of sight.

"What? Yes."

"I know they can be rough."

"I'm fine." I held up *Frankenstein*, cover toward her. "Have you read this?"

"Why?"

"Just tell me, have you?"

"Yes."

"The main character, Victor," I said. "What do you think of him?"

She shrugged. "I don't really remember."

"Well, try to."

I must have looked wild, because she leaned backward,

away from the door. For a moment, I thought she was going to walk away, but then she sucked in her cheeks and said, "I think he's thoughtless and arrogant." My heart sank, but she wasn't finished. "But I understand it. I understand why he did it. He didn't mean for things to get out of hand, and he didn't handle them well when they did."

"Do you know—maybe this sounds daft." I scrubbed a hand through my hair. "Do you know if Geisler had anything to do with it? I mean—that's ridiculous, isn't it? When I say it aloud—"

"I thought that too, when I first read it," she said.

"Truly?"

She glanced down the hallway behind her, then took a step into my room. "I think he must be involved somehow. It was all he talked about for months. Had copies shipped in from London when it was first printed there. It must have cost a fortune. He was just so . . . I'm not sure how to describe it. Feverish about it, I suppose. This sort of wild thrill, though I never quite figured out if he was excited by it or panicked. Perhaps a bit of both." She glanced down the hallway again. "Look, I have to go to the market in town and then fetch Geisler's keys from his office, but I'll be back later if you want to talk more about it."

"Can I come with you?" I asked.

She arched an eyebrow. "It's still snowing."

"I don't mind. I'd like to get out." I tried to look innocent, but it had suddenly occurred to me that if I could get into Geisler's office with her, I might be able to find something that would either tick him off the list of possible authors or confirm it.

I didn't know if Clémence would let me come along if she suspected I was planning on snooping, and for a moment she stared so intensely at me that I was certain it must be written all over my face. But then she shrugged and turned away from the door. "Get your coat."

The walk to the town seemed longer than when we had taken it with Geisler. The storm was lightening, but the bitter wind drilled snowflakes into my skin. Clémence and I kept our faces deep in our scarves, hands fisted in pockets. She had swapped out her trousers and linen shirt for a blue dress, but she still wore the gray wool coat that I was certain had been made for a man. Her hair was loose, and the strands falling from her cap twirled in the breeze like ribbons. "I've never heard of a laboratory assistant doing the shopping," I said to her as we walked.

"Well, there's no one else to do it," she replied. "The automatons certainly can't, and Geisler won't do it himself."

"He could hire a housekeeper."

"Why? He's got me."

"But that's not your job."

Clémence blew on her hands, then shoved them back into her pockets. "I don't mind. I do whatever makes me useful to him."

The market was set up in the main square, walled in by buildings that mercifully blocked the worst of the wind. In spite of the storm, there were still a fair number of people wandering about. Clémence kept her gaze on the produce she was buying and didn't speak to the merchants until she spotted a man selling baskets of strawberries from a crate.

"They grow them in the university greenhouses," she explained as she dragged me over to see. "Where else could you get strawberries in weather like this?" She had a quick exchange with the merchant, shifting from French to German and then into what seemed like a crossbreed of both of them. I didn't speak any German, so I stood stupidly at her shoulder while they chatted. The merchant held up a basket for her, and I noticed with amazement that his hand was mechanical, spindly silver fingers twitching as cogs meshed beneath them. In Geneva, a mechanical man walking openly at a market was rare, but selling goods from a university and having people purchase from him was unheard of. People spoke to this man, addressed him like a human being, and didn't run the other direction when they saw he was made of metal. I wondered if they'd treat Oliver the same way if I brought him here. Maybe not everyone would think him a monster.

Clémence handed over her money, and as the merchant gave her a basket of strawberries, he pointed to me with a thin silver finger and said something in his German-French.

"What did he say?" I asked Clémence.

"He wants you to eat one," she replied, holding the basket out to me. "He says they'll make you live long and die happy."

I took one and bit into it. I must have made a ridiculous face, because Clémence laughed. "Good?"

"Brilliant," I replied.

She took another from the basket, and for a while we just stood there in the snowstorm eating strawberries and sucking the juice off our fingers. Clémence closed her eyes and tipped her head back so that the snowflakes tangled in her eyelashes. "I can't remember the last time I had strawberries."

"When my family was in Bruges," I said, "there were good strawberries there."

"Well, you've just been everywhere, haven't you?"

I shrugged. "We had strawberries a lot when we lived there because they grew wild along the canals. Oliver and I snuck into this merchant's yard to pick some once. We took our shoes off, because it was muddy, and then a servant from the house chased us away and we had to leave them behind and walk all the way home barefoot.

Father gave us a good telling-off for that, but we got to eat ourselves sick on strawberries, so that made it all right." I realized suddenly that I was babbling and stopped. "Sorry."

"You need to stop apologizing for everything. It was a good story. I liked it. You're shit at endings, though." She sucked the fruit from a stem, then hurled it into a heap of rubbish piled against one of the shops. "I'm sorry your brother's dead. It sounds like he was a riot."

I stuck my hands in my pockets and stared up at the university spire rising above the rooftops. Halfway through the story, I had remembered why he'd taken me to steal the strawberries in the first place: it had been my birthday, and I'd wanted them. That had been Oliver's gift to me.

"Yes," I said, "he was."

We stood in the square for a while, sheltered from the wind, eating strawberries and not talking much. A group of boys from the university passed by, one of them proudly thrusting an exam sheet in the air while the others shouted and slapped him on the back. I watched them as they stopped for *glühwein*, all of them laughing and chatting like it was so easy.

That was going to be me, I thought, and the weight in my chest lifted again. It was going to happen. Ingolstadt and uni. I could be back here in weeks, in this small, remarkable town, meeting interesting people, working with Geisler, studying things that fascinated and challenged me, not doing the shop work for Father I could finish in my sleep. I would buy strawberries at the market from a man who didn't hide his mechanical bits, live in a flat all my own, and worry about exams and revision and class rankings and absolutely nothing else. I wanted it all so badly it felt like some part of me was stretching outside my body to reach for it.

Half the strawberries were gone when Clémence declared she was cold and we should head for Geisler's office. As we started to make our way between the last of the market stalls, the strawberry seller called out from behind us in German. Clémence turned and shouted something back, and he swept his hat off with an exaggerated bow.

"I told him those were the best strawberries we'd ever had," she translated for me as we turned out of the square. "I may have omitted the fact that you had better in Bruges."

"Where did you learn German?" I asked.

"I had a tutor when I was young." She slipped another strawberry from the basket and sucked on it. "Latin, English, and French as well."

"Dead fancy schooling."

She snorted. "It was."

"Is your family still in Paris?"

"*Oui*. In a large white house on the Seine."

"And what do they think of you working as an assistant to Europe's most infamous Shadow Boy?"

She looked up as we passed beneath the university gates, their gold letters muted by the spraying snow. "I don't believe they think of me at all."

She said it so casually, like it didn't matter, but when I looked over, she ducked her head and started walking so fast I had to jog to catch up. I didn't ask her any more about it—I knew families could be sharp and fragile things.

I had hoped there'd be a hunt for Geisler's keys that would buy me time and justify opening desk drawers, but they were lying in plain sight on the floor behind the desk. Clémence snatched them up. I was ready to invent some excuse to stay longer, but when she straightened, she was smirking at me. "Well, while we're here . . ."

I stared back at her. "While we're here what?"

"We might as well see what we can find about *Frankenstein*."

"We?"

"Since I'm helping you with some light burglary, I thought I should at least get equal partnership."

"What burglary? The door was wide open."

"I meant this bit." She found a key on the ring and unlocked the top drawer. A set of pens rolled forward with a clatter.

"You rascal."

"Don't pretend this isn't the whole reason you came."

When I didn't deny it, her smirk went wider. I cast a quick glance at the door, then crossed behind the desk to her side.

She shifted several books out of the way and peered in. "What are we looking for?"

"Something to do with *Frankenstein*, I suppose." I pulled a stack of papers out of the drawer as Clémence unlocked another. "No idea beyond that. Manuscript pages, maybe? Correspondence with a publisher? Does he have a laboratory on the campus where he keeps things?"

"There are student laboratories, but they're all shared."

"So nowhere safe to hide a . . ."

I trailed off. A blotched sheet had slid from the bottom of the stack. Written across it in shaky penmanship was:

12 December 1818

Male, five foot ten inches, 152 pounds, consumption

Female, five foot two inches, 104 pounds, whooping cough

Male, six foot three inches, 198 pounds, heart failure?

Male, six foot, 159 pounds, stab wound, two inches, lower abdomen

Female, five foot three inches, 102 pounds, ???

Female, five foot, 91 pounds, broken neck, some damage to skull

There were small marks in pencil next to the first two descriptions on the list.

"What have you got?" Clémence asked, and I handed it over for her to see.

"Do you know what that is?"

Her eyes ran down the list; then she folded it in half and dropped it back in the drawer. "No," she replied, but she didn't meet my gaze.

"Let me see it again."

"It's not important."

"Do you know what it is?"

"No."

"Then how do you know it's not important?"

Her mouth twisted. "Forget it, all right?"

"You do know." I made to snatch it from the drawer, but Clémence batted me away hard enough that her fingers left a red imprint on the back of my hand. "Ouch! Bleeding hell, what was that for?"

"Leave it alone, Alasdair. I thought you were here to find—"

She stopped suddenly, and I heard it too—footsteps coming down the corridor toward us. The office door was wide open, and we were standing elbow deep in a professor's papers, clearly doing something we shouldn't be.

The footsteps stopped just outside the door. We were both silent for a moment, then someone called, "Dr. Geisler?"

I started to shove papers back into the drawers, but Clémence seized me by the front of my coat and yanked me toward her. Her face was suddenly very close to mine. "What are you doing?" I hissed.

"Kiss me," she replied.

And, having no better plan, I did.

She knocked me backward against the desk, one elbow slamming hard into my chest, and I barely caught myself before I fell properly. My hand sent an inkwell smashing to the floor. "Like you mean it," she said, lips still on mine.

I didn't have a bleeding clue what she was doing, but I dug one hand into her hair while the other went around her waist. I didn't know much about what ladies wore under their clothes, but as she shimmied up against me, I could tell she didn't have much. No boning or corset or stiff stays. When she inhaled, I felt her heartbeat skip through her shirt and right up against mine, like a broken clock.

"What in God's name—"

Clémence bounced to her feet like a loosed jack-in-the-box. My hand was still so wrapped up under her coat, she nearly pulled me over. A professor in full robes was standing in the doorway, gaping at us. Me, I realized. Mostly gaping at me.

"What do you think you're doing, young man?" he snapped.

"The door was open," Clémence said breathlessly. She had somehow convinced her face to go as red as the strawberries.

"Keep quiet," the professor snapped at her, then turned his steely gaze back to me. "We expect better of our students. And in a professor's office. I should have you suspended at the very least."

I tugged at my clothes and remembered suddenly that I had a uniform on under my coat. Clémence's plan finally fell into place in my head. "Sorry, sir."

The professor took a menacing step forward. "I'll have your name, young man, and I will be reporting you to the head of your department." He folded his arms. I was reminded of Father and the big show he always liked to make of waiting for me. "Your name, please," the professor repeated.

"Victor Frankenstein," I blurted.

His eyes narrowed. "Are you being smart with me?"

"God, I wish I was."

The line of his mouth tightened. "Get out, both of you."

I reached behind me for Clémence, found her hand, and together we skirted out of the office. At the end of the corridor we broke into a run and didn't stop until we were through the university gates. I could have kept going—probably could have sprinted back to Geneva—but Clémence stopped, hand pressed to her chest as she caught her breath, and I halted too.

We stood in silence for a while, both of us breathing hard. I wasn't sure if she expected me to speak first and give some sort of permission for what she had done, so I said, "That was clever."

She shrugged. "I've been cleverer. Sorry, I didn't mean to throw myself at you like that. It was just the only thing I could think to do."

"It's all right, I worked it out." The rush was fading and I was starting to feel the cold again. I pulled my scarf up over my face. "God's wounds, I left the papers all over his desk. He's going to know we were snooping."

"I left the strawberries too," she said. "If it's any consolation."

I laughed louder than I meant to. A few people passing stared at me, and I clapped a hand over my mouth. The smirk crept back across Clémence's lips. "Let's go home," she said. "I'll go back later and tidy things up when that ass of a professor isn't prowling."

"So we didn't find anything," I said as we started walking. "A complete waste."

"Don't be so gloomy." She knocked me lightly with her elbow. "Things will come together for you."

I almost laughed again, because for the first time in years, it seemed like they might. The snow was clearing along the mountaintops. We'd be on our way to Geneva in days. Oliver would be free, and I'd be free too.

As we crossed the square toward the road to Geisler's house, Clémence asked, "Was that your first kiss?"

My heart pitched. "No," I replied. "Was it yours?"

"No." She wiped her mouth on the back of her hand, then grinned. "So I guess you haven't always been like this."

"Like what?"

"So serious. It would appear that once you knew how to have a bit of fun."

"Suppose I did," I said, though if I had, I'd forgotten now.

Clémence stretched with a wince, then rubbed the side of her rib cage.

"You all right?" I asked.

"Fine. You were just a bit too passionate for me, that's all." She kicked a snowball down the road. It skittered and then burst against a tree trunk.

"What was his name?" I asked. "The first lad you kissed."

For a moment, I thought I saw the same sort of deep sadness flash across her face that I recognized from the dozens of times I had seen Oliver wear it. But then she wiped it clean like rain fog from a windowpane and said, "Marco. It was back in Paris. He was an actor." She glanced sideways at me. "What about you? Who was the first person you kissed?"

"Mary Godwin," I replied. "Oh, not Godwin, though, she's married."

"You kissed a married woman?"

"An almost-married woman."

"My, but you were wild. So Mary Godwin, but not Godwin. Do you know what she's called now?"

We rounded the corner of the cobbled high street and crossed onto the dirt road, made muddy by the snow. I looked down at my boots, which were turning from black to brown, and tried to silence my clattering heart, which had not stopped beating for her for two long years. "If everything went according to her plan," I said, "then I'd imagine by now she's called Mary Shelley."

The night I kissed Mary was uncommonly warm for October. It was autumn heat, the sort of crisp, golden day that my mother assured me was a prelude to cold coming soon. But it was a rosy fall evening after that dreary, rainy summer.

The night before Geisler left the city. The night before Oliver died.

I was sitting on the steps to the flat in the dying light, reassembling a pocket watch I'd found smashed to bits in the street. With my head against the wall to the flat, I could hear muffled voices from the other side: Father, Mum, and Oliver, joined by Geisler. It was two days since he'd escaped prison and he had been hiding with us while the police turned over the countryside, thinking he'd fled Geneva. Tomorrow night, when their search moved back inside the city, he would make his dash for the border and return to Ingolstadt.

Oliver was meant to have some part in the escape, though I wasn't sure what. He'd been reading out on the stairs with me when Father called him in to discuss it. I kept waiting for them to start shouting, because one of them was bound to be upset over something sooner or later, but it all stayed quiet. That was somehow more alarming.

As the sun began to drop below the skyline, I heard the flat door open, and before I could turn, Oliver flopped down on the step beside me and pulled his knees up to his chest. "I'm being sent away."

My finger caught under the ratio wheel and it pinched. "What?"

He was staring straight ahead, down at the street, with his mouth set in a hard line. The sunlight splintered through his dark hair. "Once Geisler's settled in Ingolstadt, he's going to send for me so I can keep studying with him at the university there. He and Father still seem convinced they can make a Shadow Boy out of me." He said it all so quiet and calm. He didn't even look angry, though he'd spent so long being angry at Father and Geisler for nearly everything. He just looked empty.

I let go a breath, so heavy and disbelieving it sounded like a laugh. He looked over at me. "What was that for?"

"Oliver, that's . . ." He had to know. He had just been handed what I'd been wanting and working toward my whole bleeding life and nobody had ever noticed. "Studying with Geisler at Ingolstadt is what I want to do," I said softly. "That's what I've *always* wanted to do."

"No you don't," he said. "You don't want to join the mad doctor in his devil work."

"He isn't mad—"

"And how would you know? You haven't seen what he's doing. It's not *you* cutting up bodies for him in the clock tower."

"It's science!"

"No, it's insane. And I don't want you telling me I should be grateful for this. I've heard enough of that already. Hell's teeth, Ally, I thought you'd be on my side."

"I am," I replied. "I don't want you to go!"

"But you'd go, wouldn't you? If he asked you instead."

"Oliver—"

"Don't be an idiot, Ally." He stood up and stomped down the stairs, skipping the last one so he landed hard on the cobbles, then glared backward at me. "God's wounds, I thought I could count on you." Then he disappeared around the front of the shop, and a moment later I heard the bell over the door sing.

I sat there for a moment with my eyes on the spot

where he'd been. I felt clenched up and boiling and just a smidge panicked, because I'd never been apart from Oliver for longer than a night before and here he was leaving me for Germany. On the other side of the wall, I heard Father's voice, then Geisler's, and the shuffle of footsteps toward the door. I didn't want to talk to either of them, and I sure as hell didn't want to stew down in the shop with Oliver. There was only one person I could stand the thought of right then.

I stood up so fast the pieces of the pocket watch spilled off my lap, then I jogged down to the street and turned away from where Oliver had gone—across the square and toward the lake.

Mary was smiling when she came to the villa door, but I must have looked wretched, because it faded fast. "What's the matter?"

"Oliver's leaving," I said. "He's going to Ingolstadt with Geisler."

A shout went up in the house behind her, a raucous and ravaged sound. A woman shrieked. Something crashed. Mary glanced over her shoulder, then put her hand on my arm, like she was holding me back. "Let's walk down to the shore. Stay here, I'll get my coat."

We took the path through the vineyards and down to the lake, where we sat, with our shoes off, on the trunk of a bare cedar that had toppled into the water. Our feet made ripples in the dark water as I told her what had happened. "You shouldn't be angry at Oliver," she said when I was finished. "He didn't ask for it."

"But he says it's wicked work, and that I shouldn't be interested in it."

"But you are, and he can't change that. Neither can you." She dragged her toes across the top of the water, leaving a pattern like skipped stones. On the shore the cattails whispered as the wind snaked through them. "What is Dr. Geisler's work, precisely?"

"Reanimating the dead with clockwork."

"God's wounds. That isn't . . . real, is it? I mean, it can't be done."

"Not yet." She sounded so horrified I didn't dare tell her the fiery fascination the idea lit inside me—the chance it *might* be possible—in case she too thought I was mad and wicked for it. I pushed my hands through my hair and shivered. Now that the sun was gone, it felt like autumn again. "I don't want to talk about it."

"You shouldn't keep it all tucked away."

"I'm all right. Tell me about something else. Recite a poem or something."

"I don't want to recite. I want to talk to you." She said it so quietly that I had to look sideways at her to be sure I hadn't imagined it. Her shoulders were hunched as she braced herself against the fallen log, and the reflection of the first stars on the lake caught her face from below and freckled it with light. Even through my anger,

I could feel her presence ringing inside me like a tuning fork struck against my rib cage. I had been dizzy over her all summer, but it wasn't until that moment that I realized how badly I wanted her, in every way. Someone to talk to. Someone to hold and touch. It took everything in me not to reach out and touch her right then.

"It's so quiet here, isn't it?" she said. "Everything's so loud at the house all the time. It was making me anxious, being shut up with all that noise. But I feel quiet here. I feel steady." Her head was drifting onto my shoulder. I held my breath. "I feel steady when I'm with you."

"You don't like being at the house, do you?" I asked, and immediately wished I hadn't, because she raised her head.

"What?"

"At your villa—you don't like it there. You always leave like something's chasing you."

"I like it fine," she said, though her voice pitched on the word *fine*.

"So why are you always out with me and Oliver instead of your friends?"

"Is it so hard to believe I simply like being with you two?"

"Both of us?" I could have kicked myself for how disappointed those words came out sounding. I knew Mary and Oliver weren't interested in each other in any sort of romantic way—they'd both told me so, and always seemed so disinterested in each other beyond whatever antics they were daring the other into. But even knowing that, I still wanted it to be me—just me, for the first time in my life, just me and not Oliver—that she liked best.

She looked over at me and her mouth twitched. "Well, Oliver's good for a thrill, but he's exhausting. You're different. You're very . . . simple."

I snorted. "Thanks for that."

"Oh God, sorry, I didn't mean that you aren't clever. You're very clever. Much cleverer than me."

"Now you're overdoing it."

"Sorry." She laughed, one short, sharp burst. "What I meant is that I sometimes feel as though everyone around me is trying so hard to be complicated and coy all the time, but you're so sincere in everything. You make me remember people can mean what they say." And then she put her hand on mine, and pressed her thumb into my palm.

A charge went through me, and when I turned and she was right there, so glowing and lovely that I almost closed my eyes again because looking at her felt like staring into the sun. And before I knew what I was doing, before I had time to think or plan or let the part of my brain that usually kept me from doing irrational things have a chance to speak up, I leaned forward and kissed her.

And as soon as we touched, I knew I was wrong to have thought that we'd been building to this boil all summer. It wasn't what I expected it to be, not warm or splendid, no fireworks or poetry. Mary's lips were cold, and the moment we touched, she went corpse rigid. Then she put her hands against my chest and pushed me away. "Don't."

I was so mortified that for a moment the most sensible thing to do seemed to be to let myself slide into the water and drown. "I'm sorry," I croaked.

"It's all right."

"God's wounds, I'm so sorry, I thought . . . I thought you wanted it too."

"Alasdair, I'm married."

It took a moment for her words to sink in, but when they did, I felt them deep and cold, all the way down to my bones. "What?"

"I'm married," she repeated. "Well, not yet. I mean I'm going to be. Once his wife . . ." A crease appeared between her eyebrows. "He has a wife, but he doesn't love her. We eloped when I was seventeen, and we've been traveling while things . . . calmed down a bit at home. That's why I'm here in Geneva. We wanted to get away."

"That's . . ." I couldn't think how to finish, so I just gaped at her, treading silence like it was water. My ears were ringing, the twilight rippling around me as though I were seeing it from below the surface of the lake. I stared at Mary for as long as I could bear it, then dropped off the log, landing up to my knees in the frigid lake, and splashed to shore.

"Alasdair!" she called after me, but I didn't stop. I snatched my boots from where I'd left them and tried to yank them on over my wet skin as Mary skirted across the fallen tree like a tightrope walker and came to stand beside me. "I should have told you," she said.

I flung the boots to the sand and raised my face to hers. She looked so small, standing there on the shore with her arms wrapped around herself and her hair trailing in inky curls over her shoulders. "Yes. You should have."

"I'm sorry, I didn't know you felt—"

"How could you not know?" I cried, my voice ringing across the empty shoreline. "I'm so bleeding *sincere* you probably read it all over me. And Oliver told you, I know he did."

"Yes," she said quietly.

"And did you tell him about your almost-husband?" She looked away, which was answer enough. My hands curled into fists. "God."

"I only told him last week, because he saw Percy and me at the market. Please don't be angry with him, I asked him not to say anything to you."

"I am angry with him," I replied. "And I'm angry with you. You told me you were traveling with friends. What the hell have you been doing hanging around with two *boys* all summer when you've got an intended? God's wounds, Mary, why did you lie to me?"

"Because I didn't think you'd want to be around me anymore once you knew," she cried. "Everyone back home was so cruel about us traveling together without being married. I hoped things would be better here, but it's even worse. Percy and his friends have a reputation for being sordid, so everyone seems to think that's permission for them to make our lives their conversation. The papers run vulgar stories about us every week. People steal our underthings off our washing lines. Tourists rent telescopes so they can stare into our bedroom windows from across the shore, did you know that?"

"Stop it," I said. "Just stop, that doesn't matter. That doesn't explain why you lied to me."

"Then how's this: when I met you, you didn't have a clue who they were, or who I was, and I saw a chance to be free of that and I took it."

The moon had risen in earnest now, and in its light, I could see her clearly across the beach from me: arms crossed, chin raised, Mistress Mary, quite contrary, daring me to blame her for what she'd done. It nearly broke me in two. "Mary, I have told you *everything* about me. Things I've never told anyone before. Secrets that could get me killed. So why couldn't you tell me that you were engaged?"

We stared hard at each other for a long moment, and I silently willed her to say something that would take us back to just before I kissed her, some reason to return to trusting her without question and adoring her just as blindly. But when she finally spoke, all she said was, "I'm sorry."

I snatched up my boots without putting them on and stalked off, sand caving under my feet with every step. I wanted to say something more, wanted to think of something mean to throw back in her face. Oliver would have had something to say. He always did. But all I could do was walk away, trailing broken pieces behind me.

The flat was dark when I got home. I stumbled through the kitchen and pushed back the quilt strung up to divide our corner from the rest of the room. Oliver was lying on his pallet, sucking on his unlit pipe while he read by the light of a candle stub. He looked up when my shadow fell across him. "Where've you been?"

"Out," I replied, already stripping off my clothes.

"You're all wet."

"No shit." I flung myself down on my pallet so that my face was away from him. I was too hot for blankets and too exhausted to change.

From behind me, Oliver asked, "What's wrong?"

I thought about confronting him. About rolling over and letting him have all my anger, because how could he act like Ingolstadt didn't matter, how could he say

Geisler's work was wicked, how could he not tell me that Mary was married?

But instead I packed it up tight and deep inside me and said, "Nothing."

"Are you angry at me?"

"No. I'm tired."

There was a pause; then he said, "All right," and a moment later the candle went out.

And that was the last real conversation we ever had.

B y nightfall, the storm had settled into a whisper. Snowflakes wafted across the yard and a faint sliver of moon peered out from between the feathery clouds. Over supper, Geisler announced we'd be leaving the next morning.

I should have been ecstatic, with the promise of the return to Geneva to fetch Oliver, track down my parents, and end the nightmare of the last two years, but it felt as though a splinter had lodged inside me, and I couldn't shake the feeling that I was doing something wrong. I kept thinking about the list I'd found in Geisler's office, and the other pieces of this strange puzzle that I couldn't quite make fit together in my head.

Geisler disappeared after supper, muttering something

about orders to be filled, and Clémence went with him. This left me alone with that nagging, deep and persistent like an itch in my lungs. I tried to press on with *Frankenstein*, but I kept losing the thought at the end of every line, and found myself reading paragraphs over and over without getting anything from them. I finally gave up and turned in early, but I lay in bed for hours, not even dozing, staring at the window with my eyes wide open.

The moon was high when I decided if I couldn't sleep, I was going to work on something. I needed clockwork, and I needed it badly enough that I was willing to risk both Geisler and the automatons to go back to the workshop and finish reassembling the clocks I had torn apart.

I dressed in the dark, not bothering with a waistcoat and instead throwing on my coat over my shirt and braces. I remembered the empty fireplace in the workshop last time I had visited, and stuck a matchbox in my pocket for good measure. I'd have candles, if nothing else.

I padded softly through the house, peering around every corner like a burglar to make certain the automatons weren't about. The keys to the workshop were hanging beside the back door, and I eased them off the hook with my breath held, hoping they wouldn't rattle. The keys didn't betray me, but the kitchen door did—it creaked when I opened it. I stood still for a moment, certain I heard ticking machinery coming my way from the hall, then dashed out into the night. The snow between the house and the workshop was well trodden enough that my footprints would go unnoticed.

I unlocked the workshop door and peered around the frame to be certain I was alone before I went in. The room was as bare and chilly as before. I retrieved the Carcel burner from the workbench and fished a match from the box, but my hands were so shaky from the cold it was tricky to strike. When it finally caught, I tipped it against the burner wick, not realizing how close to my fingers it had burned until it singed me.

"Dammit." I dropped the match onto the floor and stuck my smarting finger in my mouth. The wick's flame wavered but stood tall as I replaced the shade one-handed and moved it to get a better look at the tools. There weren't as many out as there had been before; they'd all vanished except for two clunky spanners with bright rust creeping across their edges. I did a quick lap of the room, opening drawers and searching for more, but everything except the broken clocks had been cleared out.

I cursed under my breath, then retrieved one of the clocks and moved it to the table nearer the window, into the moonlight. I didn't have tools, but, at the risk of pinched fingers, I could still mess about. I pulled back the chair and sat down.

Next thing I knew, I was lying flat on my back on the floor. I blinked, shaking stars from my eyes, and realized the chair had tipped backward when I sat and sent me flying. I pulled myself up and examined the chair, which was now sprawled on the ground beside me. It only had three legs; the fourth, which was still sticking straight up from the floor, wasn't a leg at all. It was a lever. A dead cleverly concealed lever.

I crawled forward for a better look. There was a thin seam between the base of the lever and the floorboards, but when I pressed my eye to the gap, it was too dark to see what was below. I ran my knuckles along the wooden floor and rapped hard. The sound that returned was hollow. There was some empty space underneath the floor, tucked away and hidden.

I didn't stop to think what I was doing. I just seized the lever and pulled.

Immediately the floor beneath me began to tremble, accompanied by the low rasp of gears interlocking. Then a trapdoor sank into the floor, leaving a half-meter square of pure darkness beneath the worktable. The pale beam of my burner illuminated a set of rungs, but I couldn't see a thing beyond the pale splash of lamplight. Not how far it went, or what waited at the end.

I backed away from the trapdoor, my eyes still on it like something was about to leap out at me, then retrieved the smaller of the two spanners from where it lay on the workbench and tucked it into my braces. I didn't know what was under the floorboards, but my mind kept drift-ing to the automatons, and I felt a spanner might be a better weapon against them than anything else. I wished I'd brought the pulse gloves, but they were still stashed up in my bedroom.

I returned to the trapdoor and peered down again. The light from the burner seemed somehow fainter, though that may have been just a trick of my waning courage. Before I lost my nerve, I picked up the burner and placed my foot gingerly a few rungs down, easing myself into the hole.

My head was beneath the floorboards when I heard a creaking above me. The gears were lurching forward again, the trapdoor moving back into place. For a moment, everything inside me screamed to scramble back out to safety, but I banished that swell of panic with the knowl-edge that the gears were on my side, under the floor, and I could get them moving again if I needed to. I wouldn't be trapped.

It was a short descent, probably half as long as the stairs in Geisler's house, but the smell assaulted me immediately. It was rotten and metallic, heavy with dead flesh—I knew it from our workshop back in Geneva, but this was sharper. Fresher. I edged down, letting my feet explore the darkness for a moment before they found the next rung.

I finally reached a dirt floor, and straightened. My head brushed a beam. I held up my burner, trying to see what lay ahead, but its light barely stretched beyond the base of the ladder. Not far enough to see the room or its contents properly.

"Hello?" I called. My voice echoed faintly, but there was no reply, just the steady slither of water running down the walls.

I reached out behind me until I found damp stone and walked along it until my fingers knocked into what felt like a cold, smooth tube. I raised my lamp. A transparent half cylinder of glass about the width of my fist protruded from the wall with a thick candlewick inside of it. The tube ran parallel with the floor just below my eye level and disappeared ahead of me into the darkness.

I set my lamp on the ground and fished for the matches in my pocket. I lit one and held it experimentally against the end of the wick. It caught just like a candle and smoldered, still too faint to see into the room. But its light illuminated a knob, at one end of the tube, that connected to a rusted pipe just above it. I twisted it. There was a click like gears, followed by a slow drip, then suddenly, with a *whoosh*, the flame began to spread along the wick, stretching the perimeter of the room and bathing it all in a bloody light.

The room was clearly Geisler's laboratory, but it wasn't the workshop full of cogs and gears I had expected. This

176

was less a workshop and more a morgue, or a scene from some medieval dungeon. There were human limbs—*fresh* human limbs, I realized with a jolt—wilting on a gouged bench. Some were split down the middle, with gears spilling out between the seams as though they had been stuffed in rather than lined up to actually operate. Unmistakably human organs were stacked in pickling jars on a shelf above them, floating in a frothy yellow liquid, and skin was stretched and pinned against one wall like tanning leather. In the center was a heavy metal table, blood and rust on its bolts glinting the same flaky orange.

The glass lighting tube stopped at a spot on the wall where the darkness seemed somehow deeper. I took a few steps toward it before I realized it was a barred cell like a prison. Inside were two naked bodies, one lying facedown, the other on its side with its back to me. I reached through the bars with my spanner, hooked it around an arm, and tugged. Instead of the body rolling over like I had expected, the torso crumbled away from the legs and fell onto its back. The entire front of the chest was missing, rib cage nothing but bloody splintered stumps and the inside stripped clean. The corpse was empty.

I stumbled backward, tripped over myself, and sat down hard on the dirt floor. The thought of what might have occupied the floor before me sent me scrambling back to my feet so fast I knocked over my burner and snuffed it. I had to swallow hard several times to keep myself from being sick. I had seen bodies before, seen them gutted and stripped and reconstructed, seen metal fused with muscle and bone, even done it myself, but there was something about this, the brutality and obsession of it, that made me light-headed.

I needed to be out of here. There was no chance I'd forget what I'd seen, but I didn't have to stare at it any longer. I groped along the wall for the knob that had ignited the glass tube and turned it the opposite direction. Like the Carcel burner, the flame sank and died with a chatter of gears, leaving me in total darkness. I stumbled forward until my shin smacked against the bottom rung of the ladder and I started to clamber up, one hand groping above for the trapdoor. My fingers brushed cold gears, and I started clawing at them, feeling for the lever and the mechanism that would get them moving again and set me free.

Then, above me, the workshop door opened.

I froze, listening hard. Footsteps crossed the floor, passed above me, and stopped, followed by a soft *flump* like the sound of a heavy cloth hitting the ground.

I eased myself down onto the top rung, trying to determine who was walking above me and what chance I would stand if I made a run for it. I would risk the automatons—I was certain I could outrun them back to the house. But if it wasn't an automaton, it would be Geisler, and I couldn't let him catch me sneaking out of his underground laboratory.

A loud, hollow *thunk* on the other side of the floorboards made me jump. Something heavy had been dropped. Slow footsteps followed and the distinct buzz of machinery. It had to be one of the automatons. If I snuck out the trapdoor and hit the floor running, I could make it out.

I gave a hard tug on the cogs beside me, then yanked my hand out of the way as they started to turn, lever churning like a piston. A sliver of pale darkness began to expand above me as the trapdoor opened. I waited, my body a loaded spring, until the gap was finally wide enough, then I hoisted myself up into the workshop and ran. As I reached the door, I tossed a quick glance over my shoulder to where I was certain the automaton was waiting.

But it wasn't an automaton. It was Clémence.

Clémence was crumpled on the floor beside the empty fireplace, bare arms wrapped around herself, but I could see she was naked from the waist up. Her skin looked bone-white against the darkness. On the floor next to her, her coat and blouse lay in a heap, the large spanner from the workbench beside them.

I stopped short, one hand on the door. Clémence looked up at the same time, and for a moment we just gaped at each other. I had to focus on keeping my eyes on her face instead of letting them wander down—even with her arms crossed over her chest, her bare shoulders were enough to make the air around me feel hotter.

"Clémence," I said, her name the only word that shoved itself through my surprise.

She didn't say anything, and I realized each of her deep breaths shuddered and cracked like a static pulse.

It seemed a daft question, but I asked anyway. "Are you all right?" Her hair swung over her shoulder as she shook her head. I took a step forward. "Can I help?"

She nodded and I went the rest of the way across the room and knelt beside her. When she spoke, her voice sounded like ripping paper. "Can you fix me?"

"Can I . . . what?"

Then she moved her arms, and I saw what she meant.

The skin across her chest wasn't skin at all, but a hard steel panel that swung open like a door, and inside she was mechanical. Her rib cage on one side was gone, replaced by steel rods and a small cluster of churning gears connected to oiled paper bellows that jerked up and down as she gasped for air.

Mechanical, like Oliver.

She took another drowning breath and I realized one of her steel ribs had come undone and was sloping inward at an odd angle so that it pressed on the bellows and kept them from inflating properly. By some miracle, it hadn't punctured her skin or the oiled paper.

"I can fix it," I said. "A bolt's come loose, that's all."

She flapped her hand toward the spanner she had discarded on the floor. "Wrong size," I said, pulling the smaller one out from my braces. "I've got the right one here. Sorry."

"So this is . . . all your fault," she murmured.

"Did you actually try to fix it with that massive thing?" I nudged the large spanner with my foot.

Clémence laughed weakly. "Made it worse."

"Yes," I said. "Stop talking for a minute."

It was hard to see in the dim light, and I wished fervently for the magnifying goggles that were probably in pieces back in my father's ransacked shop. I reached down with one hand to the steel plate beneath the bellows where the bolt had fallen, then nudged the loose rib back into place with the other. Clémence gasped like she was surfacing from water.

I set the bolt and twisted it with the spanner, still holding her rib cage where it should be. "You're going to be all right," I told her as I worked. She didn't say anything, but I felt her pulse slow. It was strange, the way I could feel it echoing through her chest, so close I might as well have been holding her heart in my hand. When I worked on Oliver, it was always gears ticking, but Clémence was real and alive, flesh on top of metal.

When I finished, she took several deep breaths, each steaming white against the cold air. I watched the bellows flex, returning more to their original shape with every inhalation.

"Better?" I asked.

"Yes," she said, her voice still feathery but stronger. She shut the panel across her chest, then climbed to her feet with a hiss of pain. I looked away as she retrieved her coat from the floor and wrapped it around herself, pulling it tight at the waist. For a moment, it seemed like she was going to walk out without saying anything else and we'd be left with each other's secrets, but then, with one hand still pressed to her rib cage, she sank down again, and I slid from the balls of my feet so we were sitting side by side, with our backs against the wall.

Neither of us said anything for a while. We didn't look at each other either, just stared forward into the darkness. Then Clémence asked, "Would you like to go first?"

"First at what?"

"Asking questions. I suspect you're a bit slower to trust than I am, so I'm hoping that if I tell my story you'll be more inclined to tell me yours."

"All right, uh . . . ," I fumbled, mostly because I had so many questions I didn't know where to start, but Clémence tipped her chin to her chest and smiled sadly.

"Am I that repulsive?"

"No," I said quickly. "Not that at all. I think you're . . . remarkable."

She looked up, and her hair caught a button on her shoulder so that it fell into a swinging arc beneath her chin. "You don't have to—"

"I mean it." I said. "How did it happen?"

She took a deep breath, and I heard the bellows inside

her inflate with a crackle. Now that I knew it was there, I wasn't sure how I hadn't heard it before.

"I was born in Paris, you know that," she said. "My family survived the Revolution by selling black powder to the Jacobins, and when everything settled down, my father turned that enterprise into a business manufacturing mining explosives, and he made a lot of money doing it. It was a good life, I suppose, if you enjoy uncomfortable shoes and boring conversation." She pushed the strand of hair behind her ear. "The spring I turned fourteen, I went to Geneva to see a friend. Against my parents' wishes. Not that it matters. While I was there, I was in a carriage accident, and one side of my body was crushed. I was treated by Dr. Geisler, and he saw me as a chance to test an experiment he had been perfecting in his mind for years. Internal repairs, I suppose you could say."

"I'm familiar with it."

"He saved my life, but when I returned to Paris and told my parents, they threw me out."

"God's wounds. You'd think they'd be pleased you weren't dead."

"To them, I was. Being mechanical is as good as dead, and I'm worse because I can't survive without clockwork in me. I've never met anyone else like that."

I thought of Oliver but didn't say anything.

"So I was a girl alone in Paris with no home or family

and no money when I got word that Geisler was look-ing for me. He wanted payment for his services, and I had nothing. I could have taken debtors' prison, but that seemed like throwing away my second chance at life. So Geisler agreed to let me work for him and pay off my debt that way."

"How long are you contracted with him?"

"Fifteen years."

"So you're not his assistant?"

She gave a brittle laugh. "No, nothing like that. I don't know anything about mechanics, or medicine. I'm just paying off what I owe. Geisler doesn't like me and he doesn't particularly want me here, but I'm obligated to stay silent about the things he'd rather most people didn't know about his research. Which is a good quality in a worker, I suppose."

"So why did you tell me you were his assistant?"

"I don't know." She pursed her lips in what might have started as a smile but ended up looking like pain. "Because it's a kinder word than *slave*."

I pulled my knees up to my chest and rested my elbows on them. The cold was staring to come back now, and I shivered. "What sorts of things do you work on with Geisler?"

"You mean do I work downstairs?" She rapped the floorboards with her knuckles. "No point in pretending it isn't there."

I could still smell it, sharp and foul in the back of my throat, and I resisted the urge to spit. "What's he trying to do?"

"You saw it. And if you were in Geneva two years ago, you know. He wants to bring back the dead."

I had guessed. But I needed to hear her say it.

"He's been obsessed with it for a while," she continued. "It sort of dropped off after we first left Geneva, and I thought he'd given up. But since *Frankenstein* came out, he's been back at it, more manic than ever. I don't understand what he's so upset over. He's acting like that book's an instruction manual for resurrection, but it's just a stupid made-up story."

"You came from Geneva with Geisler?" I asked, and she nodded. "So you were with him when he fled."

"No, after he was arrested I hid out in Ornex for a while. We met up after he'd escaped and came straight here."

"Oh." The knot that had been forming in my chest loosened. She hadn't been with Geisler the night he left the city, so she couldn't refute my story about Oliver's death. I was still safe.

She arched an eyebrow. "Why?"

"My brother died that night," I said. "That's all."

"How did he die? You never told me."

"You don't want to hear that story."

"I do. If you'll tell it."

I looked down at my boots. It occurred to me suddenly that I could tell her the truth. For the first time, I could tell someone the real story of how Oliver had died. Clémence hardly knew me, and I hardly knew her. We'd probably part for good in a few days, and whatever she thought of me was of little consequence. I had gotten so rehearsed in my lie that I'd forgotten telling the truth was even an option.

"Geisler hid with our family for two nights after he escaped from prison," I began, not quite sure which version was about to come out of my mouth—they both started the same. "The police were looking for him, and security around the borders was tight, so he thought it would be safer to lie low in Geneva before he made a run for it. The night he left, Oliver and I went with him. We were meant to be some sort of cover, since the police were looking for a man alone, not three, and to be certain he made it safely to the river."

I stopped. For a moment, I had thought I was going to say it—to say what I'd done. But then, all at once, I couldn't. The words were caught inside me, too stiff and scared and soaked in guilt to find their way out.

There was no chance of telling the truth, I realized, not because of Clémence but because of me. I couldn't say it out loud. It was hard enough to admit it was truth at all. So I reverted to the same story I'd told Oliver and my parents and myself over and over in my head across the last two years. "Geisler took us to the clock tower first, where his laboratory was. He wanted to get his journals with all his notes on resurrection. Oliver didn't like the resurrection work—he'd been helping Geisler with it as part of his apprenticeship, but he thought it was mad and he was angry that Geisler wanted to keep it going. They got in a row, Oliver jumped at Geisler, Geisler pushed him into the clock face, and it broke, and . . ." My voice snagged. "Oliver fell."

"So Geisler killed you brother."

"It was an accident," I said, louder than I meant to. "Oliver thinks Geisler did it on purpose, but it was an accident."

There was a moment of silence, then she said, "Your brother died."

When I looked up, she was watching me with her head tipped. "Yes."

"So how did he tell you what he thought about his death?"

I almost laughed at my own mistake. How many times had I thought I was so guarded and ready to face any question that would ever be thrown at me? But I had spoken without thinking, the same gormless way I'd addressed her in English when we met. Something about her disarmed me. "I misspoke."

"I don't think you did." She studied me hard for a

moment, like she was trying to find some answer in my face, then said, "That's why Geisler sent for you, isn't it? You brought your brother back from the dead, and he wants you to show him how you did it." When I didn't deny it, Clémence let out a long breath and slumped a little farther down the wall. "How did Geisler know? Did you tell him?"

"No, he read it."

"Read it where?"

"In *Frankenstein*."

"You mean . . . ?"

"Geisler thinks it's about Oliver and me."

"Is it?"

I swallowed hard. Saying it out loud somehow made it feel truer than it had before. "I think so too."

"God's wounds. Are you some sort of genius, then?"

"No," I said quickly. "I understand mechanical things. That's all."

"It takes more than that to bring someone back to life. Even Geisler couldn't do it."

"I didn't know he was still trying. I assumed he gave up on his resurrections after they nearly got him executed."

"He's just gotten more obsessive. And brutal. You saw the laboratory. He tried to do that work at the university, but they shut him down. Threatened to have him arrested if he didn't stop. That's why he had this place built. The police keep an eye on it but they haven't found him out yet." There was a pause, then she asked, "Did he invite you to come do research with him?"

"Yes. He wants me to study at the university. He said I could bring my brother here if I showed him how the resurrection worked."

"How much did you tell him?"

"Just that I brought Oliver back. Nothing specific."

"Do you know Dr. Geisler well?"

"Not well. He was friends with my father. The first proper conversation we had was when I arrived here. Oliver knows him better than I do." *And Oliver never liked him*, said a small voice in my head.

"Did he tell you his bit about good men and clever men?"

"Yes."

She smirked. "It's his favorite line. He uses it at the start of every term. Dr. Geisler is . . ." She paused, fingers working at the frayed cuff of her sleeve. "Not a good man. I can't imagine that after you showed him how to bring people back from the dead he'd have much more need for you. Or your brother, who, if reports are to be believed, isn't very good either. Though I'm not sure about you yet."

"What about me?"

"Are you good, or are you clever?"

I didn't know how to answer that. I'd spent so long

living with this monstrous thing I'd done that I didn't feel either anymore. "Thank you," I said instead of answering, "for telling me."

"About my accident?"

"About Geisler. And yes, that too."

She slid her hands into her sleeves and folded them across her stomach. "I don't know much about you, but I know about the Shadow Boys, and I'm assuming you live in a way that makes secrets and lies as necessary as breathing. I think people need to be trusted every now and then with something sacred of someone else's just to understand that not everyone will turn on you."

I knew she had said it to be kind, but guilt wriggled inside me for not telling her the truth about Oliver. I stood up and offered her my hand, careful when I pulled her up not to strain her mechanical circuit. "We should go in. I think it's nearly morning."

She retrieved her shirt from the floor, then turned her back to me as she dropped her coat and pulled it on. "You go on. I sleep out here."

"What? He's got that whole big house and he doesn't even give you somewhere to sleep?"

"He thinks it's as much as I deserve."

"It's bleeding cold out here."

She shrugged. "I've got a coat."

"Come inside with me. You can sleep in my room, then sneak out in the morning before we go."

"What a sound plan, Mr. Finch."

"So let's sleep in the sitting room then. I'll stay with you. If Geisler finds us, say we were talking and fell asleep."

"What about the automatons?"

"They don't come in my room—more reason to stay up there. Come on, I'll be thinking about you all night if you don't." She paired a cocked eyebrow with her usual smirk, and I felt myself go scarlet. "I'll be worried," I corrected. "Please. I'll stay out here if you don't come in."

She stared at me for a moment, but I knew before she spoke what her answer would be.

"Fine," she said, and pulled on her coat.

As we walked back to the house, I reached out and took her hand. Her fingers were cold and chapped—I knew mine were too—but the feeling of her skin warmed me. I hadn't held anyone's hand in a long time, and it felt better than I expected.

Once inside, we made for the sitting room, but one of the automatons was standing in front of the fire and looked as though it had no intention of moving anytime soon. "Upstairs," I mouthed at Clémence. She shook her head and gestured to go back the way we'd come, but I dragged her after me into my bedroom and shut the door behind us.

The fire was dying, and it took another log and some

coaxing from the poker until it consented to burn properly again. When I turned from the hearth, Clémence was standing by my bed, trailing her fingers along the covers.

She caught my eye and smiled sheepishly. "Is it shallow to say I miss living well?"

"I don't think it's shallow. I think it's human." I glanced around the room, which suddenly felt very small, with the two of us and that massive bed in between. "You can have the bed, if you like."

"And what about you?"

"I can curl up at the end, I suppose."

"Not a chance." She pulled back the covers and patted the mattress. "Come get in with me."

My stomach gave an odd lurch. "I can't do that."

"We don't have to *do* anything," she said with a sly smile that made me blush to my bones. "We're just keeping each other warm. Come on, this was your idea."

And I couldn't argue with that.

Neither of us had nightclothes, so we just took off our shoes and crawled under the covers. I tried to keep a chaste distance from Clémence, but she wiggled up next to me, her forehead buried in my neck, so close that I could feel her heartbeat like it was inside me, thumping in tandem with mine.

Lying there beside her, thawing from the cold with her body warm against mine, was somehow both the most gentlemanly and most ungentlemanly thing I had ever done. My father would have had a fit if he'd known. Mary Godwin, on the other hand, with all her modern sensibilities, would have applauded. She would have wanted to be that girl, I thought. The girl I slept beside but didn't sleep with.

We talked for a while as the fire faded back into cinders. Clémence was delighted to learn that I had picked up my French in Paris, not, as she said, at some fancy Scottish boarding school. I told her that Scotland wasn't really the land of fancy boarding schools. She laughed, and, in spite of everything, I smiled.

"Are you coming to Geneva with us?" I asked her.

"Geisler wants me to. Someone has to carry his luggage."

"That's good. I'm glad."

She twisted her face up to mine. "Why are you glad?"

"Glad I don't have to deal with Geisler on my own."

"Oh." She looked away and pressed her cheek to my shoulder again. She smelled like smoke and iron, that faint breath of metal that pushed Oliver into my mind without warning. I tried to shove him away and focus on what Clémence was saying, and after a while I managed to pry my thoughts away from my brother, and from Geisler, and the mess waiting for me on the other side of the dawn. Exhaustion filled the space they left behind, and I started to drift off. I could tell Clémence was fading too—she kept forgetting to finish her sentences, and we both seemed more frequently unable to find the word we were looking for, let alone string it properly with others.

My eyes were closed, sleep's fingers curling around me, when Clémence's voice floated up to me like steam from a teacup. "Can I tell you one more thing? Since we've said a lot already."

"Go on," I replied, though I already had one foot in dreams and was only picking up every few words.

"When I told you about the first boy I kissed—Marco in the theater troupe in Paris . . ."

She went quiet, and I said, "Yes?" so she knew I hadn't fallen asleep.

"I lied." There was a moment of trembling silence, then she laughed, soft as a breath against a window-pane. "I don't know anyone called Marco, and my father would have murdered me if I had run around with actors. The first person I kissed wasn't a boy at all." Her body slid against mine until there wasn't an inch of us apart, and I could feel her breath, her heartbeat, her crackling paper lungs. "Her name was Valentine."

When I woke the next morning, the fire was ashes and Clémence's side of the bed was cold. I sat up, covers falling off me, and tried my best to sort out what had actually happened last night and what had been a dream.

Nothing, I realized with a sick lurch. I hadn't dreamed any of it.

And now I was going to Geneva to fetch Oliver for Geisler's mad research.

I climbed out of bed and changed into the clothes I had arrived in as I considered my choices, or rather choice, because backing out now was impossible. I had to go to Geneva—Geisler was tearing up bodies in his cellar, so who knew what he would do if I stood in the way of his work?—but I didn't have a clue what to do once we arrived. The last few days thinking Geisler would help me take care of Oliver had been glorious. The freest I had felt in years. Letting that go after coming so close made me want to climb straight back into bed and refuse to budge.

I stepped out of my bedroom and into the hallway. At the top of the stairs, a small window overlooked the front path leading to the road. Depace's wagon was parked at the gate, stacked with twice as many coffins as there had been when I'd ridden in it. Depace was leaning against the wheel chatting with Geisler while Clémence, her gray coat thrown over her blue dress, stood on the driver's seat tugging on the thick ropes that held the coffins in place. At first I thought they were unloading more bodies for Geisler's laboratory, but it didn't make sense for them to be doing it in broad daylight and just before Geisler was to leave for Geneva. That and Clémence seemed to be securing the coffins, not unloading them. I watched them until my stomach growled and I went in search of breakfast.

There were scones and coffee in the kitchen, and I took some into the sitting room and settled down to eat in front of the fire. The house felt dead quiet. The constant ticking of the clocks had blended into the silence so I could hardly hear them apart.

I had less of an appetite than I thought, and I mostly picked currants out of the scones instead of actually eating anything. After a few minutes, I heard the front door creak; then Geisler stuck his head into the sitting room. He smiled when he saw me. I nearly threw up.

"Good, you're awake," he said. "I'd like to leave within the hour."

"I'm ready," I said, then added, "Are we traveling with Depace?"

Geisler laughed. "No, he was just doing me a favor. We're traveling in a bit more style than that."

"More style" turned out to be a compact sleigh painted forest green and powered by steam and clock-work. Geisler informed me that it would be faster than a carriage after the blizzard, and would allow us to go off the road if we needed to. In spite of how gloomy I was feeling, I couldn't resist bending down to see the engine.

Clémence stepped over me as she did a lap around the sleigh to check that everything was stowed. "You look as though Christmas came early."

I stood up, scrubbing my hands along my arms for warmth. "It's amazing. I've never seen anything like it."

"The doctor made it. It gets us where we need to be faster than a carriage. The only disadvantage is, it's use-less three of the four seasons."

"What was Depace doing here earlier?" I asked as she tugged on one of the luggage straps.

"Collecting something from Geisler."

"Collecting? What's Geisler got that he wants?"

She kicked one of the runners, and a lump of wet snow was knocked free. "I don't know. I just do the lifting."

"Mademoiselle Le Brey," I heard Geisler call from the doorway. "Are we ready?"

"Nearly." Clémence glanced over her shoulder at the house, then sideways at me. "Are you all right? You look a bit weary."

I hadn't been *less* all right in a long time. The image of Geisler's bloody laboratory was still branded across my brain, and leaving for Geneva with him felt like taking a step into darkness. What I was meant to do when we got there was eating at me. I could still hand Oliver over. That thought whispered inside me in the same sly, horrid voice that had sent me to Ingolstadt in the first place. Geisler might not be a good man, but Oliver was valuable to him—too important to be treated badly. And I had spent so long putting Oliver ahead of what I wanted, trying to make up for what I'd done and only feeling worse. If we returned here with Geisler, I could study at Ingolstadt and Oliver wouldn't have to be shut up in Château de Sang tearing apart the furniture. It could be better.

But Oliver would still be an experiment, something to be studied and tested and taken apart. I'd be doing work that interested me, but he would be my work. Victor Frankenstein and his monster in earnest.

The other choice was getting to Oliver before Geisler could and then fleeing Geneva. But Ingolstadt would be behind me for good if I did that, and Geisler, and every dream I'd clung to of studying here someday, or going to university at all. Going back to Geneva was a return to Oliver and a life spent hiding and looking after him and staring him in the face and wondering where he'd gone. I'd be right back where I started—alone, with my wild brother to care for and now a madman on our tail.

So which is it going to be? I thought. Was I just the same as Geisler and Victor Frankenstein, or could I choose Oliver?

Are you good, whispered that horrid voice inside me, *or are you clever?*

Behind me, Clémence whistled. "Coming, Finch?"

I took a deep breath. I wanted to stand there forever, listening to the house tick and never moving past this moment or making a decision. But the engine was growling and the sun was on the snow, and I cut my tracks around the sleigh and joined her.

Clémence took the seat in the back without asking while Geisler climbed into the front. I hesitated, not sure where I was meant to sit, until Geisler called me over to his side. I cast a pleading look at Clémence, but she just raised her eyebrows, and I reluctantly pulled myself up next to him. As we set off in a wide loop around Ingolstadt, I turned back and took a last look at the university spire rising above the rooftops.

Geisler took a different route than I remembered. We sped along roads too narrow for a wagon, with splashes of snow spilling from the moaning pine boughs and owls swooping low between the trees. We all wore green-lensed goggles to shield our eyes from the wind and the sunlight bouncing off the snow like diamonds, but I still had to squint.

There were circulating-steam foot warmers, and the pelts of several thick-furred animals to wrap up in, but the wind still managed to find every possible route under my coat and I felt cold to my bones. I had brought *Frankenstein* with the intention of finishing it but the thought of exposing my hands, even gloved, to the cold didn't appeal to me. I was drowsy from sitting up the night before with Clémence, but when I tried to sleep, I remembered a book Oliver had read when we were both in the throes of our polar-exploration phase in Bergen. The book said that when you're about to freeze to death, you get dead sleepy, and death comes as a sort of drifting off. It didn't seem likely that I would freeze, but the thought still kept my eyes open.

That and Geisler's chatter. Now that we were on our way, a scientific expedition in progress, he seemed to feel permitted to interrogate me about Oliver and his resurrection. How long had it taken? What stock weight had

I used for the gears? How had I handled the severed arteries?

I dodged the questions as valiantly as I could, uttering "I don't remember" more than anything else. "I hope you remember a bit more once we start work," he snapped at me after what felt like hours of it. "Or else you won't be much good for holding up your end of the bargain."

"I'm sorry," I said. "I'll remember."

He grunted, eyes forward on the snowy lane. "Any more ideas about the authorship of your memoir?"

I bristled at the term but kept my face straight. "Not yet, sir. I've been thinking."

We fell into a tense silence after that. I could feel Geisler stewing beside me, but he must have consoled himself with the thought that soon the three of us—he, Oliver, and I—would be together in Ingolstadt and there would be a living experiment for him to examine.

On the fourth night of our journey, we crossed into Switzerland on an unmarked vineyard road and stopped at an inn a few miles from Geneva's walls. Traveling had left me with an aching, full-body fatigue, but I dreaded sleep. I'd had nothing but nightmares since we left Ingolstadt, and they grew worse each night. Clémence didn't seem inclined to go up to bed either, so after Geisler retired, we ordered warm wine and *chouquettes* and sat in the common room long after most people were gone.

Three drinks in, I found myself warm and airy and

talking about Oliver. I'm not sure how we arrived there—maybe it was the wine—but suddenly I was telling her stories from when we were boys, things I hadn't thought about in years, let alone told anyone. Clémence listened, hands around her mug, and it was a while before I realized she wasn't really saying anything, just letting me talk myself hoarse.

"Oliver always got up to stupid things just to be daring, like nicking sweets and sneaking us into places we shouldn't be. He had to touch everything we were told not to touch. Climb whatever said 'keep off.' That sort of thing. It got more serious when we got older. I bailed him out of jail twice. And he was so bleeding impulsive. Once, when we lived in Brussels, Oliver and I went to school, but everyone was mean because they knew what our family did. One boy threw rocks at me in the yard, so Oliver pushed him down a stairway and he broke his collarbone."

"God's wounds," Clémence said. I couldn't decide if she sounded horrified or impressed.

I tore a *chouquette* in half but didn't eat it. "The headmaster asked us what had happened, and Oliver said we'd been acting out the Bible, and he'd been playing God."

Clémence laughed. "I'm not sure if that's gallant of him to look out for you, or stupid."

"Both, I suppose. He was reckless. It's a miracle he

survived as long as he did." I stopped and took a quick drink, but that deep, permanent ache that came with talking about Oliver had already surfaced strong as ever. At some point, wasn't this meant to stop hurting so badly?

"Are you all right?" Clémence asked.

"Yeah, it's just . . ." I scrubbed my hands through my hair. "You know how when you're a child, you think you're never going to die? You've survived everything so far, so you don't realize that's going to stop. I never felt that way. I was always so aware that I wasn't indestructible—I suppose that's a side effect of living in the world we did. But it never occurred to me that Oliver might die. He was half of my whole life, and no matter what happened or where we went, no matter how shitty things got, there was always the two of us. I always had him." The candle-light reflected in the surface of my wine rippled as I worked my fingers around the mug. "And then, the week before we left Paris, Oliver cut his knuckles boxing when a man threw a bottle into the ring. It got infected, and all the travel and the sleeping on cold floors and not having enough to eat really knocked him over. When we got to Lyon, he could hardly stand, he was so ill."

I remembered it suddenly, clear as water—how pale and shaky he'd been, the slick fever sheen in his eyes, how I'd had to hold him on his feet as we stood in line to get our papers stamped because they wouldn't let us on the boat if they knew he was sick.

When we were finally on board, Father pulled me aside. He looked very serious. "We'll be in Geneva in a few hours—Geisler will have a place for us to stay once we get there. You need to keep Oliver awake until then. He'll want to sleep, but you can't let him."

"You should tell him," I said, but Father shook his head.

"He won't listen to me."

"I don't think—"

"He'll listen to you, Alasdair. He always listens to you." He clapped me once on the shoulder like it was all ordinary, but his fingers went tight just for a moment, and I felt their print in my skin even after he let go. "Keep him warm and keep him awake."

Oliver was already below deck, curled up against our trunks with a blanket across his knees. When I sat down beside him, he pressed his forehead into my shoulder. His skin was burning. Then, like he'd overheard my conversation with Father, he said, "I'm so tired, Ally."

My heartbeat jumped, and I said quickly, "Well, stay awake." He moaned and I added, "Recite something for me."

"I can't think of anything."

"Rubbish. Tell me something from *Paradise Lost*."

I felt him take a long, slow breath. *"Did I request thee, Maker, from my clay / To mould me Man, did I solicit thee / From darkness to promote me?"* he murmured, then fell silent. When I looked over, his eyes were closed.

"That's good," I said loudly. "Is that Shakespeare?"

He opened his eyes. "That's Milton, you ninny."

I knew that, because he was in his phase where he never shut up about Milton, but it seemed the only sure way to rouse him. He was so sick and pale at that point and I couldn't remember a time I'd seen him that way.

Somewhere, from a distance that felt like another world, I heard Clémence say, "Alasdair, you don't have to talk about this."

I wrenched myself back to the present and looked across the table at her. She was watching me like she was afraid I might shatter. "I'd never thought about it," I said. "Not until that moment on the boat trying to pretend I was just keeping him awake when really I was keeping him alive. And suddenly I realized that someday I might have to live in a world without Oliver. That one of us might die young and it might be him. I'd thought about dying, but never about being left behind, and that was so bleeding terrifying." I could feel something in me starting to fray, so I put my head in my hands and held it there for a long, deep breath. My throat was tight, but I didn't cry. I was afraid if I started, I'd never stop.

Clémence's fingers brushed my arm. "Alasdair."

I did my best to rearrange my face into something like calm, but when I looked up at her, I still felt shaky.

"I can't hand Oliver over to Geisler."

"Have you been trying to work that out the whole trip? You should have asked me—I would have told you that a long time ago."

"Don't be an ass, you don't understand."

"So explain it to me."

I traced the rim of my mug with my thumb and stared down at the inky surface of the wine. "All I've ever wanted my whole life is to study at Ingolstadt with Geisler. And when I brought Oliver back, I had to give that up. But coming here, and what Geisler offered me—I could have it back again. I could have Ingolstadt *and* Oliver."

"So you really were going to assume your rightful place as Victor Frankenstein."

"Never mind." I shoved my chair back and started to stand, but Clémence caught me around the wrist.

"Sorry, sorry, I shouldn't have said that. Sit down." I stood still, face away from her, until she gave another tug and I let her drag me back down. She ducked her head, staring down at the *chouquettes*, and nodded once. "All right. So you're not giving Oliver to Geisler. What made up your mind?"

I took a drink so I didn't have to answer right away. I wasn't sure how to explain that Oliver had been so good before he died—wild and impulsive and absolutely mental sometimes, but *good*. The more I'd thought about him since I left Geneva, the more I had remembered that. And if there was a sliver of that left somewhere inside of him, it was worth giving up Ingolstadt and clockwork and studying with Geisler. Because more than any of that, I wanted Oliver back the way he had been—the boy who'd stolen strawberries for my birthday and skated with me and knocked out a man's teeth when he tried to hurt a clockwork beggar. If there was even a chance he was still there, I couldn't hand him over for Geisler to take apart in his laboratory.

But instead of any of that, I said, "He's my brother." Right then, it felt like reason enough.

The clock above the mantelpiece struck two. The common room was nearly empty. Clémence glanced up as a couple down the table from us departed, then back at me. "So you go to Geneva, play along so Geisler thinks you're still on his side. Then you grab Oliver and run." That was the extent of my plan, so I nodded. "And what happens to Oliver after that? Have you thought that maybe you should let him go?"

"You mean on his own?" I shook my head. "I can't do that, he's . . ." I trailed off, remembering she had gears running inside her, but she finished for me.

"A monster?"

"I wasn't going to say that."

"You were going to use a sweeter word, but it still means the same thing."

"People wouldn't understand him. He'd never find somewhere safe to live on his own, especially not with *Frankenstein* out. Can you imagine anyone would want Frankenstein's monster renting a flat from them or working at their shop?"

"Have you ever thought," she countered, "that maybe Oliver only acts like a monster because you treat him like one?"

I frowned. "How do you mean that?"

"You keep him locked up, away from everyone. You've taught him what he is by that alone. There are places in this world that are safe for clockwork men. I've heard that in Russia they're actually employing mechanics in their hospitals to help put men injured in the war back together. Most places are better than Geneva anyways, so get him out of there. Find somewhere to settle him. It doesn't have to be far from you, but if he's on his own, he won't feel like he's something that has to be hidden. That alone might change his temperament."

"What about this?" I pulled *Frankenstein* out of my coat pocket and set it on the table between us. "Oliver's not like other clockworks—people will figure out it's about him wherever he goes."

"Maybe you need to find the author," she said. "Talk to him."

"I'm worried it might be Oliver."

"I don't think so. He would have made himself the hero of his story, don't you think?" She picked up *Frankenstein* and turned it over like there was some clue hidden in its binding. "The remarkable thing about this book is that everyone's trying to make it a political statement, but I don't think the author was. It just feels like a story. If you're lucky, most people who read it will assume it's fiction."

I thought of the badges issued to clockworks in Geneva. Frankenstein badges. People had already taken it as fact. "It's too strange to be fiction," I said. "There's got to be a reason someone wrote it."

"And there's no one else who knows?" she asked. "You're certain?"

"No one. Just me and Oliver and . . ." I trailed off.

But Clémence heard the trail. "And?"

"And what?"

"You said *and*. There's an *and*. Who's the *and*?"

I sighed. "Do you remember the girl I told you about, Mary Godwin? The first girl I kissed."

A slow smile spread across her face. "Alasdair Finch. Did you go bragging about your clockwork resurrection to impress a pretty girl?"

"No, it wasn't like that," I said. "I mean it was, she was pretty, and I . . ." Clémence's smile was going wider and I stopped before I made a fool of myself. "Oliver and I were friends with her in Geneva. After he died, I didn't know anyone else I could ask and I couldn't do it by myself, so she dug up his coffin with me, and went to the clock tower to bring him back. She was there the whole time."

"Then it's her. She wrote it."

"It's not."

"It has to be."

"No," I said. "Mary didn't write it."

"Yes she did," Clémence replied just as firmly. "You just don't want it to be her."

"And what's that supposed to mean?"

"You're still sweet on her and you can't bear the idea that she gave up your story to the world, so you've talked yourself into believing there's no chance it could be her. It's much easier to suspect Geisler or Oliver or someone who you're already not fond of."

"She wouldn't write it."

"Why not?"

"Because when you trust someone, they don't do that to you."

"And you trusted her?"

"I did."

"Do you, or did you?"

"She wouldn't write it," I protested. "She knew everything about us and what we did, but she never told anyone. She promised . . ."

I stopped. Mary had kept all her promises—that was

the way I had decided to remember her. All I'd thought about for two years was that she was gone and how much I missed her, not how she'd left. I'd forgotten the day she disappeared, the last time we spoke. The last promise she'd made me. The one she hadn't kept.

We'd taken Oliver up to the castle, and it had seemed for those early days that no matter how badly things had gone, at least I had Mary to help me through. And so when she promised I could have my first sleep in three days and she'd stay awake to watch Oliver, I hadn't even questioned that she meant it. I'd fallen asleep with my head on her shoulder and woken curled on the cold stone floor, just me and my alive-again brother, and when I went to find her, the man at her villa said they'd all gone home to London, just like that, without a word.

I didn't want it to be Mary who wrote it because I didn't want to think she could break promises to me so easily. But she already had, the day she left Geneva, long before *Frankenstein*.

"It's Mary Shelley," I said. "She wrote it."

Clémence crossed her arms. "To think I kissed you for this when you knew the answer all along."

"God's wounds." I dropped my head into my hands with a moan. "I've been such an idiot."

"You've not been an idiot. It's hard to believe that the people we love can do terrible things to us."

"But why would she write it?" I snatched up

Frankenstein and flipped through it like I might find her name somewhere I'd missed before. "It's not her story. She didn't do any of it, she was just *there*."

"That doesn't matter. What matters is, you know it's her, and you can find her and talk to her. Get Oliver out of Geneva, then find Mary Shelley. Convince her to tell everyone she wrote it and it's all a bunch of tosh, none of it real. Then people will stop looking for the resurrected man and Oliver can have his life back. You both can."

My heart was racing, but I felt steady. At the end of a long, dark road, a faint slash of dawn seemed to be finally breaking against the horizon. "That's what I'll do," I said.

Clémence looked down at her mug, then up at the clock above the fireplace. "I'm going to bed," she said. "Are you going to be all right?"

I nodded, though I still felt charged. Clémence stood and I thought she was going to leave, but instead she reached back across the table and put her hand on top of mine. "You can't make people the way you want them to be, Alasdair. Sometimes you just have to love them how they are."

And with that, she left me, and I sat up the rest of the night alone.

Once I realized Mary had written *Frankenstein*, I felt dead stupid for not letting myself believe it sooner. She knew us. She knew about the resurrection, and Geisler's work, and just enough of the stories of our lives to create these shadow versions of us in Victor Frankenstein and his monster.

And she had wanted to be a writer. The whole time she was in Geneva, she'd been fed a steady diet of gothic stories by her friends, and she had devoured them like sweets. Some of them she passed on to Oliver and me, like the legend of a castle tucked in the foothills outside the city, a hundred years abandoned and supposedly stuffed with ghosts.

So of course, she decided, we had to find it.

"I don't know exactly where it is," she confessed as we started hiking up into the pines. "I've only heard about it from my friends."

"If it's your friends who told you about it," Oliver called over his shoulder as he jogged ahead of her, "why don't *they* take you?"

Mary fisted her skirts and tugged them up out of the mud. "They don't go for that sort of thing."

"So what sorts of things do they do?" I asked.

"Oh, you know, spirit summoning and exorcisms and demon worship."

I stopped dead, at the same time Oliver turned to her and said, "God's wounds, are you joking?"

She laughed, but she didn't say she was.

The slope had barely begun in earnest when a storm broke overhead, the hard-driving sort of rain that plagued the city that whole summer. The pathway went slick and muddy under our feet, and we all slipped more than once. I kept suggesting we turn back, but Oliver was in the lead and he had never turned back from anything in his life. Between him and Mary, everything was a dare. Everything was a contest of who would give up first. Mary wasn't reckless like Oliver, just brave enough to make me feel boring in comparison.

By the time we crested the final ridge, all three of us were soaked through. The château seemed to materialize from the gray darkness, soot-stained bricks wrapped in fog risen from the rain.

I had to push my sopping hair out of my eyes to see it properly. "All right," I called over a shout of thunder. "We've seen it. Can we go back now?"

"You're very dull," Mary said. "We've come all this way, we might as well try to get inside."

I wasn't keen on that, but Oliver lit up like a firework, and before I could protest, he was already trotting off, Mary fast on his heels. I considered just sitting down where I was and refusing to go along with any more of their schemes, but Mary looked back over her shoulder at me, just one glance and a half smile and I was pulled helplessly after her, caught yet again in her magnetic field.

We circled the castle until we found a door with a heavy padlock. Mary rattled the latch like that might get us through. "Locked up tight."

"Alasdair can take care of it," Oliver offered. I glared at him, and he grinned.

"Do you know how to pick locks?" Mary asked me, but Oliver answered.

"He's brilliant at it. He could be a fantastic thief if he wanted to."

"It wasn't my idea to break into a castle," I muttered as I crouched down for a better view of the keyhole.

Suddenly Mary was right beside me, hand on my elbow to steady herself. I nearly toppled over. "Show me how. I've always wanted to learn."

"Fancy a bit of thievery yourself, Mistress Mary?" Oliver asked.

"I think it might come in handy someday, that's all."

I showed Mary how to get through the lock, first with needle files I had in my pocket and then with one of her hairpins. It gave easily when I tried, but it took her longer. Oliver kept grumbling from behind us about being wet and cold and what exactly were we doing down there with our hands out of sight. We both ignored him, but Mary's mouth kept twitching. When the lock finally sprang open, she gave a little laugh of delight. "My, but I do feel like a scoundrel. You boys make me daring," she said, and led the way into the musty entrance hall.

Inside the castle was like a museum, all the furniture from a hundred years past still in place but empty and unused, with piles of dust gathered in the corners and mold creeping through the faded wallpaper. The rain drummed its fingers against the vaulted ceilings and cast rippling shadows over the flagstones as drops slid down the windowpanes.

Mary and Oliver stopped a few paces in and looked around like we'd stepped into some grand cathedral. I stood behind them, ringing rainwater out of my waistcoat. They both seemed so impressed that I decided not to mention how bleeding creepy I thought the whole place was.

There was a hiss like a piston behind us, and we all turned in time to see the door steam shut. Oliver tried the handle, but it wouldn't give. "Dammit, it locked."

"Of course it locked, it's a prison," Mary said, and we both looked at her.

"A what?" Oliver said.

"A prison," she repeated. "Or it was, once."

Oliver scowled. "You might have mentioned that before we got locked inside."

"Don't you know the story?" Mary asked, and I shook my head. "A hundred years ago, the man who lived here killed his whole family, so the city made him serve his sentence under house arrest. They wanted him to live with the ghosts of what he'd done. I think he hanged himself before they could execute him. The family name was Sain. It's called Château de Sain but I've heard everyone calls it Château de Sang now."

"Blood Castle," I said, and I could have sworn the room got colder.

"Hell's teeth," Oliver murmured. "You and your grim stories. Think there's dungeons as well with skeletons hanging from the walls?" He looked like he was about to say something more, but his gaze snagged on me. I realized I was standing very close to Mary—*very* close, close enough to feel the damp material of her skirts brush the tips of my fingers as she shifted her weight. A sly smile started to spread across his face, and I panicked, certain he was about to say something teasing that would make me blush and her step away.

But instead he turned on his heel and started across the room. "You two stay here," he called, and shot me a knowing look over his shoulder. "I'm going to find another way out. Or the ghosts, whichever comes first."

Neither Mary nor I moved as he disappeared through a door across the room. We stood shoulder to shoulder, wet clothes dripping onto the floor and the silence between us filled by the muted echo of the storm. I could feel her next to me, an electric charge pulsing all up my side. She was still staring at the cobwebs and the dust and the peeling wallpaper with such a look of reverence on her face that I wondered if we were seeing the same thing. "What are you thinking of?" I asked her.

She took a long, deep breath, like the prelude to a sigh. *"The many men, so beautiful! / And they all dead did lie: / And a thousand thousand slimy things / Lived on; and so did I."*

I didn't know what she meant by that, but when I looked over at her, I thought for a moment she was crying. It might have been just the raindrops left on her face.

"What's the matter?" I asked.

"It's so beautiful," she whispered. "All empty and broken down. Sort of makes you want to . . ." She caught me looking at her and trailed off. I felt my cheeks get hot, but I didn't look away. Her gaze was fervent, so intense that it felt like a physical touch.

"Sort of makes you want to what?" I asked, my voice suddenly hoarse.

Between us, hidden in the folds of her skirt, her fingers slid into mine. Her skin was dewy from the rain but still impossibly warm. I felt the electric flare of her touch straight up my arm and all the way through me, our pulse points meeting like charged wires and sending up sparks.

"Sort of makes you want to write about it," she said.

I wasn't certain how we were going to get into the city, being possibly the two most wanted men in Geneva and traveling with a clockwork girl, but Geisler seemed unconcerned. He gave me a set of false identification papers that labeled me a student named Dieter Hahnel from Ingolstadt. Clémence had her own name on her papers, though I assumed they had been forged too, since nothing on them designated her as clockwork.

Geisler decided it would be better to travel apart in case one of us was recognized, so he left for the city just after breakfast; Clémence and I waited until nearly midday. The queue snaking along the city walls to the checkpoint was long when we arrived, and we waited for the better part of an hour, moving forward in shuffling steps as everyone around us buzzed nervously. The muddy snow was soaking through my boots, and I kept shifting from foot to foot to keep my toes from freezing. Beside me, Clémence kept her hands in her pockets and her gaze straight ahead. She seemed dead calm. When the girl in front of us dropped her scarf, Clémence plucked it out of the snow and tapped her on the shoulder. The girl turned, and smiled as she took it. "Oh! *Merci.*"

"*De rien,*" she replied, and ducked her head as the girl turned forward again. Clémence's cheeks went pink, and she kept glancing up at the back of the girl's head as we moved forward.

We reached the front of the queue sooner than I'd anticipated. I kept my scarf over my face and my knit cap pulled low as I handed over my papers to a tall officer. He glanced at them, then up at my face, then back at my papers. I held my breath.

"*Parlez-vous français?*" he asked.

Dieter Hahnel was supposed to be German. I didn't have a clue if he would speak French, so I kept my mouth shut and my face blank like I didn't understand. The soldier watched me for a moment with his eyebrows raised, then shrugged and flipped to the second page.

He was reaching for his stamp when another officer appeared and tapped him on the shoulder. "Your shift's up," he said in French. "I'm here to relieve you."

The first officer looked up from my papers. "Fantastic."

His hand was still on the stamp but he didn't seem like he was going to use it until his conversation was finished. I had to bite the inside of my cheek to keep from shouting, *Just stamp the damn thing!* "What happened with the protest?" he asked.

"All taken care of," the second officer replied. "A few arrests, but no one was hurt."

"Was it the Frankenstein lot again?"

Suddenly I was quite content to stand and eavesdrop.

But the officer chose that moment to stamp the second page of my papers and hand them back to me. *"Danke, Herr Hahnel,"* he said with a smile, and waved me forward.

I didn't have a clue how to respond in German, so I said in my best imitation of schoolboy French, *"Merci, monsieur."*

He laughed, and I kept grinning like an idiot as I walked past him and Clémence took my place. I was starting to relax when someone caught my arm, and I turned. It was another officer. He must have heard his fellow speaking to me in German, and must have spoken none himself, for he simply mimed instructions to me to hold out my arms. I'd gone through the checkpoint dozens of times and never had to do this before. Maybe they'd recognized me after all.

I kept my face straight as I held my arms out from

my sides, bracing myself for whatever was about to happen. But the officer didn't grab me; instead he traced my silhouette with his hands, fingers a few centimeters away from me. I didn't realize what was happening until the tin buttons on my coat wobbled, and I realized that his gloves were magnetic. He was checking for hidden metal parts.

I resisted the urge to look back at Clémence. I would make it through without a problem, but she'd be caught. And with *Frankenstein* on everyone's mind, clockwork lungs would earn her more than just a bronze cog badge.

After a quick check of the rest of me, the officer beckoned Clémence forward. I watched her from a few steps away. She said something to the officer that I didn't catch, but he laughed. She smiled, a different sort of smile than I'd seen her give anyone before. Not a smirk, just a genuinely lovely smile as she raised her arms in an elegant sweep like she was making a snow angel. They kept chatting as he ran his hands along her arms and down her back. One hand lingered for a moment on her waist before sliding down to check her knees. I hoped he'd skip any area of her body that would attract the magnets, but as his fingers passed her collarbone, they flinched to her coat. He frowned.

But before he could say anything, Clémence said, with that same sweet smile, "Oh, my necklace!" And she reached under her coat and produced a short gold chain with a heavy pendant dangling from it. The pendant tottered in midair, defying gravity as it swung toward the guard's magnetic fingertips. "Perhaps this is why you find me so attractive." And she winked at him. Actually winked, like some dopey schoolgirl.

The guard smiled. "Not the only reason, mademoiselle." He pried the pendant from his fingers and she tucked it back down the neck of her coat. "You can go on," he said, waving her forward to where I was waiting. Clémence gave him a quick bob of a curtsy, then trotted off to join me.

"That was lucky," I said when we were far enough away from the checkpoint that we wouldn't be overheard.

"That wasn't lucky," Clémence replied. "That was carefully planned."

"You knew about the magnets?"

"Geisler told me. He heard about them in France."

"They weren't doing that when we left."

"Maybe something happened."

The officer had said protests. And *Frankenstein*. I shivered.

"Is that your necklace?" I asked as Clémence tugged the pendant over her head and dropped it into the pocket of her coat.

"No, I lifted it from a woman at the inn last night. Don't look so scandalized—it isn't real gold or it wouldn't have been magnetic. I thought I'd sell it and see what money we could get." And then she smirked at me, herself again.

"Why don't you smile more?" I asked her.

"I smile all the time."

"Not like you smiled at that officer."

She knocked the heel of her boot against the base of an industrial torch to get the snow off. "Some men think a smile is an invitation to put their hands wherever they want."

"He didn't." Clémence snorted. "He was flirting!" I said. "You were flirting. I'm just saying, you look nice when you smile. It's attractive."

"I don't want to be attractive," she replied. "I don't want to smile, and I won't have you telling me I should. I don't want attention from men like him."

"But that girl with the scarf, you'd like her attention, wouldn't you?" I snapped. It felt mean even as I said it, but I didn't retreat.

Clémence went red as a cranberry, then jerked her coat tighter around her.

We didn't say anything as we crossed the river into the city center. The streets were busy, snow trampled into slush by shoppers and the spokes of omnibuses and carriages. I led the way, sticking to side streets and alleys as much as I could to avoid the crowds. It was nearly Christmas, I realized as a group of women with holly in their hair passed us, singing a wine-soaked round of "C'est le jour de la Noël." So much had changed that it felt impossible I'd only been gone a few weeks.

We found a pawnshop in Vieille Ville and I stood beside Clémence at the counter while she negotiated with the shifty-eyed shopkeeper over the pendant. As he was counting out coins from the cash box, the shop door opened behind us with a rush of cold air. Before I could turn to see who'd come in, a tiny girl with jet-black hair spilling out from under her cap popped up between Clémence and me. "Take one," she said, and thrust a battered leaflet into my hand.

The shopkeeper dropped the coins he'd been counting and charged around the counter, flapping his hands at her. "Out of my shop! Out out out!"

The girl shoved another leaflet at Clémence, then took off, skittering flat-footed across the shop and flailing out the door with her hair flying behind her. The shopkeeper stopped on the threshold and glared after her, then shambled back to the counter with his head bent. "Apologies," he murmured.

I glanced down at the crumpled paper the girl had forced on me. Printed on it was an illustration of a man, half mechanical, half human. His chest was drawn to look like an open clock, and a long scar ran the length of his face. Above the illustration, in heavy, bold letters, it read FRANKENSTEIN'S MONSTER LIVES!

Next to me, Clémence drew in a sharp breath. I held up the leaflet for the shopkeeper to see. "Do you know anything about this?"

He didn't look up from his cash box. "I've told her to stay away, but she keeps coming in and harassing my customers."

"Does she work for someone?" I asked. "Or do you know—"

The shopkeeper shut the lid of the cash box so hard the change inside rattled, then slid our coins across the counter and turned toward the back room. "Excuse me."

I didn't wait for Clémence. I spun on my heel and dashed out of the shop, looking both ways down the street for the tiny girl with the black hair. I spotted her a few shops down, thrusting leaflets at passing pedestrians. Behind me, the bell jingled as Clémence followed me out. "Alasdair, what are you—"

"Oi, you!" I called as I started down the street. The girl looked up and for a moment I thought she was going to bolt, but instead she flung her hands in the air, one still fisted around her leaflets. I jogged forward to meet her, Clémence on my heels. "Don't run," I called as we drew closer.

"I can't," she replied.

"Can't?" I looked down. One of her bare feet was wrapped in muddy strips of cloth. The other was tarnished metal, connected to the socket around her ankle with a heavy bolt rusted orange.

"Can't," she repeated. "It's too stiff. But I'll take the leaflet back if you don't want it. Printing's expensive."

Clémence appeared at my shoulder. "She needs a mechanic," she said as she stared down at the rusted foot. Then, to the girl: "Where are your parents?"

"In a grave," she replied, straight-faced.

"Do you stay at the orphanage?"

"They wouldn't have me." She knocked her metal foot against the ground for emphasis. "The woman told me they only take human children."

"Bleeding hell." I shoved the leaflet into my pocket and tugged my gloves off. "Sit down, let me look at your foot."

She didn't move. "I can't run, but I'll scream."

"He won't hurt you, he's a Shadow Boy," Clémence said. "He takes care of people like you."

The girl stared at us for a moment with her chin up, then sat down hard on the frozen street. I crouched beside her and took her foot in my hands. The ball joint in her ankle had gone stiff, rust creeping along the socket welded to her leg and invading her skin.

Clémence leaned over my shoulder, though I wasn't certain she knew what she was looking at. "What do you need?"

I needed my tools, and my files, and my magnifying goggles—all smashed up in our shop. I needed to know why this girl who looked like she could be knocked over by a winter breeze was handing out leaflets with my brother's picture on them. I needed to get Oliver out of Geneva and I needed Geisler gone.

"Vinegar—it takes rust off. It's not ideal, but it'll work."

"There's a market around the corner," the girl piped up. Then she added, "I haven't got any money."

"I do," Clémence said. "Stay put, I'll be back."

Neither of us said anything for a while after Clémence disappeared. The girl was sucking on her bottom lip while she traced patterns with her finger in the muddy snowbank next to her. Her nails were black around the edges, and the chapped scrape of frostbite decorated her knuckles.

"You keep doing that, your fingers will fall off," I said.

She glared at me, then stuck her hand up to the wrist in the snow. I sighed and turned my gaze upward, over the rooftops to the golden clouds settled above the chimneys. At the end of the alley, above the houses and shops, I could see the outline of the clock tower cut against the sun. "Do you know what day it is?" I asked her.

"Don't you?"

"If I did, I wouldn't ask," I replied through gritted teeth.

"December the twenty-second," she answered. Her

eyes followed mine to the tower. "The clock strikes again on Christmas Eve. Did you know that?"

"Yes." I pulled my gaze away from the clock tower, then took the leaflet out of my pocket and spread it flat against my knee. "Why are you handing these out?"

"They asked me to."

"Who asked you?"

She crossed her arms. "I'm not supposed to tell because you aren't made of metal. You aren't like me."

"If I fix your foot, will you tell me?"

She considered this, teeth still working on her bottom lip. She didn't say no.

Clémence returned a few minutes later with a bottle of vinegar. I poured some onto my glove and scrubbed at the rusted joint until it consented to bend again. It badly needed to be replaced and the whole foot could use a good cleaning, but I didn't have the means for either. The girl watched me with her elbows resting on her knees and her nose wrinkled at the smell.

"You need shoes," I told her.

"No money."

"Then you need to wrap your feet up better. When the metal gets wet, it rusts, and that gets under your skin."

"And then your foot's going to fall off and probably take your leg with it," Clémence said. I hadn't realized it was meant to be a joke, but the girl giggled.

The gears in her foot snapped against each other, and I slid my finger along them to guide the track for a few rounds. When I let go the girl straightened her leg so fast she almost knocked me in the face. "I can move my toes," she said. "I've never been able to move my toes before."

"Here, keep this." I handed her the vinegar bottle. "In case it rusts again."

She shoved the bottle into her hat, fingers snarling up in her black hair. "I'm Mirette," she said.

"I'm Alasdair," I replied. "And this is Clémence. And it would be magnificent if you could tell us who you're handing out leaflets for."

Mirette rotated her foot in its socket, watching it work with her head cocked to one side. She was so filthy and fragile, like a china doll dug up from the soil. "They said if I'm going to stay with them, I have to do my part."

"Stay where?" Clémence asked at the same time I said, "Part of what?"

"The Cogworks," Mirette said.

Clémence looked at me, and I explained, "It's a factory in the north quarter of the city. They make the clockwork parts for the carriages and the omnibuses there."

"That's where I stay," Mirette said. "With Frankenstein's Men."

"What does that mean?" I asked.

She glared at me, and for a moment I thought I'd lost

her, but then she looked down at her foot again. "People don't treat us right, so we're going to make them. We won't be pushed down and stepped on anymore." It sounded like she was reciting something she'd heard, words that meant little to her, though she knew the feeling behind them. "This man"—she tapped her finger against the drawing of the resurrected man on the front of her leaflet—"is going to come for us, and he is going to lead us. We show him that we're ready for him, and then he'll come and save us."

"*Frankenstein* is a book," I said. "This man"—I thrust my leaflet at Mirette—"he isn't real. He's just in a book."

She shook her head. "You're wrong. We're waiting for him. Me and Frankenstein's Men."

That made everything inside me go cold and shaky. I couldn't decide what was more unfair—that this small, pale girl had nowhere to go, or that she wanted to use Oliver to do something about that. I creased the leaflet and shoved it in my pocket as I stood.

Mirette grabbed my coat sleeve and used me to haul herself up. I resisted the urge to shake her off. "I wasn't supposed to tell anyone about the Cogworks," she said.

"We'll keep it secret," Clémence replied.

Mirette tugged on my sleeve again, and I looked down. "Thank you for fixing my foot, Shadow Boy," she said. Her hand slid into mine and gave one quick pulse, then she trotted off down the street, steps big and buoyant on the cleaned springs of her foot.

I watched her go, my fingers worrying the edge of the leaflet in my pocket as I turned it over in my mind. I forgot Clémence was there until she nudged her fist against my arm. "Here, take this."

I opened my palm and she dropped half the coins from the pawned necklace into it.

"What's this for?"

"Something to eat; you look wretched."

"'Course I look wretched," I snapped. "Apparently all the clockwork men in Geneva are waiting for my resurrected brother to come lead their uprising against the city."

"You make that sound like a bad thing."

"Isn't it?"

"People are fighting back. It's brave."

"It's bleeding stupid."

"Says a boy who's never been thrown out on the streets because he's got metal pieces in him." She swiped her hair out of her face and glared at me so hard I looked away. "Do you know the address for where we're meeting Geisler?"

"Yes."

"All right, then, I'll meet you there."

"What?" I looked up, but she was already walking away from me, hands in her pockets, in the same direction Mirette had gone. "Where are you going?"

She didn't turn. "There's something I need to do."

I thought about chasing her down and demanding to know exactly what that something was, but I was still annoyed with her for nothing in particular, and being apart after days together was sort of appealing. So I turned in the opposite direction and started off alone. The coins in my pocket danced against the crumpled leaflet.

Geisler had chosen a run-down public house sloping into the Rhone for our meeting place. The sunset had collapsed into the foothills by the time I arrived and darkness had taken its place across the copper rooftops. Geisler was already there, finishing supper at a table by the fire. "No problems?" he asked as I slid onto the bench across from him.

"None."

"Good, I got in smoothly as well. Perhaps the city's security is not as tight as they like to boast." He glanced around. "Where's Mademoiselle Le Brey?"

"She . . . We got split up," I said. "She should be along soon."

"I've got work for her."

"You knew about the magnets," I said before I could stop myself.

He looked up from his supper. "Of course."

"She could have been caught."

"But she wasn't. Alasdair, is something wrong?"

234

"Is it because of *Frankenstein*?"

His brow creased. "I hadn't thought of that. Did you hear something?"

"No," I said quickly. "I was just wondering if you knew."

He frowned at me, and for a moment I was certain he saw straight through my lie. Then he picked up his knife again and said, "Do you want supper? You look half starved."

"I don't—"

"Go get something to eat. Your parents wouldn't forgive me if I let you waste away."

He tucked back into his plate, and I sat in stupid silence for a moment before I stood up and wandered over to the bar. I was so sick with the weight of everything, I wasn't sure I could keep any food down, but I didn't want to go back and sit with Geisler, so I just stared at the board for a while. I could feel the barkeeper's eyes on me.

After a while I heard the inn's door open, but I didn't turn until a tight hand closed on my arm and started pulling me away from the bar. I yelped in surprise and whipped around, ready to fight or run. But it was Clémence.

"What are you doing?" I hissed at her, but she didn't answer. She tugged me after her to the opposite side of the room, then put her hands on my shoulders and twisted me sharply so I was facing away from the door.

Her cheeks were very pink. "God's wounds, what was that about?" I demanded.

"Don't turn around." Her voice was low and fast, and her eyes darted behind me as she spoke.

"What's wrong? Where have you been?"

"Keep your back to the door."

"No, tell me what's going on." I started to turn, but she grabbed my face and pulled me back toward her.

"Alasdair." She put her hand on my cheek. "Trust me."

I swallowed hard and held her gaze. She looked more serious than I'd seen her before.

"All right."

We stood for a moment, eyes locked, then I felt a rush of cold air on my back as the door opened again. Clémence glanced toward it, and I felt her fist close on my arm. Around us, the room went quiet, like everyone had stopped what they were doing and was holding their breath. I couldn't see what we was happening, but I held my breath too.

Then, from behind me, I heard someone say, "Dr. Basil Geisler, you're under arrest."

My heartbeat was suddenly so loud it was hard to hear anything over it. Geisler said something I couldn't make out; then there was the sharp scrape of a bench being pulled back. Someone near us gasped.

"He's not fighting," Clémence said quietly. "He's going with them."

Heavy footsteps crossed between the tables and passed by where we were standing. I glanced over my shoulder and saw the backs of two police officers as they led Geisler away. He looked startled, and somehow old and harmless between the two tall men in their greatcoats with rifles slung over their shoulders. In the doorway, he looked back and his eyes found Clémence and me. It was good the police had hold of him, for he looked like he wanted to leap across the room and skin us alive.

But then they were out on the street, swallowed by the darkness. There was a flurry of noise beyond—the raised voices of more officers, the shrill hiss of a steam-powered carriage—then one of the officers slammed the inn door and the noise in the room returned at twice the level it had been before. I took a deep breath, and Clémence's grip on my arm relaxed. I hadn't realized how tightly she was holding me until she let go.

We stood in silence for a moment, both of us breathing hard. Then she said, "You're shaking," and I realized I was. "Do you need to sit down?"

She didn't wait for me to respond, just led me by the hand to a bench against the wall, and we both sank down onto it. Everyone was going wild around us. One of the servers looked like she was about to faint, and the barkeeper kept saying, "Geisler . . . Dr. Geisler . . . here! I made him a drink!"

"You turned him in," I said to Clémence.

She shrugged. "Slavery doesn't really breed loyalty."

"Bleeding hell." I still felt sort of unsteady, and I put my head in my hands.

"I thought it would make things easier." She paused, then added, "For both of us."

"It does. That was . . ." I looked up at her. "You really are something."

"I like to think so. Damn, I think we've been spotted." I followed her gaze across the room. One of the servers had leaned across the counter to speak to the barkeeper and was pointing in our direction. "We don't have much time," she hissed. "Geisler will return the favor first chance he has and tell the police about us, and probably your brother as well. We need to get you and Oliver out of Switzerland."

"What about my parents? I think they're in prison here. I need to help them."

"I'll stay. See what I can do about that."

"You don't have to."

"There's no danger for me here, not like there is for you."

"No, I mean . . . you don't have to do that for me. They're not your concern."

She fiddled with a loose thread on her coat sleeve, then turned her face up to the ceiling. "I have to tell you something. But you have to promise you won't hate me after I do."

"I think I owe you too much to hate you for anything."

"Don't make any promises yet." She snapped the thread, then tugged her sleeves down over her hands and took a deep breath.

"Just say it."

"I'm the reason your parents were arrested."

I blinked. "What?"

"I mean, I didn't . . . It was Geisler. He told me their names and said I was to give them to the police when I arrived, then find you. He wanted to be certain you didn't have any reason to stay in Geneva. I'm so sorry, Alasdair, I was only doing what he told me to." When I didn't say anything, she knocked me with her elbow. "See, I told you you'd be angry."

Part of me wanted to be—I could feel a hot fist tightening inside my chest, and it would have been so easy to loose it on her. But I had so few allies at that moment that it felt stupid to push her away. And she had turned Geisler in, and kept the police from finding me, and now she was looking at me with her eyebrows knit together and her mouth tight, like she didn't know what she'd do if I stormed off and left her behind. And she was still here. She hadn't run from me yet. "I'm angry," I said, "but not at you."

"Are you sure?"

"It was Geisler. You worked for him, I understand, you were only doing what you were told. At least we got to return the favor."

Her mouth twisted into a half smile. "Bastard got what was coming to him."

"Something like that."

"I want to help get your parents out of prison. I can't make what I did right, but I can at least do that." When I didn't say anything, she added, "I know you're not used to people being on your side, but I am. I swear to it." She put her hand on top of mine, and when she squeezed my fingers, the knot inside me loosened a bit. "You should eat something."

"No, I'm all right. I need to go see Oliver."

"When was the last time you ate?"

"Sometime in Germany?" Other than the *chouquettes* the night before, I couldn't remember the last meal I'd had.

"Let's have some supper and then we can go see your brother. You'll feel better once you've eaten."

I didn't like the idea of waiting a moment longer than I had to, but it didn't seem likely Clémence would back down. "Yes, Mother," I muttered. She laughed.

We left the inn and followed the Rhone as it wound its way through the city, across Vieille Ville, purposely avoiding the lit braziers and the music rising from the

Christmas market. Above it, the black hands of the clock tower stood out like a shadow puppet show against the illuminated glass face.

Nearly everything outside the Christmas market was closed, but we found a man selling questionable-smelling cabbage and sausage off a cart on the rim of the financial district and sat on the steps of a church while we ate. I still had no appetite, but I choked it down because Clémence was watching to make certain I did. I felt better afterward, but I didn't tell her.

"It's a long climb to the castle," I said as we finished. "You don't have to come."

"I want to."

"Oliver's not really . . ." I wasn't sure how to explain him, so I just said, "He's not used to people. He might be difficult."

She sucked a spot of grease on her thumb, then looked over at me. "Your brother thinks he's the only mechanical man of his kind, and maybe I didn't come back from the dead, but he and I are different from the other clockworks in the same way. It's damned inconvenient to live without an arm or a leg, but you can manage. Oliver and I . . ." She hesitated, and her fingers traced the shape of her metal panel over her coat. "We'd be dead without machinery. It's what we're made of. So maybe if he meets me—if he knows there's someone else like him—he won't feel so alone." She paused, then added, "It would be good for me as well. If that matters."

She ducked her head when she said it and a curtain of her white hair fell between us so I couldn't see her face. I realized with a sharp smart that I'd been so caught up in myself since we arrived that I had hardly thought of what being here and knowing Oliver existed must mean to her, a girl with gears beneath her skin who'd thought there was no one else in the world who lived and breathed by clockwork. I felt like apologizing, but I wasn't sure what I'd say when she asked what for. So instead I said, "You can come."

By the time we set off again, the first sparks of starlight were beginning to burn between the wispy clouds. "Should we go down by the river?" Clémence asked as we neared the checkpoint. "Might be safer."

"I think we're all right." The river trail would be slower, and suddenly I felt like sprinting the whole way to the castle. We were so bleeding close, it almost didn't feel real.

I held my breath as we passed through the checkpoint. The officers on duty glanced up, but neither of them stopped us or even seemed interested.

When we reached the foothills, the path turned steep. I was worried that Clémence wouldn't be able to make it with her damaged lungs, but she didn't complain or ask for help or a rest. It was hard to see, the darkness made deeper by the thick forest, and I kept glancing over my shoulder every time a shadow shifted. I stopped dead twice when I thought I heard footsteps crunching the snow behind us. Clémence stopped too. "What's wrong?" she asked.

"I heard something."

We both stood still for a moment, and the silence of the foothills caved in on us. I searched the darkness, but there were too many shadows from the pines and cliffs to make out anything properly.

Then Clémence said, "Alasdair, there's nothing there."

"I must have imagined it," I said, though I was certain I hadn't. We started climbing again, but I couldn't convince myself it was just the two of us and the night. The lines from the Coleridge poem started darting through my head: *Because he knows, a frightful fiend / Doth close behind him tread.*

As we crested the hill and Château de Sang appeared against the black sky, Clémence finally halted, and I stopped as well, relieved to have an excuse to catch my breath.

"That's it?" she asked.

"Yes."

"It's beautiful. Was it a home?"

"Once. Then a prison."

"So which is it now?"

I pulled my coat tighter around me. "Come on, let's go."

I led her across the abandoned courtyard and around the back to the servants' entrance I used. After a few seconds of fumbling with the bolts, I realized with a sick lurch they were all undone. I bent down to the lock and ran my fingers along the latch. It was hard to see by only the slivered moonlight, but I could feel scratches on the keyhole—the marks of sloppy lock picking done in the dark.

"What's wrong?" Clémence whispered.

"I think someone was here," I replied, "or Oliver's gone."

"Which is the better option?"

"Hell if I know." I fit my key into the lock and propped the door open. Somehow, the darkness seemed deeper inside. I reached behind me for Clémence.

We took the stairs up from the kitchen into the deserted entry hall. I'd rarely come to see Oliver at night, and I was surprised by how shadowy and silent the whole place was. The vaulted ceilings disappeared into the darkness and every footstep cracked loud as a splitting avalanche. I was dead jumpy, but if Clémence was afraid, she didn't show it. The only time she started was when her foot went through a rotted beam on the stairway and I had to grab her hand and pull her back up.

"Sorry, the stairs are a bit treacherous," I murmured. "I should have warned you about that."

"Would have been nice."

I started climbing again. Then from behind me I heard her say, "You can let go of my hand."

"Oh." I was surprised to find I was still holding it, and even more surprised by how badly I didn't want to let go. "Do you think maybe . . . ?"

I trailed off, but she worked out the rest. Her fingers flexed against mine. "Keep going, then," she said, and we started again, still linked. As we reached the second landing, Clémence said, "It smells like gunpowder."

"It's from the basement," I said. "The city keeps explosives here."

"It reminds me of Paris."

"I don't remember Paris smelling of gunpowder."

"My father was a bomb maker there, remember? Gunpowder smells like home."

At the top of the stairs, I spotted an open doorway down the hall with golden firelight dancing from beyond it. The wallpaper peeling away in long strips looked like thorny spikes in its shadow.

The room was a large, open antechamber connected to what was once a bedroom. The barred windows overlooked the moonlit rooftops of Geneva far below, with the illuminated face of the clock tower hanging above them like a halo in an Annunciation painting. A fire was blazing in the grate, flames leaping up into the chimney, and a figure silhouetted against it. Not Oliver, I realized. A woman. She turned when we entered, her dark profile framed by the firelight so I didn't know who it was until she spoke.

"Alasdair," she said, and her voice made my whole being go still.

"Mary Godwin," I replied.

Mary took a step toward me—out of silhouette and into the firelight so I saw her in full like an apparition raised from smoke. She was . . . *different*. That was the only word that came to my mind. The Mary I had known two years ago was round faced, with rosy cheeks and full lips, and a body even a shapeless gown couldn't conceal.

But this woman, this specter of a woman, looked so much older than I thought anyone could become in two years. Her cheeks were hollow, the skin beneath her eyes shadowed, and she looked frightened, something I had never known Mary to be.

"Alasdair," she said again, and she took another step toward me. Her eyes flitted to Clémence's and my linked hands, and a stab of vindictive satisfaction tore through my surprise.

"What are you doing here?" I asked.

"I came to find you. I told you I was coming to Geneva. It was in the letter."

"I never read it."

"I know that now," she said, and my stomach dropped.

"Where's Oliver?"

"I'm here." There was a creak from the darkness and Oliver stepped into the firelight. His pipe, lit and smoking between his teeth, cast a bloody glow across his face and turned his eyes black. "You came back," he said.

"You thought I left you?"

"It seemed the only logical conclusion." He looked around at Clémence, Mary, and me in turn. "Well, this is the most visitors I've had in two years. We should call it a party."

"Why's Mary here?" I demanded. I wasn't in the mood for games. I wanted to know what was going on, and how long I had before he erupted.

Oliver took a long pull on his pipe, then tipped his head back and released the smoke into the air. The mechanic in me—the Shadow Boy that would always be Oliver's maker—flinched when I thought of the damage he was doing to his oiled-paper lungs. "When you didn't come for days," he said, "I assumed you'd finally grown tired of playing mother to your creation and had left me locked in here to die."

"I'm back now."

"To dispose of my corpse before someone found your resurrected man?"

My hand turned to a fist inside my pocket. I hadn't expected him to be pleased to see me, but I had hoped he'd be a bit less openly hostile. "I came back to get you out of here."

Oliver crossed his arms and stared me down. His pipe bounced as he clenched his jaw. "So where'd you go?"

I glanced at Clémence, wondering whether it was worth lying, and suddenly wishing I hadn't brought her. "I went to Ingolstadt," I said. "Our parents were arrested and Geisler offered me protection."

"Oh good, so you've been chumming it up with my murderer as well."

"I needed somewhere safe," I said over him. "I didn't abandon you, Oliver, I was always going to come back. I *have* come back."

"To fetch me for the mad doctor's experiments?" Before I could deny it, he clapped his hands together in mock delight. The gears in the metal one whined. "Oh, and look who came to visit while you were gone! Mary Godwin, the long-lost poetess of the year I died. Her sweet little letter saying she was coming for a visit was tucked in one of the books you gave me, and that helped me find her in my own memory. She"—he pointed a silver finger at Mary—"didn't think I had memories at all, but there they were, just waiting. I remembered that you two had a bit of a flirt, and you'd been sick over her ever since she left." He glanced at Clémence. "Seems you're moving forward, though."

I felt Clémence's hand try to abandon mine, but I clung to her. I was afraid if I didn't have something to hold on to, I'd tip over. "Why did you come here?" I asked Mary.

She glanced at Oliver, and he spread his hands. "Go on. You can tell him."

"I went to your shop," Mary said, her voice quavering, "and it was all torn up. I thought if you'd made it out, you'd be here with Oliver, so I came to find you. But you weren't. And then I couldn't get out." She glanced sideways at my brother. "Neither of us could."

"It's a brilliant prison, Ally," Oliver added. "Doesn't keep people out, but it certainly keeps them in."

I ignored him and instead asked Mary, "How long have you been here?"

"Four days."

"She's good company," Oliver interrupted again, like he couldn't keep his mouth shut for more than a second. "My first company in years. Mrs. Shelley—did you know she was Mrs. Shelley?" He seized Mary around the wrist and held up her hand so the gold ring around her finger flashed in the light. She flinched. "Are you devastated?"

I was grateful the darkness covered my blush—I was so hot I thought my face might catch fire. "Stop it," I snapped, but Oliver just laughed. He let go of Mary's wrist and dropped into a chair beneath the window, crossing his legs in a crooked way that came from only having metal-hinged joints. "Why are you angry at me?" I asked.

"Because you left!" he cried, voice suddenly sharp-edged, and he flung his pipe. I dodged, but a few flecks of hot tobacco still licked my cheeks. "You left me here to die, to rot!"

"I didn't leave you to die. I didn't have a choice! The shop was raided. The police were hunting me. I had to get out. Why else would I leave you? I've got no life but you!"

"Apparently you have a whole other life I didn't know about." He pressed his metal finger against a piece of glowing tobacco that had landed on the arm of the chair so it smoked against the upholstery. "All this time I thought you were working in the shop, you've been out chasing literary pursuits."

"Literary pursuits?" I repeated, dread creeping through me. "What do you mean?"

"You didn't think I'd notice? How insulting." Oliver snatched a book from beside the chair and tossed it at me. I knew what it was, but I made a show of looking at the spine. *Frankenstein, or The Modern Prometheus*, with that empty space below the title where the author's name should have been. So I *had* left it with him.

"What's this for?" My voice wavered in spite of my best efforts, and I fought the urge to look at Mary.

"I was hoping I could trouble you for an inscription," he replied. "I've heard books are worth much more when they're signed by the author."

This time I did look at Mary. She looked away. "I didn't write it," I said.

Oliver continued as though I hadn't spoken. "I thought it was Geisler at first. I couldn't believe a boy with so much clockwork in his blood would write something that elegant. You never told me you were a writer." He stared at me like he was waiting for me to crumble and confess. When I didn't say anything, he dropped his head back over the arm of the chair with a groan. "Come on, Ally, are you really not going to admit it was you?"

"I didn't write it," I said again.

"Of course you did, it's us!" he cried, and suddenly he was across the room and towering above me. I'd never realized how much taller he was until that moment. He seized me by the front of my coat, wrenching me away from Clémence and nearly lifting me off my feet. I could see the puckered scar along his hairline flex as a vein in his forehead tightened. "It's about me, and you, and bringing me back to life—it's about us!"

From behind us, Mary said quietly, "It wasn't Alasdair."

"You don't think so?" Oliver called to her. "All just a big coincidence? A young man who brings back the dead with clockwork to gain the notice of a famous university and what he makes instead is a monster. Doesn't that sound a bit like our Alasdair Finch? And what a chance—it's Geneva, and it's Ingolstadt, and it's my bleeding life!" He shoved me backward and I had to grab the windowsill to keep from falling. I looked to Mary and then to Clémence. They were both staring at me, and I realized that out of all of us, Oliver was the only one who didn't know the truth.

When I spoke, my voice tripped over my heartbeat. "I know it's about us, Oliver, but I swear to you, I didn't write it."

"They're looking for me," he said, shoulders shaking. "Mary told me all about it. There's a manhunt going on for this resurrected man. The police are pulling clockworks off the street to make sure they aren't me, and all the clockworks want me to rise up and lead them. People are rioting in my name."

I took a step toward him, not sure what I was going

to say but almost certain he wouldn't listen. "Oliver, I didn't write—"

He was so fast I didn't realize he was moving until his fist crossed my face. He used his mechanical hand, and it hit me hard ennough that I collapsed, blinking stars out of my eyes as my vision tipped.

He'd never struck me before. Not since we were children and didn't know better.

Mary shrieked. I braced myself as Oliver came at me again, but he reared back suddenly with a yelp of pain. Clémence had grabbed his mechanical arm at the socket and twisted. He thrashed, and his elbow knocked into her chin and sent her stumbling backward. A trickle of blood ran from her lip, but she swiped it away and turned to face him, her knees bent like she was ready for a fight.

Oliver rounded on her now and began to advance. I tried to stand, but my vision darkened again and I sat down hard instead. "So who are you, exactly?" he asked with another step toward Clémence. She didn't back away. "I don't think we've been introduced."

"I'm someone like you," she replied.

Oliver gave a short caw of laughter. "No one in this whole world is like me."

"I am." Clémence seized his mechanical arm around the wrist and slammed it against her own chest. There was a hollow clang of metal on metal.

Oliver started, and looked up from his clenched fist to her face. "Bleeding hell."

With one hand still around Oliver's wrist, Clémence tugged down the neckline of her dress and showed off the gleaming panel beneath. "You are not alone in this world," she said softly.

For a moment, Oliver looked like he might kiss her. I'd never realized just how lonely he was until I saw that rush in his face, cheeks all at once bright with a color they had missed for years. "So you're not his sweetheart," he said. "You're his experiment."

"I'm not Alasdair's," Clémence replied. "I don't belong to anyone."

"But someone made you."

"Geisler," she said. "He's the one you should be fighting, not Alasdair."

"My dear brother," Oliver said, and he choked on the words, "has turned against me."

I finally managed to pull myself back onto my feet. "I haven't, Oliver, I swear."

"I don't believe you."

"He didn't write it," Clémence said.

"How do you know?" He was shouting again, and his voice screeched against the high ceiling and bounced back. "If it wasn't Alasdair, then tell me who it was!"

"It was me," Mary said.

Oliver froze, gaping at her with his misshapen mouth

half open. I froze too, every hope that we would all walk away from here in one piece shattering inside me. It was in my defense, I knew, but there couldn't have been a worse moment for her to say it out loud. She'd taken what little control I had left over Oliver and set it on fire.

Mary seemed to take the silence as a cue to say more, for she started speaking, fast and reckless. "After I left Geneva, I wrote it all down, everything I could remember about the resurrection, and I showed it to my husband."

Just shut up, I pleaded with her silently. *Shut up, shut up!*

But she kept going. "I wasn't planning to do anything with it, but then—" Her voice hitched. "Oliver, I'm sorry. I didn't think."

Oliver didn't say anything for a moment. He stood still, firelight glinting off his mechanical pieces, and I swore I could see through his skin to his metal skeleton, bars and rods that joined like tributaries of a river to form the twisted shape of him.

"You sold us out," Oliver said, his voice so low I had to strain to hear it over the snapping fire.

"I'm sorry," Mary whispered. Her hands were clasped before her like she was praying. "Please, I never meant to hurt you. I didn't think—"

Her words fell into a shriek as Oliver lunged toward her, as fast as before, but this time I was expecting it. I sprang forward too and grabbed him around the shoulders, trying to hold him back, but he wrenched me straight off my feet.

But my added weight was enough to slow him down, and he halted, too far from Mary to strike her. Then he twisted sharply, and I was thrown to the ground. My elbow hit the stone with a sharp blossom of pain. Clémence was coming forward now—I could see her from the corner of my eye, but she didn't seem to want to stop Oliver. She hovered, reaching out to no one in particular.

Oliver seized Mary by the shoulders, pressed her against the wall, and pinned her there with his mechanical arm. He was shouting at her, words lost in volume and ferocity, and she was crying, tears streaming down her cheeks. Oliver raised his fist, and the firelight caught a flash of something in his hand. As his arm came crashing toward Mary, I flung myself to my feet and leapt between them so that his fist landed on my shoulder instead of hers.

I didn't realize he had stabbed me until blood started to pool along my collarbone. We both watched as the dark stain stretched its fingers across my shirt. Then Oliver looked up and I thought I caught a glimpse of panic or remorse, a smidge of someone that I hadn't seen since before he died. He looked, for a moment, almost human.

It may have been longer than that, but the pain set in then, sharp and sudden, and I swooned. Mary caught me before my head cracked against the floor, and we sank to the ground together. All the sound in the room seemed to funnel and close, flushing me into silence with a weight like a collapsing tunnel. I looked up at Mary. Her lips were moving, and I realized she was saying my name. "Alasdair!" She had one hand cupped at the back of my neck. "Alasdair, stay here with me!"

I wanted to tell her I wasn't going anywhere, but instead I murmured, "Sorry." It was the only thing I could think to say. I tried to sit up, but my head felt too heavy. Mary pulled me up the rest of the way, then held me there with my cheek against her shoulder. She kept saying my name, like she had forgotten every other word she knew.

Oliver was still standing over me with his mechanical hand pressed to his forehead and his mouth contorting. In his good hand, his flesh-and-bone hand, he was gripping a pair of needle-nose pliers, blood sliding from their tip. *My* pliers, I realized, the set I'd left with him the last time I came. My pliers, and my blood.

Clémence alone kept her wits. She was at my side, wrenching her scarf off and pressing it to my shoulder. I didn't know I'd made a sound until she said gently, "Shut it, I know it hurts."

I could feel my heartbeat throbbing across my skin like an electric current as it worked to make up for the blood I was losing in hot waves. Pounding, pounding, pounding through my skull, in my ears, over every inch of me like I was a drumhead.

I didn't realize it was more than my heartbeat until Oliver and Clémence both looked to the door. "What was that?" she said.

It sounded like gears and machinery, like some engine in the belly of the castle had woken, and it was getting louder. It was coming toward us. Oliver's hand tightened on the pliers as he faced the door.

Then suddenly the room was full of people. Dark shapes flooded in, and I recognized their halting, stiff-legged walk and blank faces. They were the automatons, Geisler's automatons, six of them here and striding toward us. And in their midst was the inventor himself, Dr. Geisler, with the police chief Inspector Jiroux at his side, sweeping in like a storm in his greatcoat and black cornered hat. The sound of the gears grinding inside the automatons seemed magnified twofold by the room's high ceilings, but I still heard Geisler say to Jiroux, "That's him, Inspector. That is Frankenstein's monster. The resurrected man."

Beside me, Clémence swore under her breath; then her hand left my shoulder as she stood. I wanted to stand too—didn't want to face them from the floor—but Mary was clinging to me, and I heard her whisper, "It's all right now," like she thought they'd come to save us. *It's not all right*, I thought. It was not bleeding *all right* because there were the police and the automatons and

259

Geisler and I had led them straight to Oliver.

Oliver may not have remembered Jiroux, but he recognized Geisler—I could see it in his stance. His shoulders rose, his knees bent. Then he said, dead quiet—which was far more frightening than his shouting—"Get away from me."

Geisler took a step forward and raised his hands like he was approaching a feral dog. "We're not here to hurt you, Oliver."

"No, you're just here to take me away and disassemble me in your laboratory."

Geisler took another step. Oliver seized a chair from beside the fireplace and raised it like a shield. Jiroux reached for his pistol, but Geisler shook his head. "He's not to be harmed."

"So are you going to take me away?" Oliver called. "Or are you just here to kill me again and be done with it?"

My pulse spiked as Geisler turned back to him. "I did not kill you, Oliver."

Oliver laughed, shrill and cold.

"And I am glad," Geisler continued, "so very glad that you're alive."

Beside him, Jiroux growled, "Hurry up, Doctor."

"Look at you," Geisler continued, his voice rising over Jiroux's. "You're a marvel. A scientific wonder."

Oliver's fists tightened on the chair, and the leg in

his mechanical hand splintered. "I am not your science, Doctor."

"You are a threat to the safety of this city," Jiroux interrupted.

"You know nothing about me!" Oliver cried.

"I know you are an unnatural creation, and an abomination," Jiroux replied. "If you will not come quietly, we will use force."

"He's not to be harmed," Geisler said again. He tried to drag Jiroux's hand away from his pistol, but Jiroux threw him off.

"I will do what needs to be done, Doctor."

"That was not our arrangement."

"What arrangement?" Jiroux snapped. "What power do you think you have here? You are a prisoner of the city."

Geisler turned back to Oliver, his arms held out in front of him. "I swear to you, Oliver, you won't be harmed."

"You have no power!" Jiroux roared at the same moment Oliver shouted "Liar!" and flung the chair at Geisler, who ducked so it shattered against the wall. Geisler and Jiroux both shied.

Oliver tried to make a break for the door, but he had gone only a few steps before Jiroux drew his pistol and fired twice. The first shot went wide but the second struck Oliver in the chest with a *clang* and he was thrown backward into the wall. I cried out, but Oliver was back on his feet in an instant and running again.

Geisler knocked the pistol out of Jiroux's hands and it skidded across the floor. "I told you not to shoot!" He whirled on the automatons. "Bring him to me!"

The automatons flickered to life and began to advance, stepping in front of Oliver and facing him away from the door. I thought for a moment they had him, but then Clémence dodged into their path. One of the lead automatons made to bat her out of the way, but she threw up her hands before it could touch her. There was a flash of light and the automaton slumped with its chin against its chest, arms dropping to its sides.

Clémence kept her hands up, and I saw the glowing plates on her palms. Pulse gloves. "Get behind me," she shouted at Oliver, and flicked her wrists again. There was another flash, and two more of the automatons dropped. She tried again, but this time there was only a static flicker along the rims. She rubbed her palms together, fast and hard, but the automatons were closing in. Oliver thumped one in the chest and it toppled over onto its back. Another seized Clémence around the throat and lifted her off her feet. She grabbed it, her hands on either side of its skull, and pale light scribbled across its metal skeleton. It faltered, and she slid free.

Then its arm rose sharply and knocked her in the face. She staggered, hand rising to her cheek as the automaton plunged its fist into her chest with a clang of metal on metal. Her feet left the ground as she was tossed backward by the blow, then she hit the floor again with a grinding gasp. *Get up*, I thought, but she lay still where she'd landed.

It was Oliver against them now, Oliver backed into a corner and screaming like an animal. Everyone was shouting—Jiroux and Geisler and Oliver—and the automatons' gears were jangling and it was so much noise.

I had too much blood gone by then to make sense of it anymore. The room was going cold around me, and time seemed to be jumping about as if I were in a dream, seconds holding still, then leaping ahead with a burst. My head was still pounding, heartbeat reverberating through me all the way to my teeth. I had to close my eyes because it hurt too badly.

From somewhere, leagues away it seemed, I heard Jiroux speak. "Sedate the creature, and be certain he's properly restrained before we move him. Doctor, would you care to handle that?"

The gears in the automatons chattered as they moved, metal steps like gunshots against the flagstones, but Geisler's voice was still audible over them. "We will come through this together, Oliver, you and I. I will protect you. Just trust me."

I heard Oliver give a shout like a battle cry, and I opened my eyes again, just in time to see him tear himself from the two automatons that held him, slam Geisler into the wall, and bury the pliers in his throat.

Maybe that was what pushed me over the edge. I don't know. But that was when I fell backward into Mary, and I was gone.

I'd only blacked out once before in my life.

It was the beginning of the summer in Geneva, four days after I met Mary—strange I remember that—and the end of the first week of Geisler's trial. People from both sides had been picketing all morning, and when the proceedings at the courthouse ended, things started to get scrappy. The police had their hands full trying to keep riots from breaking out on every block.

Oliver and I had gone to see the trial, and we got sucked into some mess on the way home. The police came to break it up, and an officer thumped me with his baton when he passed and knocked me out cold. I remembered standing on the street, hearing someone running up behind me, and turning around. Then next thing I knew I was waking on my straw pallet in the flat with my head pounding. It was dark, and Oliver was sitting beside me like he was keeping vigil. He had his hand on my wrist, fingers fit into my pulse point. He must have been waiting for me to wake up, but I didn't move, so we just stayed like that, side by side, until the sun came up.

I didn't dream then. I didn't even realize I was out. It was like closing my eyes one moment and opening them somewhere else the next. It was the same way this time. Falling backward in Château de Sang, and next thing I knew, a pale, steady light was pushing its fingers under my eyelids and prying them open until they snapped. I gasped.

Sunshine. I was awake and alive and there was sunshine, and Mary at my side with her cold hand against my cheek.

"Mary." I tried to sit up, but her hand slid down to my chest and she pushed me back.

"Don't strain yourself."

I'm only sitting up, I thought, but then the throbbing ache began to rise in my shoulder. And I remembered everything. I twisted my head as far as I could and saw the wrap of white bandages around my collarbone and chest. Then the pain stabbed so hard that my vision blurred, and I closed my eyes.

"Here, drink this."

I opened them again. Mary was holding out a mug.

"What is it?"

"Tea."

The bitter steam curled toward me. "What's in it?"

"Tea." Mary glanced down at her lap. "Laudanum."

I shook my head. "I don't want it."

"Alasdair, you need to rest. This will help with the pain."

"I'm not in pain," I said, then tried not to wince as I looked around the room. It was bare and institutional: whitewashed stone walls and a single barred window letting in the sunlight. There was a fireplace, ashy with coals, in one corner, as well as the bed I was in and Mary's chair. At several spots along the wall, closed metal hooks had been drilled into the stone. "Am I in prison?" I asked.

"Sort of," Mary replied. "You are in *a* prison. And there may be some chains involved." Her eyes flitted down to my feet. A heavy iron manacle was locked around my ankle, its chain fastened to one of the wall hooks. "And there's a guard outside the door, so be careful what you say. But you haven't been arrested," she said, then added, "Not yet."

"Hell's teeth." I scrubbed at my eyes, trying to force the fog to clear from my brain. "How long have I been out?"

"A day and a half, nearly. You were running a bad

fever when they brought you here, and you lost a lot of blood." She rubbed her hands along her skirt like she was trying to wipe something off them. "How much do you remember?"

"Too much. Geisler . . ."

"Is dead," she finished.

The image of Oliver jamming the pliers into Geisler's throat flashed before my eyes and for a moment I thought I might be sick. "And Oliver?"

"He got away."

"He made it out?" I asked, and she nodded. "Bleeding hell—How? With all the automatons and the chief of police?"

"It was your friend, actually," Mary said, her voice suddenly clipped. "What was her name?"

"Clémence."

"Yes, Clémence. He got away with her."

"God's wounds." I reached up for the bandages on my shoulder and began to tug them off, but Mary caught my hand. A tremor ran up my arm.

"What are you doing?"

"I want to see how good a prison surgeon's sutures are."

"It wasn't a prison surgeon," she said. "It was your father."

I stopped. "My father? He's here?"

"They brought him in to treat you, then took him

back to his cell as soon as he was finished."

"What about my mother?"

She shook her head. "I don't know."

"I want to see my father."

"You need to rest," she replied, some of the bossiness I remembered returning to her voice. "Sleep now, while you can. I don't know how much peace they'll give you once they know you're awake."

"I can't sleep," I said, finally succeeding in pulling myself into a sitting position with the assistance of the iron bed frame. "I need to find Oliver."

"Alasdair." Her hand caught mine, and she looked at me very seriously. I could feel the cold line of her wedding band against my skin. "They're not going to let you go."

There was a heavy thump on the door; then a moment later a stocky man in a blue policeman's uniform entered. He looked from me sitting up in bed to Mary with her hand in mine, then cleared his throat. "I'm meant to collect Mr. Finch when he's awake."

Mary scowled. "He needs to rest."

"Inspector Jiroux wants a word."

"Well, the inspector can wait." She glared at him, and he seemed to shrink a bit beneath it.

"I'm meant to bring him as soon as he's awake."

"He's in no fit state—"

"I'm fine," I said, and they both looked at me like they'd forgotten I was there.

The officer looked relieved as he crossed the room and unfastened the chain on my ankle from the wall. Mary stood up, scowling firmly at him all the while. "He needs rest," she insisted.

"He said he's fine." The officer let the chain fall with a clatter. "Your clothes are under the bed," he told me as he left. "Get dressed. I'll be back in a minute."

Mary helped me into my shirt and tied a sling around my arm to keep me from tearing the stitches in my shoulder. My boots had vanished, and I had to walk barefoot beside the stocky officer as he led me down the hallway beyond the infirmary. He hadn't undone the manacle from my ankle, and the chain dragged behind me, clanking against the floor.

The officer steered me into a windowless room and shut the door behind us. Patches of the dark walls were stained darker by something I didn't want to think about, and there was a single chair in the center, ancient and gouged but sturdy looking. It was bolted to the ground.

I sat down on it without being instructed. The officer fastened the chain on my ankle to one of the bolts. "Sorry about this," he muttered. "It's procedure."

"I don't mind," I said. I wasn't planning on running.

It was only a few minutes before the door opened and Inspector Jiroux strode through, dressed in a dark greatcoat and tall black boots that made me sick with envy.

He stopped in front of me with his hands behind his back. His salty hair was ruffled and his face was puffy and pale, as though he hadn't slept properly. I felt a surge of satisfaction as I imagined him turning the foothills upside down for Oliver and coming up empty.

Exhausted or not, when he spoke his voice was buoyant and strong. "Good morning, Mr. Finch." When I didn't reply, he added, "How's your shoulder?"

"Fine," I said.

"Not in the mood for pleasantries, are we."

"I'd like to know what's going to happen to me," I replied. "That's all."

He watched me for a moment, his smile so tight it trembled. "How direct," he said, then began to walk in slow circles. "I'm not sure if you remember, but I knew your brother before he died. Or I should say, I knew of him. He had a reputation among the officers. We arrested him once for brawling at some pub. Isn't that right?" He glanced over his shoulder at me, and I nodded. "It took three men to bring him in. We only wanted him to pay for the damage, but he was so cheeky. Then he bit one of my officers, so we held him overnight." He stopped before me, his hands still behind his back. "Do you remember?"

"Yes."

"You're much calmer than him."

"I'm not my brother."

"That's quite clear. Though, based on the incident two nights ago, I don't believe your brother is your brother anymore." He started to pace again, back and forth like a swinging pendulum. The cross on his watch chain bounced against his waistcoat with every step. "When I first heard rumors of the resurrected man, I discounted them as fanatical ravings. I even read that book—*Frankenstein*, isn't that what it's called?—and thought there was no chance any of it was real. No deed could be so unnatural as the resurrection of a human being with clockwork and circuitry."

I made a noise before I could stop myself—something halfway between a laugh and a snarl.

Jiroux stopped again and glanced at me over his shoulder. "Are you a churchgoing man, Mr. Finch?" When I didn't answer, he nodded and said, "No, I didn't expect someone like you would be."

Someone like you—he said it without any trace of mockery. It sounded like he pitied me. I bit the inside of my cheek.

"But I hope you at least know the story of creation," he went on. "*On the sixth day, God created man in His own image.* So why do you and the other mechanics who share your work feel that you can improve upon His design with the addition of clockwork pieces? Do you think you are equal to God?" He rubbed the gold cross between his fingers, then looked me dead in the eye.

"The Bible is clear on the subject, Mr. Finch: men with mechanical parts and those who make them such spit in the face of the divine creator. And that's damnation."

I thought that was shit logic, from someone who'd never seen a body in broken pieces, but I didn't dare tell him so when I was chained to a chair.

"We have been unable to capture your brother and the young woman who assisted his escape," Jiroux continued, "but we're certain that when they left the castle, they returned to Geneva. Oliver Finch can't be allowed to roam free in the city. He is a threat to the general safety and a rallying point to an already unruly subset of our population. If the public becomes aware of the presence of Frankenstein's monster, it's likely to cause a panic."

"I don't know where Oliver is," I said, but he pressed on like he hadn't heard.

"Our force has never dealt with anything quite like this before. Dr. Geisler told us your brother's clockwork parts had given him some superhuman qualities that would make him hard to capture and detain, but I hardly expected—"

"Geisler didn't know anything," I interrupted.

"He led us to you and your brother," Jiroux replied, and the corners of his mouth turned up. It might have been a smile, but on his face it looked like a sneer. "So it would appear he wasn't entirely ignorant."

Of course it had been Geisler who'd told them about us, just like Clémence had said he would. I cursed myself for not being more careful when we'd gone to the castle, not trusting that gut feeling that someone was following us. "There's no special way to find Oliver," I said. "He's just a man on the run."

"Well, now that we're in possession of the Clock Breakers—"

"The what?"

"Geisler's automaton soldiers. They were confiscated when he was arrested. He told us he called them Clock Breakers."

A shiver went through me with the name. "You're going to use them to catch Oliver?"

"Geisler informed us that he designed them specifically for capturing and restraining mechanical men, in case his own experiments got out of hand. But now that Geisler has left us, the Clock Breakers are the property of the police. I have no doubt they'll be a valuable asset to our force, both for detaining your brother and for keeping the city's clockwork population in line."

I thought of Depace's wagon outside the house the morning we left. It hadn't been bodies in the coffins—it had been the automatons. Clock Breakers made for Oliver. "So what do you want from me?" I asked. "You've got your mechanical soldiers. What can I do?"

"The automatons cannot find your brother for us," Jiroux replied. "Without your help, we have no sure way of locating him. In spite of your protestations, you know him better than we do."

The wound in my shoulder throbbed. "I don't know where Oliver is, and even if I could find him, he wouldn't come easier because of me."

"Are you certain?" Jiroux reached into his greatcoat and withdrew a crumpled piece of paper, which he held up for me to see. It was the leaflet that had been in my pocket—the illustrated clockwork man with the words FRANKENSTEIN'S MONSTER LIVES! above it. "We think your brother has taken refuge with the group of radicals who call themselves Frankenstein's Men. They've been a thorn in my force's foot for a few weeks, but we're afraid that with your brother's added support they may be inspired toward increased action. And it seems you've been in contact with them as well."

I swallowed the urge to curse.

"We don't know where they are," Jiroux continued. "And we don't know where your brother is. But I suspect you do, and if you help us, we're prepared to reward you for your services."

I kept my mouth shut, hoping he would let me in on what sort of reward he had in mind, but he was looking at me just as intently, waiting for me to ask. I swallowed, then said, "What do you mean?"

"If we are able to capture your brother and suppress this rebellion based on information or aid you provide us, we will release both you and your father. We'll give you time to get out of the city. No charges attached to your names. You'll be free."

My heart leapt, but I kept my face blank. "And if I don't?"

"As a convicted Shadow Boy, the best your father can expect is life imprisonment. With the evidence that you've been helping your brother, I'd imagine it would be significantly worse for you."

They'd kill me if I didn't help them, that's what he was saying. But they'd kill Oliver if I did. "How do I know I can trust you?" I asked. "You made some deal with Geisler that you clearly never intended to deliver on."

"Geisler was a fool," Jiroux snapped. "His bargain was a desperate plea made by a desperate man. But you will trust me for the same reason he did: because it is your only choice." He looked deliberately down at the chain on my ankle. I fought the urge to look down too.

"How long will you give me to find Oliver?" I asked.

"Twenty-four hours should be sufficient."

"A day? That's it?"

"I have a sense you're not as ignorant as you claim, and I hope that a deadline will encourage you to work quickly before the rebellion has a chance to act." He crossed his arms, his eyes narrowing as he studied me. "I know you don't think much of me, Mr. Finch, but I hope you can see that I am simply trying to do the best for the city I have been charged to protect. Surely you understand that your brother and his rebellion are a threat to the safety of Geneva, and I hope we can count on your assistance to see that the threat is counteracted."

He was staring at me like he was waiting for an answer, but I didn't have a clue what to say. It felt like a trap. He was asking me to choose between Oliver and Father, so whatever I did, I lost something important, and that felt so unfair it made my blood boil.

I had to swallow hard several times before I found my voice. "Can I see my father?"

Jiroux blinked. "Excuse me?"

"I want to see my father," I said, louder this time. "He's here, isn't he?"

"He is." He considered this for a moment; then he turned to the stocky officer still waiting by the door. "Go on, Ottinger, take him down. Five minutes, Mr. Finch," he instructed as Ottinger came forward to unshackle me. "Then we'll continue this discussion."

My feet had gone so numb against the cold stones that I almost toppled over when I stood. Ottinger caught me by my unslung arm. "Easy."

"I'm all right," I murmured, stamping my feet against

the floor a few times to get my blood flowing again.

"Here." Ottinger cast a quick glance at the door to be certain Jiroux was gone, then bent down and unfastened the manacle from around my ankle.

"Thank you."

He shrugged. "That way you aren't clanking like a machine the whole way."

We left the interrogation room and took a flight of narrow stone steps down. This was the police station, I realized as we walked. It wasn't a proper prison, but there were holding cells below ground and the interrogation rooms above. And it seemed I was going to have the privilege of seeing both.

Ottinger walked a few feet behind me, and at my side when the halls were wide enough. He kept one hand on my elbow, but his grip wasn't strong. When I looked over at him, I realized he couldn't be more than a few years older than me—maybe the same age as Oliver.

Out of nowhere, I missed Oliver so badly. I wanted him here with me, by my side, holding on to me and steering me the way I should go like he always had when we were young. Not the Oliver that had stabbed Geisler in the throat. The Oliver I'd grown up with. The Oliver I'd killed and meant to bring back. I felt his absence deep and aching inside of me, the piece of myself that belonged to him broken off and buried. I could have cried from the hurt of it.

We descended a short set of stairs that opened into a dark hallway lined with cells. Ottinger stopped outside a door at the end of the row. "I can only give you five minutes," he said as he unlocked it. "But my watch is sometimes slow." He smiled, and I tried to return it but I think mine ended up looking more like a grimace.

The interior of the cell was barren and dark, the only light coming from a slotted window on the far wall. Matted straw was scattered across the floor, and there was a wooden bench shoved in one corner with a ragged blanket draped across it. I stood still for a moment, letting my eyes adjust to the gloom.

Then, from one corner, came a voice. "Alasdair?"

I turned, and there was my father. He looked sick and pale, but he pulled himself onto his knees when he saw me.

"Father!" I was worried he'd tip over if he tried to stand, so I dropped down beside him.

"God's wounds, Alasdair." His hands were chained, but somehow he managed to maneuver me into a hug. It was the first time I could remember him holding me since I was a boy, and my body went stiff with surprise for a moment before I relaxed into it.

"I didn't know what had happened to you," I said.

"I'm all right." He leaned back and peered into my face. "And you're all right. How's your shoulder?"

"It's fine."

"What happened?"

I hesitated. I wasn't certain how much he'd been told. "Someone stabbed me."

He didn't press me on that one. Just nodded, like this was ordinary, then said, "I've been worried sick over you."

"Well, don't sound so relieved. I'm in prison."

"Yes, but I thought . . . I thought it might have been worse. At least you're alive."

"What about Mum?"

"She made it out," he replied. "Morand came to see me—she's with him in Ornex. She's all right."

"I should have helped," I said before I could stop myself. "When you were arrested, I shouldn't have run, I should have—"

"You did the right thing," he interrupted. "You always . . . you always do the right thing." His face darkened, and he slid down the wall. I sat beside him. I was trying to shore up my courage to tell him what was going on, but he spoke before I could. "I saw Miss Godwin."

"Mrs. Shelley," I corrected.

"Yes, Mrs. Shelley. She told me . . . Oliver's alive." He shuffled his hands, and the chains around his wrists clattered against each other. "He was dead, and you brought him back, that's what she said." He paused for a moment, like he was waiting for me to tell him that was wrong, but I didn't say anything. I'd gone suddenly breathless. Father tipped his chin to his chest, eyes downcast. Then he said, "That's incredible, Alasdair."

I hadn't expected that. "What?"

"You brought him back. You did what even Geisler couldn't."

"But he's not Oliver anymore," I said. "I did something wrong and I ruined him. I made him into a monster."

"I doubt that very much. From what Mrs. Shelley said, you made a human being. And humans are, by nature, monstrous." He turned like he was going to meet my gaze, then changed his mind at the last second and leaned back against the wall so that he could stare up at the ceiling instead. "That's the thing no one seems to understand. I'm not even sure Geisler did. There are monsters inside all of us, clockwork men no more so than the rest. None of us are made to be one thing or another."

"I should have told you," I said. "I'm sorry. I didn't know how."

He nodded once, and a vein in his neck flexed. "Oliver was always a bit of an unexploded firework, we knew that. But you . . . I can always count on you." And then he reached over, clumsy in a way I chose to blame on the chains, and put his hand on my knee.

I didn't know what to say to that—probably couldn't have spoken if I tried. All I could think about were the things I could tell him that would change his mind about me right then. That I'd abandoned Oliver to run away to Ingolstadt. That I'd nearly handed him over to Geisler's experiments. Why he'd ended up dead in the first place. All the horrible things I'd done between that day and today. I should have at least told Father about Jiroux's offer and asked him what I should do—that was the whole reason I'd come. *Don't count on me*, I thought. *I'll let you down.*

But I didn't want to spoil the moment.

Now it was me staring at my bare feet with his gaze on my face—I could feel it. I could feel, too, the seconds of our time left together falling away, but I couldn't think of a thing to say.

After a long minute, Father said, "You need a haircut, Alasdair." In spite of everything, I laughed. It was feeble, but still a laugh, and I heard the smile in his voice when he spoke again. "Your mother won't like it if I return you to her all scruffy looking."

Something about the impossibility of that hope stung deep, and my throat went tight. Father's shoulder brushed mine. "Look at me, Alasdair," he said. I did, and as our eyes met, I realized—maybe for the first time in my life—that his were the exact same color as Oliver's. "We're going to be all right," he said. "*All* of us."

It was a stupid promise. The sort that couldn't be kept, and I think we both knew it. But right then, that didn't really matter. It was something to hold on to.

15

They let me out that afternoon. Jiroux came to the infirmary with Ottinger and explained clearly the terms of my release: I had twenty-four hours to sort out my loyalties and find where Oliver and the rebellion were hiding out, then deliver that information to the police. If Oliver was caught and the rebels stopped thanks to me, Father and I would be freed and given passage out of Geneva. If not, we'd both be kept in prison, likely executed. If I didn't come back before the end of my allotted time, they'd kill Father.

It was December the twenty-fourth. Christmas Eve. On Christmas Day, I'd have to decide who I was going to sell out.

The last provision, and my only say in any of it, was

I walked barefoot beside Ottinger down to the waiting room where Mary was standing, wrapped in a fur-lined cloak with her hair pulled up beneath a bonnet and my scuffed boots in her gloved hands. Seeing her again made my insides tighten. I took the boots from her without a word, and she stood at my side while I struggled to pull them on and then lace them, with one arm useless in its sling. Ottinger noticed, and he bent down to help, leaving me standing stupidly while a police officer did up my boots for me like I was a lad. But my shoulder hurt enough that I let him.

When he was finished, he gave me my coat, and I turned without putting it on and walked out of the station. I didn't say a thing to Mary, but I heard the door catch as she followed me out.

The day was gray and foggy, with a canopy of sparkling mist blotting out the sunlight and making the snow look silver. The streets were crowded with holiday shoppers, and I could hear sleigh bells down the way. *Christmas Eve*, I thought again, and my eyes found the clock tower silhouetted against the sky. I started down the street, pulling on my coat as I went with my head bent against the wind. Behind me, I heard Mary call my name. "Alasdair."

I didn't stop. Her bootheels clattered on the cobbles. "Alasdair, wait."

She managed to catch up, and suddenly she was in front of me, blocking my path. Her dark hair whipping out from under her bonnet trailed behind her like a kite string.

I stopped. "What?"

She crossed her arms, breath steaming white against the air. "How's your shoulder?"

"It's fine."

"If you're lying to me, I'll skin you alive." I couldn't stop myself from laughing, but I was so weary and sick it came out sounding meaner than I meant.

Mary scowled. "What are you laughing at me for?"

"If I'm lying. What a joke coming from you."

"And what's that supposed to mean?"

"You know damn well what I mean. Mary—" I broke off. The two years between us were building at my back, the weight of all those unsaid, unexplained things, and it felt so heavy that I nearly sat down where I stood. I was angry—at her for *Frankenstein* and the way she was looking at me like she didn't understand, at myself for this whole tangled mess, at Oliver because I had been certain there was something inside him worth saving but then he'd put the pliers in Geisler's throat.

Mary looked away from me, up at the sky with the clock tower cut like a cameo against it, then down at the cobblestones, muddy snow congealing in the cracks between them. "I'm sorry about your parents," she said.

"And Oliver. And . . . everything." She reached out and took my hand, just for a moment, and squeezed it. A bolt went through me, somehow both ice and electricity, and I pulled away. Mary looked up. "I need to tell you what happened."

"I know what happened," I said. "You took my life and Oliver's life and you made them into this book. You made us into monsters, both of us. I don't see much more than that going on here."

"That's not it, Alasdair, I never meant—"

"Mary, I don't have time to talk to you about this."

"Well, maybe I need to talk about it!" she cried, and for a moment she was the same fierce, beautiful creature who had captivated me two summers ago. Then she looked down, face shadowed, and I lost her again like a reflection in a lake cracked by ripples. "Will you listen to me, please? There are some things I need to tell you."

I only had a day. It felt like no time at all, like I didn't have a second to waste on Mary Shelley, but there were answers I needed whether I wanted them now or not. It didn't feel like the right place—three doors down from the police station, on a street corner in Geneva on Christmas Eve—but I couldn't think of anywhere that would ever be right for this.

I sighed and sank down onto the stoop of a watchmaker's shop. Mary hesitated, then eased herself down beside me. She pulled off her bonnet so I could see her face, and her dark hair unfurled across her shoulders. Our arms brushed. For a moment, we both sat completely still as pedestrians and carriages clattered by. Cathedral bells were singing from the square.

Then Mary said very quietly, "Here's the truth of why I spent so much time with you and Oliver that summer. All my life I thought I was a wild and brave girl who was not afraid of anything, but then I came here with Byron and Shelley and they were so much wilder than me. With them, everything felt so real and dangerous—all that free love and opium and acting as though we were living inside dark stories. I was frightened of the things they did, and I started to feel cowardly, like perhaps I wasn't who I had always thought I was. Perhaps I wasn't brave at all. But then I found you and Oliver, and you were . . . different. You were danger without ever feeling danger-ous. You did adventurous things and I shocked you by doing them with you, and you made me feel wild without my ever having to do anything that truly frightened me. You especially—I always felt so daring with you. And I loved you for it, because it was like you gave me myself back when I thought I'd lost it."

She pressed two fingers to the bridge of her nose and closed her eyes like she was drawing these mem-ories from a deep darkness inside of her. "But then Oliver died, and it was so messy and complicated and the realest thing that had ever happened to me. I was so frightened because I was a part of it. It wasn't me doing the work, but I was there. I was complicit. My God, Alasdair, look at what you did. You changed the rules of the universe. I think you were so caught up in the fact that it was Oliver, you didn't realize that. But I did, and I didn't know what to do with it. After it happened, you wouldn't talk about it, and I couldn't tell anyone else and I needed to make sense of it somehow. I tried to leave it behind—I went back to London, but it was still haunting me. You can't hide from the things inside your own mind. So I wrote it all down, just to try and be free of it. It started with just you bringing your brother back from the dead."

"On a dreary night in November," I said, the first line of the resurrection scene in *Frankenstein*.

She winced, like it was a jab. "But then my husband found it. I couldn't tell him it was real, so I said I'd made it up. They were all writing horror stories while we were here, and I told him that was mine. And he liked it so much he wanted me to write more. If I had said no, I'd have had to tell him why, so I kept writing. And it felt so *good*. It was like I was finally making peace with what we had done."

"So you should have burned it."

"I couldn't have done that. I'm its creator, same as you're Oliver's."

I hated that word, *creator*. I wanted to spit and stomp on it. I hadn't *made* Oliver. He'd done that himself.

"Then Percy showed it to his publisher," Mary continued, "and they wanted to print it and I didn't know what I was supposed to do. So I hid you as best as I could." She looked over at me. "I wrote it because I couldn't keep it inside of me. You were always so good at that, but that was never who I was. I needed some way to work out how the rules of God and man and creation changed after you brought your brother back from the dead." She pulled her legs up next to her on the stoop as a group of carolers shuffled past us, singing softly. "Do you know the story of Prometheus?" she asked. I shook my head. "It's from Greek mythology. He's a Titan who makes mankind from clay. It's a creation myth, a way to explain the creation of man."

"I know what a creation myth is," I snapped.

"Then you understand that *Frankenstein* is mine. My creation myth, for men made of metal and gears. The only way I knew to explain what happened. It's not your story, though," she added. "It started that way, but I didn't know what happened after I left Geneva. It's all made up."

"It doesn't matter that it isn't true, Mary, because it's us. It's me and it's Oliver—that's where it started, and people will recognize that. They already have."

She tucked her chin into her collar and said nothing.

"Are you in it?" I asked. "I thought maybe you were Victor Frankenstein's wife, but I don't think so anymore."

"I think I was Henry at first. The observer. The best friend. The least clever out of everyone." She smeared a patch of snow with the toe of her boot. "I don't know. Perhaps I'm the monster. Perhaps we all are."

I closed my eyes, trying to convince myself that speaking to Mary was poison flowing from my veins, but it was still poison, and it still burned. "Do you think I'm horrid?" I asked.

"What?"

"Victor Frankenstein is horrid. He's arrogant and he's cowardly and he puts his own cleverness ahead of anything else. Do you truly think that's the way I am?"

She didn't say anything for a moment, and her silence made my heart sink. "The night it happened," she said slowly, "you weren't yourself. You were so fixated on bringing Oliver back because you knew you could. You kept saying that to me, *I know I can do it.* You didn't care about creation or morality or any of that. And that frightened me, because it was like I didn't know who you were. That night, I thought I'd lost you both." She held her breath for a moment, then asked, "Do you know where Oliver is?"

I couldn't find my voice, so I just nodded.

"And you're going to tell the police."

She sounded so sure of it that I looked up. "You think I should?"

"Don't you?"

"He's my brother, Mary."

"You really think he's still your brother? That man who stabbed you, who killed Geisler and tormented me for days? I knew Oliver, and that creature isn't him." Her voice pitched, and she put a finger to her lips for a moment before she finished. "He never came back, Alasdair. We both know it."

Something inside me splintered when she said that, and I pressed the heel of my hand against my eyes. Her fingers ran a whispered track along my spine. "You need to tell the police where he is," she said. "You can save yourself and your father. If you see Oliver again, he'll kill you."

"Well, he'll have to get in line, since Jiroux seems quite keen on it as well." I stood up and brushed my unslung hand off on my trousers. "I've got to find Oliver. I have to be certain I know what the right thing is before I do anything."

Mary stood too, shaking out her skirt. "I can't talk you out of it?"

"No."

"Then come see me after, so I know you're all right. I'm at the villa in Cologny again."

"I can't leave the city."

"Then I'll meet you somewhere. We'll find you a room for the night. The Christmas market—meet me there." She reached out for my hand again, and this time I didn't pull away. "Please be careful," she said, and when her fingers pulsed, mine responded with a spark.

We parted on the corner. Mary started back the way we'd come, into the sunset, and I went in the opposite direction, toward the Cogworks and the only place I could think to look for Oliver. If he wasn't there, I didn't know what I'd do.

I crossed the Rhone to Rive Droite, the north quarter of the city where the factories churned. The buildings here were all industrial brick, stained black by soot and grime, and the belching steamstacks made the air sweat. There were no casings on the industrial torches, just open flames tearing at the sky. Everything smelled damp and foul, and the shadows all around me seemed to stretch and curl like smoke.

If Oliver and Clémence had fled into the city like Jiroux thought, I was certain it was so she could take him to the rebels in the Cogworks. I could find him there, though I didn't have a clue what I'd do once I did. When I closed my eyes, I could still see Oliver jamming his pliers into Geisler's throat, and his fist on my shoulder when he stabbed me, and I couldn't wed those images with the boy I'd grown up with, wild and reckless but good straight to his core. Perhaps Mary was right and I was foolish to try again. Perhaps he truly was gone.

The Cogworks was a single-floored, sprawling structure made of cut gray stone and grimy windows. The door was bolted, which rendered my lock-picking skills useless, but there was a window that opened without much coaxing. I managed to hoist myself up with only my good arm, grateful for once that I was so bleeding skinny, and dropped onto the factory floor with a stumble. The darkness made the room look as though it stretched for miles, all haunted shadows and impassable shapes. Black outlines of workbenches lined with saws and factory tools cut through the gloom, their edges made molten by the pale dregs of the day's coal still smoldering in the forges. The air was heavy and metallic, so sharp it almost smelled like blood.

I started forward cautiously, unslung arm extended so I wouldn't smash into anything. Rust and metal shavings crunched under my feet. My heart was slamming like a piston, and I kept waiting for someone to grab me. If they were kind, they'd cut my throat right there and spare me from having to sort out the wretched mess I'd gotten myself into.

But there was no one. The factory seemed well and truly deserted. I walked the floor end to end and found not a soul, nor any hint of a revolution being built there. No rebels. No clockwork men. No Oliver.

Then, just as I was about to give up, I found a gated

set of spiral stairs that led underground. At their base, a pale light flickered. I hopped the gate and jogged down, a bit unsteady without a hand to put on the rail.

The stairs opened onto a storeroom a quarter the size of the floor above. The air was different here, sulfurous and chalky instead of metallic. In the center of the room was a Carcel burner with a glass shade—not a fine piece, but too delicate for a factory—and the flame cast a sheen of pale light across the low ceilings and the cracked stone. Beside the burner were a few loose sheets of paper, and when I picked one up, I realized it was a leaflet, same as the one Mirette had given Clémence and me. The paper was brushed black with something that looked like soot but felt coarse when I scrubbed at it. It was on the ground too, I realized, a light dust like something had spilled. I held my fingers above the burner shade and rubbed them together. A bit of the powder wafted down into the lamp, and the flame sparked with a loud pop. I jumped back, realizing what it was. Gunpowder.

I dropped the leaflet and crouched down, trying to figure out what I was meant to do with this empty room and a few leaflets laced with gunpowder, but the only thing I could think about was Oliver with his wild heart and, if Jiroux was right, devoted revolutionaries at his command, ready to let himself and his men loose on Geneva. I looked down again at the leaflet, black powder gathering in its creases—FRANKENSTEIN'S MONSTER LIVES!

There was a soft patter from behind me like scuttling footsteps on the stone. I looked up just as a brass gear the size of my fist was lobbed out of the darkness and clattered to the ground at my feet. "Hello?" I called.

Silence. Then a small voice replied, "I know you, Shadow Boy."

And from the corner came Mirette, black hair striped amber in the lamplight and another gear in her hand.

I kicked the one on the ground. "Did you throw that at me?"

"I meant it to hit you."

"Bleeding awful aim."

"It's heavy." A pause as she took a step closer to me, head cocked so her tangled hair raked over her shoulders. "Were you crying?"

"No."

"I didn't know boys cried."

"I wasn't . . ." And then I stopped, because the light from the burner had sliced across her face and I realized *she* had tears on her cheeks. "What's wrong with you?"

"They told me to stay hidden down here, but I wanted to help. Then I heard someone upstairs and I thought it was the police come for me." She dragged her hand across her face and gave a throaty sniff, then added, "You were wrong, you know."

"What was I wrong about?"

"The resurrected man." She pointed at the drawing

on one of the leaflets. "He's not just in the book. He's real. I saw him with my own eyes."

I sat up. "So he was here?"

"He came to lead us. I told you he would."

"Where have they gone?" I asked. "Where's he taken them?"

Mirette sucked her bottom lip. "I'm not supposed to say."

"It's important, Mirette, please." She turned away from me, her face out of the lantern light. I crawled forward so I was right beside her, and nudged the burner into the space between us. "How's your foot?" I asked.

"I can still move my toes," she replied, then thrust out her foot to demonstrate for me. She'd wrapped it in rags so that the socket fused into her skin was covered. "And I'm going to nick some shoes soon as I can. You fixed it good."

"I wish I could do better." I picked up one of the leaflets and held it between us. "The resurrected man," I said, "he's my brother. I'm trying to find him. Please, Mirette, will you help me?"

Mirette pressed her metal foot hard into the floor, leaving a clear print in the black dust. Then she said, "First we went to the castle."

"The castle?"

"Up in the foothills. They let me come along to carry the lantern."

"All right, then what?"

"Then they brought the crates back here."

"They brought what?"

"Crates. All the crates. That was yesterday."

"What did the crates . . . ?" And then I realized. Oliver was running around with Clémence, the daughter of a bomb maker, and they had gone back to Château de Sang for the gunpowder packed in the basement and left a trail of it here between the stones. "Mirette, where've they gone?"

"The tower. The clock strikes again tonight."

I could have hugged her for that, but I was worried she'd whip another gear at me if I tried, and I was a much easier target with just a few feet between us. "You have to promise me you'll stay here tonight. Don't go anywhere near the clock tower."

"But I want to help."

"You can't help. You need to stay put."

"Are you going?" she asked. I hesitated, which answered the question, and she grabbed my coat sleeve. "Take me too!"

"No, it's dangerous."

"But *you're* going. That's not fair."

"Mirette, if you follow me, I'll tell the resurrected man that it was you who blabbed about where he and his men had gone and you'll be in trouble."

Her fist twisted on my coat sleeve, so tight the material

tugged at my skin. "No, please don't!"

"Then promise me you'll stay here and stay hidden."

Her mouth puckered into a scowl. "Fine. I'll stay here."

"Good. And for God's sake, put the light out before you blow yourself up."

Mirette twisted the knob on the side of the burner and the flame died into nothing. She was gone before I could stand—I heard her footsteps fade into the darkness—and I went in the opposite direction, fumbling my way back to the bottom of the stairs, the powdered remnants of my brother's bombs crunching under my feet.

I left the Cogworks and sprinted through the north quarter until I came to the river and crossed back into the financial district. Every inch of me was buzzing. I knew I should have gone to the police first, but there wasn't time. All I could think about was Oliver and his army somewhere in the crowd in the clock tower square, waiting to make their move, and Mary there too, waiting for me, not knowing that something was about to happen.

The noise from the square reached me from streets away, the sounds of the market and so much happy chatter and the voices raised in carols. When I turned the corner into the square, I found Place de l'Horloge packed. The Christmas market stalls were walled in by people shopping and eating and staking out their spots to watch the clock strike for the first time in years. The frosty air was spiced with wassail and sweet smoke from the braziers. I shoved my way through the crowd toward the base of the clock tower, hoping that by some miracle I'd smash into someone I recognized—Ottinger or Oliver or Mary, especially, so I could drag her away from here.

I searched the sea of upturned faces pinched red by the cold, and across the square I spotted Clémence.

She was standing in the middle of everything, looking straight ahead instead of up at the clock like everyone else. Perhaps she sensed my gaze, for she turned her head and I caught a glimpse of the left side of her face, where the bruise from the automaton's fist was blushing violet. For a moment I thought she was looking right at me; then I realized her attention was on someone else across the crowd. She tapped two fingers to her lips like a greeting or a signal and started to move. I changed course and followed her.

Clémence was smaller than I was and she moved easily through all the people. I kept getting whacked by elbows and shopping bags and scarves as they were whipped over their owners' shoulders. I stopped apologizing after stepping on a man's foot nearly cost me the sight of her.

She broke from the rows of market stalls and trotted around the side of the clock tower, away from the crowd. I followed, but when I rounded the corner, she was gone, as suddenly as if she'd vanished into thin air. It was only me standing at the edge of the river, trying to work out where she went.

Then, from high above me, there was a flash like a sudden sunbeam, accompanied by a coarse grinding sound. A cheer rose from the square, and I looked up. Someone inside the clock had given it a pulse, and I could hear the gears starting to churn, weights sinking and rising on heavy chains as the chimes began to sing. I heard it all, and I felt it inside of me, like my own heart syncing to the clockwork.

Then a murmur ran through the crowd, cheers turning into a collective gasp. Something was wrong.

I jogged back to the edge of the market and looked up at the clock face. The minute hand, poised to strike when the clock was started, had moved one step backward instead.

Then the doors to the glockenspiel under the face opened, and the platform began to roll out. The clockwork figures that were meant to be there had gone, and in their place was a single crouching form. I knew him before he stood, but stand he did. Stood and looked out across the city like a grotesque gargoyle from a cathedral buttress.

It was Oliver.

He was wearing nothing but trousers, and it seemed a miracle that his metal joints hadn't frozen at that height in this cold. He raised his chin as the wind teased his dark hair, the light from the clock face shafting through it like veins of gold in obsidian. He had his shoulders thrust back, his twisted clockwork body on display.

For a moment, the crowd didn't seem to realize that the strange brass form gleaming above them was not a clockwork figure from the glockenspiel but a living man made of stitches and steel. Then people began pointing and shouting. Someone screamed, high and shrill.

"Geneva!" Oliver cried, his voice carrying over the wind and the river and the crowd. "You have tried to silence us, but we cannot be silenced."

A man in front of me bolted, knocking into my shoulder as he ran. My stitches flared. "What's going on?" a woman nearby whimpered.

"Your monsters are unleashed," Oliver cried, raising his arms before him. "And they come for the men who beat them and broke them."

He looked down, and the crowd followed his gaze to the archways at the base of the clock tower. Shadows were breaking from the darkness, joining the cobblestone square and taking the shape of people. Clockwork people, I realized, with their mechanical parts proudly showcased. Men and women with brass legs and iron fists and silver shoulders and kneecaps, trousers and skirts and coat sleeves rolled up so their limbs could be seen. They walked toward the crowd, with Oliver shouting above them, reciting:

"'Thou didst seek my extinction, that I might not cause greater wretchedness; my agony was still superior to thine, for the bitter sting of remorse will not cease to rankle in my wounds until death shall close them forever.'"

Frankenstein, I realized. He was quoting *Frankenstein* in the cawing oratory voice he used to adopt when he and Mary read Milton aloud on the shores of Lake Geneva, and birds scattered from the grass before him.

Now it was the crowd scattering before him as his army advanced. A woman stepped backward on top of me and I almost lost my footing. Someone shoved me from behind. People were starting to run.

The first explosion went off then. Somewhere in the back of the crowd there was a bang and a flash, and the screams multiplied. One of the market stalls had caught fire, sending a tongue of flame blazing into the air. Then there was a second bang from close behind me, and a gust of hot, sulfurous air hit me so hard I stumbled.

And then everyone was running and coughing and shouting. It was hard to make out anything amid the noise, though I swore I could still hear Oliver reciting *Frankenstein*, like a scripture, at the top of his voice. The clockworks were shoving back at the crowd, pikes and hammers and fists ready for a fight.

Through the haze, I could see blue-uniformed police officers streaming into the crowd. They had their rifles raised and were making for the tower, but the ring of clockworks held them off. Shots were fired. More people screamed. I saw a splash of blood in the river—washed away so fast it was like blinking away sunspots.

My eyes were burning from the smoke and it was hard to keep them open. Ahead of me, amber flames were clawing at the air, jumping from one stall to the next along the garlands. I staggered forward and tripped over something. A body was sprawled at my feet, blood trickling into the cracks between the cobblestones. I stopped dead for a moment, too shocked to move, but I knew I didn't have time to waste being afraid. Mary was somewhere in the crush. My brother was swearing vengeance against her and her book in her own words, and I had to find her.

"Mary!" I called, not certain if anyone but myself could hear. I started to shove my way back, against the crowd and toward the clock tower base. It was a fight to not get sucked under and stepped on. The crowd was funneling toward the mouths of the streets and across the bridge, which was jammed up too tight for anyone to move.

"Mary!" I shouted again, so loud I felt something tear in my throat. *"MARY!"*

And, miraculously, I heard someone shout back, "Alasdair!" I turned. Mary was struggling toward me, scarf pulled up over her nose and tears streaming down her cheeks. She reached out. I snatched at her hand, just the tips of our fingers brushing, but the second time, I caught her and pulled her against me. Our arms tangled, and I held as tight as I could to her as we started fighting our way out.

We were shoved sideways, away from the square and toward the clock tower. A line of policemen had formed a perimeter around one of the arches at the base; they stood shoulder to shoulder with their rifles trained forward, but they weren't firing.

"Out of the way!" someone bellowed from behind us, and Mary dragged me to the side as another battalion of officers pushed through the crowd, Jiroux in the lead. He threw up his hand and his men stopped, rifles raised.

"Stay back or it goes up!" I heard someone shout, and it sounded like Clémence. In spite of everything, I stopped and turned to look.

It *was* Clémence, standing under the clock tower with her face illuminated by a blazing torch in her hand. She was surrounded by other clockworks, all holding firm as they stared down the police. In the light from her torch, I could make out barrels and crates packed in tight rows along the walls.

Oliver's men had filled the clock tower with explosives.

The police weren't getting any closer, but they kept their rifles up.

"Lower your weapons and back away!" Clémence bellowed at them.

"Just shoot her!" one of the policemen shouted.

"Shoot her and the whole tower goes up!" one of the clockworks behind Clémence hollered back.

"No!" Jiroux screamed. "Do as she says! Lower your weapons and do as she says." The rifle barrels began to drop. Jiroux set his own rifle on the ground and took a step forward, arms raised. Clémence kept her torch high but came out from under the tower to meet him.

"I speak for the rebellion," she called. She had to shout, and even then I almost couldn't hear her. "We are led by Oliver Finch, the resurrected man. Your clock is running backward, and when it completes one full rotation, if our demand has not been met, our explosives will detonate and the heart of your city will be destroyed."

"What demand is that?" Jiroux called back.

Clémence held his gaze. She didn't look frightened. She didn't look brave either. Just determined, like a girl with something to do. "We want Mary Shelley, the author of *Frankenstein*, turned over to us for our justice."

Mary's fingers clenched around mine.

"We will not give an innocent life to appease you," Jiroux called back to Clémence. "You will be stopped before you have the chance to act."

"We are capable of great damage, Inspector," she replied. "So take whatever risks you want, but know that you will not get through. Any person who comes near the tower will be shot. We'll only give passage to Mary Shelley."

Jiroux held her eyes for a moment, then turned to the line of blue coats behind him. "Empty the square!" he bellowed. "We need everyone out!"

Most of the crowd didn't need to be told, but the officers turned and began shoving the stragglers back toward the streets as fast as they could. I whirled on Mary and grabbed her by the shoulder. "You have to give yourself up," I said. "Then we can get inside the tower and talk to Oliver."

She shook her head. "Alasdair, I can't."

"We can make him hear reason. We can end this, please, Mary!"

"Keep moving!" an officer shouted just behind me. "The square is being evacuated."

I didn't move, but Mary was tugging on me. "Alasdair, we have to go."

"We can't go, we have to get to Oliver!"

"Keep moving, sir!" The butt of a rifle knocked into my back and I stumbled.

Mary grabbed me before I fell. "Come on," she said. She was leaving me behind and there was nothing I could do but follow, because suddenly she was the only chance of stopping this. As the crowds and the police pushed us out of the square, I looked up at the clock tower, hoping for one more glance at Oliver, but he was already gone.

The streets were packed almost too tight to move. Everyone was pushing and shouting and coughing as the smoke from the bombs seeped through the streets, tripping over each other as they tried to get away from the square. Omnibuses were stopped dead, clogging the roads, and I saw a carriage overturned, luggage spilled into the mud and wheels spinning slowly like some invisible hand was pushing them forward.

Mary kept a tight hold on my arm, pulling me through the mob and away from the clock tower. "We can go to the villa," she called to me over her shoulder. "It's outside the city, we'll be safe."

"Mary, we can't leave." I stopped, and rather than let go, she stopped as well and turned to face me.

"The police will take care of it."

"No, Mary, *we* have to do something. We need to get to Oliver; you're the only one who they'll let through."

"*We?* Alasdair, he wants to—" A man smashed into her so hard she staggered into me, and I grabbed her before she fell. For a moment, she was still, forehead against my shoulder and her nails digging into my arm. Then she turned and dragged me sideways through the crowd. "Where are we going?" I called, but she didn't answer, just pulled me after her off the street and up the steps of Saint Pierre Cathedral.

Inside, the cathedral was deserted. The sound of our footsteps carried all the way to the top of the dome before returning to us in whispers. "What are you doing?" I hissed at Mary as she led the way into a chapel off the aisle. A saint's statue glared down at us from a raised dais in the center of the room, praying hands intertwined with the chain of a dangling pocket watch. Saint Pierre. Patron saint of clock makers.

Mary sat on the pew in front of Saint Pierre and closed her eyes. I didn't know what she was doing or what to say, so I just sat down beside her. My whole body felt like a loaded spring, tight and about to snap. I kept waiting to hear an explosion from the square, even though Clémence had promised an hour. I didn't have a clue how loud it would be, or if we'd feel it from here. Maybe the whole street would go up with it, I thought.

Maybe we'd die and never feel the blast.

From beside me, with her eyes still closed, Mary said, "Do you remember when you kissed me?"

I felt that blast. All the cold left me in an instant and I was hot with shame and furious that she dared bring that up, especially when there were so many other things conspiring against me. "I don't want to talk about that now."

"It was at the lake, in the moonlight," she said, like she hadn't heard me. "The night before—"

"I don't want to talk about that."

"That was the bravest thing I'd ever known anyone to do."

I didn't think it possible, but my face got hotter. "Don't patronize me."

"It was brave," she continued, opening her eyes, "because you were scared but you did it anyways."

"I wish I hadn't."

"You don't mean that."

I didn't say anything, because she was right—I didn't. I would have kissed her again.

She reached out like she was going to touch me, but stopped halfway there, her hand raised and wavering between us. Then she said, "I'm not brave like you, Alasdair. I am not brave, and I am not good."

"You are," I said, but she shook her head.

"I'm not going to give myself up."

I closed my eyes. "Please, Mary."

"We could go," she said, and when I opened my eyes again, she was staring at the doors. A pale sliver of candlelight guttered across her face like a scar, and for a moment she looked cleaved in two. "We could run, you and I. Right now, run away. Leave all of this."

"I can't do that."

"You don't owe Oliver anything," she said.

"We can go to the clock tower together," I pressed on. "I'll stay with you, every step. Never leave you."

"He wants to kill me."

"I won't let him. I'd die before I let him."

She laughed, but it fractured halfway through. "Find a better thing to die for."

"Think how many people will die—"

"The police will stop them."

"Then think how many *clockwork* people will die. They are Frankenstein's Men—Frankenstein's army, those are your words, Mary. You have ruined so many lives with your book—people are going to die if you don't come with me and talk to Oliver. Can you live with that?"

She swiped at her cheek with the heel of her hand. "I'll be all right."

"How can you say that? You would never have said that two years ago. You would never have done this to everyone. To me."

"Yes, I would have," she replied, and suddenly she

sounded angry. "You don't know me, Alasdair. We had a few months together and you have spent every moment since then creating some make-believe version of me in your head, but whoever you think I am, I am not. I am not clever and I am not good and I am not brave. I am not any of those things I pretended to be to keep you interested in me."

Footsteps cut through the silence, and we both turned to see a minister hurrying into the chapel, hands clasped before him. "You have to go," he called, weaving his way through the pews toward us. "You can't stay here. The police are evacuating the area."

Mary stood up. "We were just leaving."

"No, Mary, please." I reached out for her hand but she snatched it away. The moonlight through the rose windows fell between us in pastel fragments. She didn't look back at me as she turned and walked past Saint Pierre and the minister, straight through the doors and out into the swelling streets.

By the time I followed, she was gone. Just like that.

I broke free of the crowds of evacuees streaming away from the square and jogged in the opposite direction, back toward the clock tower. With or without Mary, I had to get through to see Oliver. Darkness and the lingering smoke from the explosions gave me good cover, but the police were everywhere and it was a tricky business staying out of sight. I managed to make it to the main road unseen, but four officers were patrolling the entrance to the square at its end, and it didn't seem likely I'd get past them unnoticed.

I was lurking in the shadow of an omnibus, weighing my chances if I made a run for it, when someone grabbed me by the collar and dragged me backward, off the street and around the corner. I tried to fight, but I was slammed against a doorway so hard my head spun. The man holding me pressed an arm against my chest to keep me in place, then raised his lantern, and as the beam fell between us I realized it was Ottinger. There was soot smudged across his cheeks, and a thread of blood was running from beneath his cap, but under it all, his glare was fierce. My stomach dropped.

"What are you doing?" he hissed.

"Let go of me." I tried to shove him away, but with only one good arm, it was like trying to knock over a brick wall.

"Get out of here," he said, and suddenly he was speaking very fast. "There's hardly anyone at the station; you can walk right in. Get your father and go."

I stopped fighting and gaped at him. "What are you saying?"

"I'm saying you should run. You've been given a free pass out of the city, so get out before they find you."

"I can't go."

"Why the hell not?"

"Because that's my brother!" I cried, louder than I meant to. Ottinger glanced down the street; then his grip loosened. I slid free and faced him head-on in the pale beam of his lantern. "I have to get into the clock tower. I can talk to Oliver."

He shook his head. "No one can get through. Jiroux had his men shoot three of the clockwork sentries and then try to force their way in, but they were massacred. We have a girl from the clockworks who says they'll let her pass, but she won't go without Mary Shelley. That's our only way."

"Mary's gone," I said, and the realization caved inside me all over again.

"Jiroux's been operating under that assumption. It doesn't matter. He wouldn't have turned her over. He won't do anything that might be interpreted as compliance."

I closed my eyes, trying to put together some sort of plan, but my brain was a mess of stuck cogs, rusted and wound down and refusing to turn fast enough.

Then I realized what he had said.

"The police have a girl from the clockworks?" I asked, and he nodded. "The blond one? Clémence?"

"I think so. They're holding her in the square."

"Can you take me to her? She can get me through to see Oliver."

"She said she won't go without Mary."

"She'll take me, I know she will." I saw the hesitation in his eyes and before he had a chance to say no, I said, "I know you aren't as thoughtless as them. If I can talk to Oliver, I can help."

"You truly think you can call him off?"

I wasn't anywhere close to certain, but doubt wouldn't do me any favors, so I nodded.

Ottinger held my gaze for a long moment, and then he nodded slowly. "All right, I'll take you. Come on, stay close."

As we crossed back into the street, a low clang echoed from the square, loud as a cannon blast. We both jumped and then turned in its direction. The clock was striking the half hour.

Half our time was gone.

The police had created a spotty perimeter around the square, using the abandoned market stalls for cover. The whole force seemed to be crouched behind the barricades with their rifles trained on the clock tower base, waiting for whatever would happen next.

Ottinger gave me his cap. It was hardly a disguise, but it kept my face in shadow. "Walk like you know where you're going," he told me. "And let me talk if we're questioned." But no one stopped us as we skirted the square. Hardly anyone even looked our way. They were too busy watching the clock tower.

The police had thrown Clémence in one of the stalls at the edge of the market, near the river. Ottinger unlocked the door, and as he pushed it open, I heard her say, "And here I thought you were going to let us blow a crater in your city." I stepped past Ottinger and went inside. She was sitting on the floor with her back against a shelf of broken nutcrackers, smirking until she saw me, and then her face straightened. "Alasdair."

"Mary's gone," I told her. "She left the city. She's not going to give herself up."

She blinked, and for a second, a sliver of surprise blazed through her well-worn veil of defiance. Then she swiped her hair out of her eyes and said very calmly, "So we're all dead."

"Not if you let me talk to Oliver. You're the only one his men will let through, and if I'm with you, they'll let me through too."

"They said it could only be Mary."

"Well then, we're going to have to figure something else out, but I need you. You are the only way we can stop this."

She glared up at me. "Who says I want to stop this?"

"Do you understand what you're doing?" I cried, loud enough that Ottinger shushed me from the doorway. I slid to my knees so I was right beside her and dropped my voice. "This won't change a bleeding thing. You've proved them all right! All those people who think that metal parts make you violent and cruel and less than human—you've gone and shown them that's exactly what you are. You could have demanded anything and you called for someone's death. What's killing Mary going to change?"

"We don't have to *change* anything," she hissed back. "What could we have asked for—equality? Tolerance? Those aren't things you can claim to want with a tower full of explosives at your back. They would have made promises until they were hoarse and then shot us all the moment we put our hands up."

"So you'd have Mary shot instead?"

"I didn't say I wanted her dead," she replied, and suddenly she looked angry.

I was angry too; angry that here was someone else I thought I knew and now she had thrown her true self into sharp relief. Perhaps I didn't really know anyone. Perhaps everyone was just a fiction inside my head. "But the exploding clock tower—you're all right with those casualities?"

"I didn't say that!"

"Then why are you here?" I demanded. "What exactly do you want?"

"I don't want to live this way anymore!" She dropped her head backward against the shelf, and a nutcracker fell to the ground with a soft clatter. "It's just unfair," she said, and when she took a breath, I heard her lungs pop. "All of it."

I slid down from my knees so I was sitting cross-legged in front of her. "Why'd you take Oliver to the rebels?"

"He wanted to go. And I was looking for something to fight for. I've been a prisoner for so long, fighting for freedom seemed rather appealing." She kicked the nut-cracker at her feet and it splintered as it bounced across the floor. "Oliver's not going to walk away."

"Just let me talk to him."

"I can't promise they'll let you through. They might . . ." She trailed off, but I filled in the silence.

"I'm dead either way."

"Well then," she said, and she sounded herself again, "might as well go down fighting." She climbed to her feet, reached out a hand, and pulled me up beside her. Our eyes met, and she smirked at me, that stupid twist of a smile, and the knot in my chest loosened just a smidge.

Ottinger, Clémence, and I slipped out of the market stall and took shelter near the banks of the Rhone beneath an abandoned carriage. Clémence said we could access the tower by the river path, but there were police-men blocking the stairs we needed to get there. We were arguing softly over the best way to pass them when they abandoned their post and started to jog to the other side of the square. I followed their progress, and through the spokes of the wheel I could make out a pair of police wagons that had just arrived and a large group of officers clustered around them. I spotted Jiroux near the center, the red feather on his cornered hat standing out like a splash of blood. He was shouting orders and gesturing at his men, overseeing a fresh batch of policemen filing out of the wagons.

Then the light from the industrial torches hit their bodies and I realized they weren't policemen—they were Clock Breakers.

"He's sending in Geisler's automatons," I hissed at Clémence.

"It'll be a massacre. There's no chance Oliver will listen to peace once he sees them."

"Then we need to stall them."

"I can do that," Ottinger said from my other side.

I twisted around to face him. "Are you sure?"

"I can try, if you tell me how."

"Here." Clémence dug in the pockets of her coat, elbowing me in the process, and pulled out a pair of pulse gloves. "You have to rub them together to get a charge," she explained as she handed them to Ottinger. "Then just grab onto one of the automatons and they'll be disabled. Better if you can use both hands; they take a good shock to shut down. And if one of your fellow policemen tries to stop you, just grab him too. Pulse gloves can knock a grown man out cold if they're fully charged."

Ottinger took the gloves from her and fastened the leather straps around his wrists. "They'll spot me fast with these. I can buy you some time, but not a lot."

"Some is better than none," Clémence replied.

"Are you sure you can do it?" I asked him.

"Yes."

"Sure you *want* to do it?" I corrected.

He raised his face to mine, elbows splayed to keep his balance. "I didn't tell you this, Mr. Finch, but my sister's clockwork. She was born with a bad leg, and your father gave her a new one a few years ago and kept our secret. So I've got a stake in this too." He looked past me to Clémence. "I thought you should know, not everyone's against you."

"Thank you," she said.

He gave an awkward salute, careful not to touch his skin with the plates, then rolled out from under the carriage and took off at a run toward the automatons.

"Let's go," Clémence hissed, and I followed her as we crawled back toward the riverbank.

The stairway leading to the waterfront path was submerged halfway up, but there was no chain here like when we left Geneva. Instead we had to walk along the top of the retaining wall, bricks slippery with moss and water. My boots were so wide that only half my foot fit.

Ahead of me, Clémence skirted as gracefully as an acrobat, though I thought I saw her waver a few times. I gritted my teeth, struggling to keep my balance, but the arm I needed most was useless in its sling. After nearly falling twice, I decided there were worse things than torn stitches, and ripped the sling off and tossed it into the river. I stretched my shoulder cautiously. The sutures pulled, but they held. I placed both hands against the damp wall and began walking again, steadier than before.

One of the clock tower struts moored on the riverbank was hollow, with a ladder running up the inside. Clémence went up first and I followed, close enough that I had to keep ducking to avoid getting kicked in the head. Water dripped down the metal walls, and the whole thing shook as the cogs churned above us. My shoulder was starting to burn, but I kept going, pulling myself up hand over hand through the damp darkness until a small circle of metallic light blinked into view above us. I pressed down the pain by focusing on that spot and counted the rungs as it got larger and larger, and then suddenly Clémence had her hand around my elbow and was hoisting me out.

We were on a narrow metal walkway that stretched like a bridge across the clock tower from end to end, nothing below it but a long fall broken by support beams and struts. Level with the bridge but a good six feet away were the glockenspiel chimes and the horizontal wheel where Oliver had stood when he called his army into the square. Clockwork figures as tall as I was were lined up and frozen along its edge. Above us, the clock face was obscured by grinding cogs, the underbelly of the giant timepiece now running in reverse. Sparks jumped between the teeth as the wheels turned, and the air was metallic and charged like the prelude to a lightning strike. I remembered this from the night Oliver died, and the resurrection. My stomach twisted sharply.

I pulled myself to my feet with the help of the iron railing that ran along both sides of the walkway. Beside us, a weight dropped from between the cogs, a beam of white electricity skittering up its chain. The whole tower was charged.

"Do you know where Oliver is?" I called to Clémence over the chatter of the cogs. She nodded and started across the bridge, but stopped suddenly.

Three people were coming toward us, two men and a woman, all with guns. "Le Brey!" the man in the lead shouted at Clémence. He had long, scraggly hair and a bad limp from clockwork in his left knee. The woman's mechanical arm was in poor repair. It ended in a hook rather than an actual hand, but she kept it on the trigger of her gun, and I was certain it could have fired just as well. I didn't see any clockwork on the second man, but I knew it must be there, out of sight.

"We need to see Oliver, Raif," Clémence called across the bridge.

"You said you'd bring back Mary Shelley or you wouldn't come back at all." Raif took a step toward Clémence. She put a hand on either side of the railing. "Who's this?" he asked, pointing his pistol at me.

"This is Oliver's brother," she replied.

Raif let out a crackling laugh. "The brother who sold him out to the police?"

"I didn't!" I shouted, but I wasn't sure he heard me.

Clémence raised her chin as Raif took another step forward, pistol still raised. "Out of the way, Le Brey."

She didn't move. "Alasdair's one of the Shadow Boys. He's on our side."

"Then why wasn't he here fighting with us?" Raif demanded.

"He's here now," she said. "Let him see his brother."

"Who's there?" someone called from behind Raif and his companions, and they all turned. I had to lean around Clémence to match sight to the voice I recognized.

Oliver. It was hard to see him properly in the darkness as he dropped from a ladder onto the end of the bridge and straightened. All three of his men stepped back, a sort of fearful reverence in their posture toward him. "Le Brey brought your brother," the woman said.

"Did she?" Oliver came forward slowly. I could feel his footsteps ripple across the bridge and resonate up through the soles of my feet. "Where's Mary Shelley?" he called to us.

"She's gone," I said before Clémence could speak. "You can't have her, Oliver."

The shadows of the cogs fell on his face, turning him in and out of darkness as they spun. He looked smoldering, a lit fuse burning into a powder keg. "Then we haven't got long left."

"You don't have to do this!" I called. I tried to get past Clémence but she kept her arms in place and I was worried that if I shoved past her, one of us would fall. "Mary isn't your martyr, and she isn't your enemy. She didn't sell you out."

"Mary took my life and used it against me. Now her life belongs to me."

"That's not how—"

"This is retribution!" he shouted over me. "For Mary Shelley, and *Frankenstein*, and for every wrong done to every clockwork man in Geneva."

"This isn't retribution, Oliver, this is suicide!" I cried. I saw Raif's pistol rise, but I pressed on, unafraid. I was startled by how unafraid I was. "You're throwing away your life, and the lives of all these people who worship you. The only message you'll send Geneva is that clockwork men are monsters!"

"Can I shoot him?" Raif asked Oliver, finger flexing on the trigger.

"That's all they'll remember you for," I said. "You're proving them right."

Oliver's metal fist tightened on the rail, and he turned his face away from me. For a moment, the shadows from the gears matched the pulse of the ones beneath his skin. "If they want monsters, we shall be their monsters."

Clémence's shoulders shrank, and I sidestepped her so that Oliver and I were face to face, so close our shadows were the same. "You are not a monster," I said, as quietly as I could and still be heard.

I could see him clearly now, even in the dim light—the stitches across his forehead, gears pushing back against his skin, body that didn't fit right—but more than that, I was seeing him. *Really* seeing him, clearer than I had since the resurrection, and I knew him. It was Oliver, my brother, the brother I'd grown up with, who'd stolen strawberries for me, and given me his coat when I was cold. Who couldn't sing in tune and who spoke Dutch with Scottish vowels and wrote poetry in charcoal on the school walls and taught me how to skip stones and cuss and survive. Who he had been, and who he still was, the dark-haired boy with the wild heart who just felt everything so deeply.

"You are not a monster," I said again, and this time, I meant it.

"I am a monster!" He shouted it, as loud as I had been soft. "I was murdered by a madman and resurrected by his devil work. I was damned to be inhuman from the moment I was reborn."

"Geisler didn't kill you," I said. My hands were shaking, but my voice stayed steady. I knew what I was about to do, and I didn't flinch from it.

"He pushed me off the clock tower," Oliver replied through clenched teeth. "You can say it for the rest of your life, Alasdair, but I will never believe it was an accident."

"It was an accident," I said, "but it wasn't Geisler who killed you."

Oliver looked up, as though he finally heard me. "You told me—"

"I know what I told you," I said. "I lied. I've been lying to you since I brought you back." I felt lightheaded, dizzy with what I was about to say, and I had to plant my hands on either side of the railing to steady myself. My shoulder was burning. "Oliver, Geisler didn't kill you. He wasn't even there; he was halfway across the city trying to get out. I convinced you to take me to his laboratory. We came here because I wanted his journals. Oliver," I said, and my heartbeat shook, "I killed you."

He took a step back, like I'd thumped him in the face. I had never known him to retreat from anything, and I had never known him to look at me the way he did now. He *stared* at me, like he'd never seen me before, and perhaps he never had until that moment.

It might have been all wrong to tell him then. I

thought of Mary in Château de Sang, blurting at exactly the wrong moment that she had written *Frankenstein*; of sitting by Lake Geneva with her and kissing her at exactly the wrong moment; of Oliver in the clock tower the night we'd found Geisler's journals, shouting at me that I was mad and wicked at exactly the wrong moment. Perhaps we all said the right things at the wrong time; perhaps we couldn't help it. Perhaps words became too heavy to haul, and the moment we let them loose was always the wrong one, but they needed to be free. And I had carried this like a lead weight around my neck for years, feeling it get heavier and heavier every time I saw him, and suddenly I had dropped it down into the chasm of the clock tower. No matter what happened next, no matter if the timing was all wrong, no matter if everything was wrong, Oliver knew, and that was right.

I don't know what I expected him to do. It wouldn't have seemed strange for him to pick me up and hurl me over the side of the bridge right then.

I didn't expect him to run, but he spun on his heel and bolted back the way he'd come, up the ladder and out of sight. I started to chase after him, but I felt Raif's pistol in my belly. The barrel shuddered as the bullet clicked into its chamber.

I didn't move, didn't back away or try to fight him. It seemed sort of fitting if he killed me after that confession. A life for a life.

But then, from behind me, Clémence shrieked, "Look out!"

A shadow moved over Raif's shoulder, then something smashed into the side of his head. Blood slapped me across the face as Raif pitched sideways over the bridge and fell, his body striking the beams below with a hollow clang.

Clock Breakers were swarming onto the bridge, each stiff-legged step rattling its length. The lead Clock Breaker took a swipe at me and I stumbled backward, tripping over Clémence. She seized me by the collar before I fell and dragged me after her, back toward the ladder we'd come from. Two of the Clock Breakers had made quick work of the others who'd been with Raif. One had ripped the woman's clockwork arm out with such force that her shoulder had been wrenched from its socket and was spraying blood as she screamed. The second man was on the ground, twitching with a Clock Breaker's foot on his throat. And there were more, coming now from both ends of the bridge and trapping us in the center.

"Do you have pulse gloves?" I shouted to Clémence.

"Ottinger's got my only pair," she replied. "Anyways, I don't think they'd be enough." Between us, her hand snatched at mine. I could feel her heartbeat galloping in her wrist.

"Do we surrender?" I asked, though I wasn't sure the Clock Breakers knew the meaning of the word.

"Not yet," she replied.

There was a groan above us and we both looked up. The balance wheel was shifting, teeth slipping another step on the track as its airbreaks began to spin. The clock was striking the quarter hour, I realized, and a moment later the gong boomed in confirmation, the noise so low and loud that I felt it shudder straight through me. From between the gears a weight began to drop toward the bridge, and I wasn't sure if it would hit us or just miss. Perhaps that would be a better way to go than being left to the mercy of the Clock Breakers.

Suddenly Clémence grabbed me by the shoulders. "Jump over to the glockenspiel platform."

I looked over at the wheel and all the empty space between it and the bridge. "I won't make it."

"Don't think about it, just jump."

Before I knew what I was doing, she shoved me toward the rail and I hoisted myself onto it. The weight was dropping toward us and a Clock Breaker was near enough that I felt the skeletal tips of its fingers against my neck as Clémence yelled, "Jump!" And I jumped.

I landed half on the platform, my stomach and the bottom of my rib cage smashing into the edge and knocking all the wind out of me. My fingers found a hold in the track the figures ran on, and I managed to heave myself up and roll onto my side, trying to get out of the way for Clémence to follow, but she didn't.

She was balanced on the rail, her knees bent to spring, but when she jumped, she jumped straight upward toward the dropping weight and caught it, arms wrapped around it like an embrace. The momentum of her body carried it sideways so that instead of passing by the bridge, it crashed directly into it. Metal slammed against metal and the electric current rushing through the entire clock tower funneled through the weight and into the bridge like a magnified shock from a set of pulse gloves.

The flash was so bright and strong I threw my hands up over my face. All the Clock Breakers were flung backward as the electric pulse hit them—some off the bridge, some down the ladder, some just blasted off their feet and crumpled like broken toys, their circuits overwhelmed by the current.

Then darkness fell into place again. The weight began to rise, and Clémence's arms dropped away from it. Her body slumped backward, landed softly on the bridge, and curled like a feather of cooling ash.

"Clémence!" I scrambled to the edge of the platform and screamed her name over the noise of the gears, hoping, praying, willing her to leap to her feet and smirk at me. To sit up. To just bleeding open her eyes. "Clémence! Clémence!"

She didn't move.

My vision flinched and for a moment I couldn't see

anything clearly, like I was looking through etched glass. I pressed a hand against my eyes and let them burn, but even behind my lids all I could see was her body, so small and still, and that flash of light. I didn't want to leave her there, crumpled on the clock tower bridge. I was here because of her. I was *alive* because of her.

But I could feel the tower throbbing around me, the charged air trembling as each second left before the explosives detonated passed. Somewhere above me, I knew, Oliver was waiting, ready to take the city down with him. I had to find him.

I gave myself ten seconds—counted them backward in time with the ticking clock—then opened my eyes again and looked up into the tower.

A rope ladder with wooden rungs stretched between the glockenspiel and the clock face. I had to jump to catch the bottom and then pull myself up, arms shaking with the effort. I managed to loop my leg around the last rung and began to climb, hand over hand, until the glockenspiel below me shrank, its clockwork figures as small as the windup toys we sold in the shop. The ladder wobbled, swaying as the tower shook with the strength of the gears, but I clung on, arms wrapped around the rungs.

The ladder ended at another walkway, similar to the bridge from below but shorter and leading to a semicircular platform beneath the luminescent clock face. On the other side of the glass, the black hands loomed, seconds running like water through my fingers. Somewhere nearby, I heard a cog kick into place. A weight dropped. Then the black hands shuddered, one step closer.

Thirteen minutes to go.

17

The platform below the clock face had been Geisler's workshop before he was caught, and it looked almost the same as it did in my memories of when I resurrected Oliver there. The workbench was still in place, and the cabinets, and Geisler's green leather chair with a book-case at its arm. But everything was empty—the shelves were bare, the workbench stripped of tools and beakers and bell jars. As I crossed the bridge, the moonlight shifted so that the clock face shone semitransparent like the frozen surface of the lake. This close, I could see the faint lines where the cracks had been patched over, veins and seams like scars left behind.

Oliver was sitting on the platform with his back against the spot where the shards met. His knees were pulled up to his chest, face buried in his arms and shoulders shaking. It was a moment before I realized that he was crying. I'd never seen him cry.

I stepped off the bridge and onto the workshop platform. The metal wailed beneath my feet, and Oliver looked up. He didn't try to pretend he hadn't been crying—just swiped his face with the heel of his good hand and said, "Tell me what happened. What *really* happened. No more lies."

"No more lies," I repeated, but I stayed silent. I let Oliver ask again, to be certain he wanted to know.

"Tell me," he said.

I took a breath, so deep I thought it might burst my rib cage. "The night you died," I said, "was the night Geisler escaped Geneva. That part was true. You and I saw him from the flat to the river—I don't know what the plan was after that, but that was our role. But before we left, Geisler pulled me aside and he told me his journals were still here in the clock tower. He asked me if I'd find them, and keep them safe for him, and I said yes. I was so proud he asked me. Me and not you. I thought maybe he was starting to notice me, and if I found them, it'd impress him, and he'd want me as his student instead." I closed my eyes for a moment and let the memory spread through me like wet watercolor, released at last. "So on our way back home I begged you to bring me here. I told you it was so we could nick some things from the workshop before the police cleared it out, because I knew you wouldn't come if I told you it was about the journals." I pointed to a spot just over his shoulder. Oliver didn't look. "There's a panel in the rim around the clock that comes away. They were hidden there."

We stared hard at each other for a second. I kept waiting for him to stop me, but he didn't.

So I went on.

"I found the journals," I said. "But you saw me with them, and when I told you I wanted to give them back to Geisler, you said you wouldn't let me because it was wicked work, and if I wanted any part in it"—something tore inside my throat like paper, but I pressed through it—"then I was wicked too. And I was so angry about that. I was so angry about so much. That you were Geisler's apprentice and you were going to Ingolstadt and you didn't even want it. That you knew Mary was engaged and you didn't tell me. And I'd pushed it all down for so long, but something about what you said . . . I just let it all go."

"What happened then?" Oliver asked softly.

"You grabbed the journals," I said, "and you started ripping pages out, so I jumped on you. Right on your arm. I think I must have snapped your wrist. You let go of them, anyhow. And you were in pain and off balance for just a second. And I didn't even think. I don't remember deciding what I was going to do, I just did it."

"You pushed me off the tower."

"I pushed you into the clock face, and the glass cracked. And then it broke." I looked up at him. "And then you fell."

Fell from the same spot where he sat now, staring at me with his face blank. The clearest I'd ever seen it.

The strength went out of me then, like all my gears had run down, and I sank to my knees in front of Oliver so that our eyes were level. I waited for him to strike me or kill me or do whatever it was he was about to do to me now that he knew the truth.

But all he said was, "I'm so tired, Ally."

I swallowed. "Me too."

"And I'm scared." He pressed his mechanical hand to his forehead, leaving an imprint of the bars and cogs like a new set of scars when he moved it away. "I can't remember the last time I was this afraid."

"I didn't think you were ever afraid," I said with a weak smile.

"I think I was afraid when I fell. And when I woke again. When I was a boy, I remember reading books and thinking the monsters weren't afraid, but they are. They're more frightened than anyone." He glanced up at me. "You're bleeding."

I looked down. My front was speckled with Raif's blood, but a thicker crimson stain was spreading into my shirt. The wound in my shoulder had opened back up and I hadn't had time to feel the pain. "I'm all right."

"Did I do that?"

"I think I deserved it."

"You didn't," he said. "You don't. No one deserves anything I've set on them." He closed his eyes, his jaw tightening like a fist. "You should have told me how I died."

"I know," I said. "But I thought you already hated me for bringing you back and keeping you locked up. You'd have hated me more if you knew what I'd done."

"I don't hate you."

I held those words tight for a moment, pressed them deep and hard inside me until they left an imprint there, a brand to carry and run my fingers over when I didn't believe it. "Do you think it would have changed anything?" I asked. "If I'd told you the truth from the start?"

"I don't know," he replied. "Probably not. I still would have been a monster."

"We're all monsters," I said. "We're all careless and cruel in the end."

"I don't want to be."

"Then don't do this. You can still surrender."

"I don't know what to do," he said, and the words came out in the middle of a sob. "If I walk away, they'll put me in prison and do experiments on me until they finally shut me down. Maybe it would be better if I just . . ." His voice hitched, and he ducked his head. "If I asked you . . . would you just end me now?"

My heart splintered. "Oliver . . ."

"You killed me once, so just do it again," he said, and it almost sounded like he laughed. "Ally, please. Just shut me down. You can do it quicker and kinder than they would, I know you can."

For a long, tight moment, I couldn't think of a thing to say. There hadn't been a day since I'd brought Oliver back that I hadn't wanted to be rid of him, and now here he was, asking to leave me. But instead of feeling relieved or free or any of that, I was hurtled back to the night I had stuck gears and cogs into his skeleton and put him back together. I hadn't done it to be clever, or right, or to see if I could—I wasn't Geisler, and I wasn't Victor Frankenstein. It was because a piece of me had gone into the coffin with Oliver, and there were bits of him I'd carried too, like shrapnel in my skin, and I couldn't bury that. Not then. Not now. We were locked so tightly together, he and I. It would always be us—dead or alive or alive again—knit like gears so that neither could turn without moving the other as well.

"I don't think you want to die," I said. "I think you want to live. Just not like this."

He took a deep breath. I heard it crackle through his paper lungs.

I kept going. "It's only you they want—the rest of

your men can walk away if they're quick and clever about it. If you dismantle the explosives, I think I can get you out of here." The platform shifted underneath us as the hand of the clock moved another minute. My heart jumped. "You can start a new life, somewhere no one knows about *Frankenstein*."

"I'll never be free of that."

"I can call off Mary. Get her to undo some of the damage. She'll help, she owes us that much. And then . . . then you can go somewhere. Somewhere things are different."

"Don't you have to come along and make sure I stay out of trouble?"

"I think . . ." I faltered. I'd spent so long certain my future was a prisoner of Oliver that I'd never realized he was chained just as tightly to me. "I think you need to be free of me. You need to be on your own. Make your own life."

He looked up. "You mean that?"

"'Course I do. If we give the police something else, something to distract them, you can get away from here tonight. And you can have your life back. Properly this time. No more hiding. No more running. No more fear."

"No more fear," he repeated. "That would be good."

He climbed to his feet and offered me his hand. I took it, and he pulled me up beside him. We stood like that for a moment, his mechanical hand clasped with my flesh-and-bone one, in the same place we had stood two years ago when I pushed him and he fell.

"I know it's too late," I said, "but I'm sorry. For everything. Everything I've done since that day to today."

"Me too." He looked down, then back up at me. "There were so many times since you brought me back that I just wanted to give up and rip myself apart. What kept me alive was knowing that once I was someone worth saving. Worth bringing back. I'm sorry I haven't been able to come back to who I was. But I'm trying, Ally. I really am."

The clock gave another shudder. Another tick of the minute hand.

And together—locked gears that we were—we began our descent into the trembling belly of the clock tower.

The square had been cleared when the clock began to strike the hour, but there was still a line of officers left behind their barricades, waiting for the gong. When it finally struck, they started, turned their eyes to the full-moon face as one, and waited for the bombs.

But nothing happened.

Then the gong struck a final time, and this is what they saw:

At the base of the tower a figure appeared, rising from the fog-fringed darkness like a ghost. A cornered hat was tipped over his dark, curly hair, casting his face in shadow, and his walk was stiff-legged and slow, the limp of a man with cogs for knees. The moonlight shivered along the silver mechanical hand trailing from his coat sleeve.

The policemen's guns all leveled on the man, who stopped and raised his hands to his head, then collapsed forward onto his knees as though he was too exhausted to stand any longer.

"Oliver Finch!" one of the policemen called, his rifle steadier than his voice. "Oliver Finch, stay where you are!"

The mechanical man didn't move. He stayed on the ground, arms above his head, shoulders slumped.

The police surrounded him, their rifles trained on his chest, but kept a skittish distance as though afraid he would attack. Then, in a fit of courage, one officer kicked him hard in the back and he fell face first onto the cobblestones. He didn't fight, or try to stand. Just lay there, still and silent, while they put irons around his wrists and ankles, blindfolded and gagged him, knocked his hat into the snow and left it behind as they dragged him, blind, stumbling, and bleeding, to the waiting police wagon. They threw him in so that he landed hard on his side, unable to move for the journey across the city.

They hauled him through the station, up the stairs, let him trip over his manacled feet, let the blood from the nose they had broken course down his face and splash onto the floor. If any of them thought it strange that this reportedly wild man didn't fight, they didn't say. Perhaps their triumph at catching Frankenstein's monster made them forget everything else. They chained him to a chair and stood guard, eyes and guns fixed on him, until heavy footsteps signaled the approach of their commander.

Jiroux strode through the door and stood still for a moment, staring at their prisoner with his face unreadable. Then he stormed across the room, tugged down the gag, and ripped off the blindfold with such force that the resurrected man's head snapped backward, revealing his dark eyes.

"Alasdair Finch," Jiroux said.

I looked back at him, bleeding and chained and certainly not Oliver. "Inspector Jiroux," I replied.

J iroux's face contorted with rage, cheeks flushing fever red. I kept my expression as blank as I could, though my mind was buzzing, trying to work out whether I'd given Oliver enough time to take the ladder down to the river. There were no police at the checkpoints or patrolling the borders—they'd all been at the clock tower or trying to keep the city calm. If he'd moved fast, there was a good chance he was already gone.

"Where's your brother?" Jiroux demanded. "Where's Oliver?"

I didn't say anything. A trickle of blood ran from my nose and dropped onto the floor, just missing the toe of his boot.

Jiroux struck me across the face. Starbursts erupted

over my vision and I bit my tongue hard enough to taste it. "Where is he, Finch?" he bellowed, his spittle joining the grime on my cheeks.

I looked up at him, struggling to focus, but still didn't say anything.

He struck me again, so hard I was certain the chair would have tipped if it hadn't been bolted down. My consciousness stumbled, and for a moment I thought I was going to black out. Through the fog, I heard Jiroux slam his fist into the wall with a screech of frustration. "Get him up," he barked, and someone grabbed me by the collar and hauled me to my feet. "Get his father, then take them out back and shoot them both."

My legs gave out at his words and I slumped against the officer holding me. He grabbed me before I fell, and the mechanical arm Oliver and I had stripped from a disabled Clock Breaker slid out of my coat sleeve and hit the ground with a clatter. I had no feeling left in either arm—one was numb from holding the metal arm in place, the other from the torn stitches still bleeding into my collar.

"Sir—" I heard the officer say, but Jiroux cut him off.

"I don't care which of you does it, Krieg, but there's to be no record they were here. I don't want to see either of them again." And then he spun on his heel and stomped out.

Most of the men followed. A few stayed behind,

watching me warily and glancing at each other like they were silently arguing over who was going to pull the trigger. "What are we—" one began, but the officer holding me—Krieg—instructed, "Go and fetch Mr. Finch." When none of them moved, he snapped, almost as fierce as Jiroux, "Do it now." Two of the officers departed, leaving Krieg and one other. My legs were still shaking, and I felt myself start to tip over again. "Help him," Krieg grunted, and the other came forward and pulled me back up by my injured arm. Another hot surge of blood slipped free.

The officers unchained my ankles, then led me down through the station and out into the alley behind it. They stopped in the splash of lamplight, each with a tight hold on me, and waited. As they shifted from foot to foot to keep warm, the butts of their rifles knocked into the back of my legs.

After a few minutes, the station door opened with a gust of hot air and the two officers reappeared with my father pinned between them. As they dragged him forward, his eyes met mine, and I knew no one had to explain to him what was happening.

One of the officers reached for his rifle, but Krieg shook his head. "Not here."

And suddenly we were moving again, and I was counting down the seconds left in my life like the tower clock running backward.

With Krieg half carrying me in the lead, the officers

marched us through the network of connecting alleys behind the station, which were dark but for the moonlight and rank with piss and mud. I didn't have a clue where they were taking us—I'd never seen this part of the city before. The only light came from the whittled sliver of moon and Christmas candles flickering from behind the windows, glass turned black by the darkness. Streets over, from what felt like worlds away, I could hear cheering, and the bells from Saint Pierre's ringing like it was Sunday. People were singing. Carols and hymns rose above the wind in celebration that the city was still in one piece. Krieg had a tight hold on my arm, but he kept glancing in the direction of the noise, then down at the chains around my wrists. I stared at him, but he wouldn't look me in the eyes.

They led us through a checkpoint and outside the city walls until we were standing at the edge of the lake. At our feet, the water lapped hungrily at the shore. I wondered for a moment why they'd brought us here rather than just finishing us off behind the station, but I figured it was probably easier to throw our bodies into the lake and be rid of them. A bitter wind snapped off the waves as Krieg pushed me forward so that my face was toward their rifles with Father beside me. I shivered.

I am going to die here, I thought.

I wondered if it was a luxury, knowing the end was coming, or if it was better for it to knock you down out

345

of nowhere, like Oliver crashing from the clock tower. Everything felt like it was crashing—the waves behind us, the raucous carols mixed with laughter from the city, the sound of my heartbeat as it clawed at my chest. But then I thought of Oliver, alive and free, and it all quieted a bit.

I took a breath and closed my eyes.

The officers' rifles clattered as they swung them off their shoulders. I waited to hear the shots or feel the pain or at least the impact. To feel *something*. But long seconds stretched to a minute, and nothing happened.

I opened my eyes. The officers were standing shoulder to shoulder in front of us with the butts of their rifles still on the ground. They were all staring at me. Then Krieg said, "You stopped the explosions."

I didn't know what would come out of my mouth if I tried to speak, so I just nodded.

He took a step forward, hands outstretched, and I flinched. "It's all right," he said, and I realized he was undoing the chains from around my wrists. When I was free, he unfastened Father's too and tossed them into the water behind us. Their splash was swallowed by the waves.

Krieg turned to the other officers. "Gentlemen," he said, and they all raised their rifles to the sky and fired once. I knew it was meant as a decoy, but somehow—madly—it felt like a salute.

Then the officers turned. They began to walk back to the station. And Father and I were left alone.

I couldn't move. Couldn't get my breath back. I was standing there like I was made of stone, shaking and gasping and wondering how the bleeding hell I was still on my feet. More than that, how I was still alive. We both were.

"Alasdair." Father's voice seemed to come from far away. "Alasdair, we need to go." I felt his hand on my arm. I think he meant to pull me toward the road, probably to run, but instead I turned and fell against him, my face pressed into his shoulder. After a moment, he reached up, and we stayed there for a while with my face in his coat and his hand on the back of my neck.

Far behind us, buried deep within the city streets, I heard the tower clock strike.

Ornex was the first town across the French border, and it was where Mum was hiding at Morand's boarding-house. It was a few hours' walk there on a clear day, but it took us most of the night to reach it. We had to cross the foothills to avoid the checkpoints at the border, which involved a fair amount of scrambling up rock faces slick with ice. The striped shadows from the pines made it nearly impossible to see where we were going, and I kept sinking into snowdrifts that I barely had the strength to pull myself back out of. It was the coldest I could remember being in my whole life.

I was stumbling more than walking by the time we crossed into France and rejoined the road. My shirt was soaked through with sweat and blood and snow, and I kept swiping at my nose and coming back with fistfuls of scarlet. Father had a tight hold on my arm to keep me up, though he wasn't much steadier than I was.

Ornex was a tiny town, and with dawn just beginning to bleed across the sky, it was nearly as dark as the foothills. We staggered through the streets for a while before Father spotted the half-timbered boardinghouse painted bright blue, with Morand's name on the hanging sign. "Just here," I heard him murmur. "Come on, stay awake." I wasn't certain which of us he was talking to.

Father dragged me up onto the stoop beside him and unwrapped his hands from my coat so he could hammer on the door. As soon as he let me go, I started to sink. "Alasdair—" He grabbed me around the waist, but instead of him getting me back up I dragged him down as well. My knees connected hard with the stones.

And that was how we were, tangled on the ground like unstrung marionettes, when the door opened. The faint light from a fire beyond felt like staring into the sun, so bright it made my vision blur.

"Finch! God's wounds, how did you get here?" That was Morand's voice. I felt his metal hand pulling me up, but I couldn't see straight enough to stand—everything was tipped and darkening. Father and Morand were both holding on to me, trying to get me on my feet, but then a wall of the warm, boozy air from inside hit me hard as a slap. All my strength surrendered, and I passed out cold.

This time, I had a sense of sleeping far longer than I should have. I knew there was something I had to do, some pressing reason for me to wake, but it was like being underwater with stones tied to my ankles. When I finally clawed my way up to the surface with a gasp, it took me a moment to make sense of my surroundings. I was in bed, in a tiny, bare room with no idea how I got there. I was still cold, but I wasn't shaking anymore, and the pain in my shoulder had dropped into an ache. And sitting beside me, white hair glowing like sun-gilded snow, was—

"Clémence." Her name left me in a breath.

"Good morning," she said, and the corners of her mouth turned up. "You look gorgeous."

I didn't know what to say, so I blurted, "You're alive."

"So are you. That seems a bit more miraculous just now."

"I thought you were dead."

"I thought I was dead too, if it's any consolation."

"Bleeding hell, I left you. I should have gone back. I thought—"

"Alasdair, calm down. It's all right."

"No, it's not, it's not all right. I *left* you—"

"Alasdair, stop." She put a hand on mine, and the feeling of her skin—of her, real and true and alive—stilled me. "It's all right," she said gently, the softest she'd ever spoken to me. Something inside my chest unclenched, and I slumped backward again with a shaky breath. Clémence dropped her hand with a smirk. "Look at that. You've only been awake a minute and you've already worn yourself out."

"How did you get away?"

"Oliver came back for me while you were putting on your show for the police and he brought me here. You only missed him by a few hours."

I didn't know who to ask about first, my parents or Oliver, but then, like an answer, the door opened and Mum entered, Father on her heels. "God's wounds, Alasdair!" She didn't cry or make a fuss, but she put her hands on either side of my face and held on for a long moment, like she was making sure I was truly there.

Father stood behind her with his arms crossed. He didn't look quite himself yet, but he was standing steadier than before and some of the color had come back to his face. "How do you feel?" he asked.

"I'm all right." I thought about sitting up as proof but decided that would be too exhausting, so I just stayed slumped against my pillow while he took my pulse and pressed a hand to my forehead.

"Your fever's gone down. Do you think you could eat something?"

"How long have I been asleep?" I asked.

"Most of the day," Clémence replied. "Happy Christmas."

"Hell's teeth." I made a valiant attempt to sit up but barely made it to my elbow.

Father stopped me, but I wouldn't have made it all the way if he hadn't. "What's wrong?"

"I have to go."

"Alasdair, it's all right," Mum said. "We're safe here for now, we don't have to leave. As soon as you're feeling—"

"No, I have to go. I have to find Mary."

"Absolutely not. You're not well," Father said at the same time Clémence said, "What do you want with her?"

"It's something I have to do. For . . ." I swallowed. "For Oliver." Father didn't say anything, and Mum looked at the floor. Father must have told her, but I wondered if she'd seen Oliver when he brought Clémence here. She didn't say anything, but reached out for my hand, and I met her halfway. "Please, just trust me," I said. "If I wait too long, I may not be able to find her again."

Mum nodded, but Father kept his arms crossed and stared me down with his mouth set in a firm line. "You'll be careful?"

"Always."

"You're not going anywhere for a few days."

"I know that."

"Your mother and I were thinking we might stay here until things have calmed down. Help Morand." He paused, then added, "You don't . . . you don't have to stay with us. But we'd like to know you're all right."

"I can do that."

He gave a small *humph*, then nodded shortly, and I knew that was as close to permission as I was going to get.

We talked for a bit longer, in a roundabout way where none of us actually mentioned anything that had happened over the course of the past few weeks. There would be a better time for that. The conversation wore me out, and after a while they left me to sleep. Mum kissed me on the cheek, then tugged on one of my curls. "You need a haircut, Alasdair. You're getting scruffy."

Father stopped in the doorway and looked back at me. His eyes met mine, and we both smiled.

As soon as my parents were gone, Clémence made to sit down again, but I grabbed her hand and tugged her onto the bed. "Come here, will you?"

Her mouth twitched, and after a quick glance at the door, she lay down beside me, on top of the blanket with her face away from mine. I slid my arm around her waist and pressed my forehead into her shoulder. Her hair still smelled like sulfur from the bombs, and for a moment I was back in the clock tower. "Do you know where Oliver went?" I asked.

"North," she replied. "He said something about Russia."

"Was he all right?"

"Yes," she said, and she sounded sure. "He was very calm, which was surprising after everything. More than anything, he just seemed ready. Ready to go somewhere new. Try again." There was a pause, then she added, "He asked me to go with him."

"So why didn't you?"

"I wanted to find you. Make sure you were all right too." She shifted, and I could feel the gears on the other side of her skin thrum. "Are you all right?"

"Yes," I said, and I realized that I was. My whole body hurt and I couldn't remember ever being so tired, but I felt better than I had since Oliver died. I still missed him, but not in the way that I had for the past two years, when he was standing right in front of me and still not there. It was the way I used to miss him, on the nights he didn't come home or when he'd go boxing and leave me alone at the shop. The way I'd missed him in the days right after he died, missed him so much I had to bring him back.

I didn't know what was going to happen now—to him, or to me, or any of us. But that didn't matter so much right then. My brother was out there: alive, and whole, and himself.

"Do you think things will be better?" I asked.

"For Oliver, or for clockwork men and Shadow Boys in general?"

"Either. Both."

"The clockworks that stayed in Geneva won't have an easy time after what happened. I don't think your brother will either, no matter where he goes. It probably won't be good for any of us for a long time, but I like to think that things have a way of falling into place."

"Someday," I said.

"Someday," she repeated. "And what a world that will be."

Sleep was closing in, but I focused on the feeling of Clémence beside me, her skin against mine, her heart beating through her shoulder blades and into my chest. "Will you come with me to see Mary?" I mumbled.

She didn't answer for a moment, and I was afraid I was going to miss her answer. Then she said, "If you want me to."

"I do," I replied, and I fell asleep just as her hand fumbled its way into mine.

A week later, I sat in the front room of the Shelleys' house in Turin. It was warmer in Italy than it had been in Switzerland, and the combination of clear winter sunlight coursing through the windows and a roaring fire made the room stifling.

January 1, 1819. The first day of the new year.

I had cleaned up as best I could. There was nothing to be done about my bashed-up face, and my arm was back in a sling, but before we left Ornex, Morand had found a jacket that nearly fit me, and my boots had shined up nicely. I still felt shabby. The Shelleys weren't living as well as they had in Geneva, but it was a good deal finer than what I was accustomed to.

Mary was on the chaise across the room, her shoulders sagging so that she seemed to sink back into the upholstery. Percy Shelley stood at the fireplace, staring pointedly away from anyone. His dirty-blond hair was pulled into sleek pigtail and he wore a well-tailored coat in midnight blue. Silhouetted against the fireplace in his fine clothes, he looked like a figure in a painting. When I'd arrived and Mary had introduced us, he'd gripped my hand harder than I thought he needed to, and his gaze had almost been as sharp as Jiroux's. Perhaps he recognized me as Victor Frankenstein, or had heard other, truer stories about me. Or perhaps he hadn't known I existed until Clémence and I showed up on their doorstep, the same way I hadn't known of him until I kissed Mary on the shore of Lake Geneva.

The Shelleys had been easy enough to find. Gossip followed them like a rank odor, and we hadn't even left

Ornex before someone told us that Mary had traveled from Geneva to Turin on Christmas Eve. Our arrival had been uncomfortable, to be generous about it. Mary had hidden her shock poorly; Shelley hadn't even tried to hide his, or the anger that came close on its heels. He'd objected to my proposition and laughed at my poor attempts at extortion. As much as I knew about Mary, I had little ammunition against them. Their reputation was already so wretched that I could hardly do it further damage. Shelley had shouted at me for a while, and I'd endured it with a blank face in spite of the fear sitting heavy inside me that I wouldn't be able to keep the promise I'd made to Oliver.

Mary had said very little while Shelley raged, and she'd made no move to stop him. But she caught me at the door as I left and asked me quietly to come back the next day. When I arrived, there was a small, round man sitting in the armchair beside the fire, clutching a notepad while a white-faced Shelley stood at the mantelpiece. He was a reporter, Mary explained to me, from an English newspaper, stationed in Turin. She had invited him—without asking Shelley—to report on what she had promised him would be the story of the year. Which was a big claim, considering we were only a day in.

"Mrs. Shelley," the reporter prompted, and Mary looked up at him. She had broken off midsentence and was staring out the window.

"I'm sorry," she said, and tugged at her necklace. "Could you repeat the question?"

"What was your intention when you wrote *Frankenstein*?"

"I had no intention but to tell an imagined story," Mary replied. "I never meant to cast my allegiance to one side, or for my novel to be such a rallying point for oppression and fear." Her gaze flitted to me, the moment too brief to be called eye contact.

The reporter scribbled something down on his pad, then dipped his pen again. "Why did you choose to publish the novel anonymously?"

"That was my suggestion," Shelley interrupted. "We wanted to see if the book had merit on its own without my surname attached to it."

Mary's mouth tightened into a frown, but she said nothing.

The reporter made a note, then looked back to her. "And now you will be republishing under your own name?"

"Yes," Mary replied. "I want everyone to know I wrote it."

"There has been a good deal of speculation, Mrs. Shelley, particularly with the recent uprising in Geneva, that your novel was based on an incident surrounding the late Dr. Basil Geisler and his work."

My hand flexed on the arm of my chair. There had been no mention of Mary or the resurrected man in the official reports out of Geneva, and only a hint that the rebellion might have been sparked by *Frankenstein*. The unofficial reports had ranged from laughable to shockingly close to the truth. In Ornex alone, I'd heard stories that included the resurrected man and *Frankenstein*, as well as Mary. But no mention of my own name, or Oliver's.

Mary pursed her lips but managed to keep her tone light when she spoke. "I don't know anything about the uprising."

"Really?" The reporter leaned forward with his elbows on his knees, and his mustache twitched. "Because I heard that you were seen in Switzerland just before—"

"Move on," Shelley growled from his post at the mantel.

The reporter sat back with a wary glance at Shelley, then ran his finger down his pad like he was finding his place again. "Could you tell me, Mrs. Shelley, where precisely the inspiration for the novel came from? If not from truth, that is."

Mary looked to Shelley, but he kept his back to her. For one gut-twisting second, I thought she was going to change her mind and leave me with the shards of another broken promise. But then she said, so softly the reporter and I both leaned closer, "It came to me in a dream."

"A dream?" the reporter repeated, and he sounded disappointed.

"While my husband and I were in Geneva, some of our friends were having a competition to see who could write the best ghost story, but I couldn't think of anything. Then one night I dreamed of a student, kneeling, with a corpse made of gears and cogs stretched out before him. And then by the working of the engine placed inside, the monster came to life."

"So none of it is based on true events?" the reporter asked. "There is no Dr. Frankenstein, and no resurrected man?"

"No," Mary said, and this time she looked at me. Met my eyes, and touched her fingers to her heart. "It's only a story."

There were a few more questions after that; then the reporter stood up and shook hands with all of us. "I don't think I caught your name," he said when he reached me.

"He's a friend of the family," Shelley interjected.

"Well, good to meet you, friend of the family." I could see him reaching for his pad again. "Would you care to comment on anything?"

"No," I said flatly. "No, I would not."

Shelley watched the reporter leave through a gap in the drapes. Then he twitched them shut and rounded on

Mary and me. "How dare you go behind my back," he snapped at Mary.

She smoothed the front of her dress and said calmly, "It's not your choice, Percy. It's my book, and I want people to know that."

"This had nothing to do with credit, it's because of *him*. And you—" He swiveled his gaze to me. "You have no right to be in my house. You've done your damage, now get out."

"Don't be cruel," Mary said.

"I want him out," Shelley snapped, and he stalked from the room, coattails swinging.

Mary looked like she might cry, so I said quickly, "It's all right. I need to go. We've got a journey."

Mary helped me into my coat and followed me out onto the front step. Clémence was waiting at the end of the drive, sitting with her back against one of the gateposts. When she saw us, she stood up, but didn't come closer.

"Is Oliver all right?" Mary asked me.

It was such a stupid question after everything she'd done that I was tempted to say something just as thoughtless back, but I swallowed that and said instead, "I hope so."

"Will you see him again?"

"I don't know. Maybe." A gust of wind caught me under my coat, and I shivered. I looked down the drive at Clémence, who raised her hand. I nodded, then looked back at Mary. "I should go."

She glanced at the house, then back at me, and tugged at her necklace. "I have to tell you something. I probably shouldn't . . . but this may be my last chance, and I need you to know that when we first met, you weren't wrong in thinking I was a bit in love with you. I was. And I think . . . I think I still am. Being with you again reminded me of that. And I think we could make each other happy. You could stay here in the city. We could see each other. See what happens. And I just think it would be good . . . for both of us . . ." She paused, and took a deep, shaky breath. "I want you to stay with me."

I had waited two years to hear her say that, but my heart didn't swell like I expected it to. It didn't even stir. It was two years later than it needed to be, and there was too much between us, too many dark, jagged things filling the holes she'd left behind.

So I said, "No, Mary. I can't."

"Oh. That's . . . unexpected." She looked away, face turned into the wind so that it tugged her hair backward in a thick spiral. "Is it her?" she asked, and I followed her gaze down the drive to where Clémence was still standing straight as a soldier, watching us but out of earshot. "It's all right if it is," she added. "I just want to know."

"It's not Clémence," I said, and it wasn't.

Mary pressed her chin to her chest, and I thought for a moment she was crying, but when she spoke her voice was steady. "I'm sorry, I shouldn't have said anything. I'm an idiot."

"You're not an idiot," I said. "You're just . . ." I paused, not sure how I meant to finish. *You're not who I thought you were* was the first thing that crossed my mind, but instead I said, "You're just too late."

She took my hand and squeezed it. "Take care of yourself, Alasdair."

"You too," I said.

She nodded once more, eyes still down, then turned and retreated back inside the house. The door shut behind her, so softly it barely made a sound.

I walked down to where Clémence was waiting. The wind whipped her hair around her face, but she made no move to push it away.

"Everything all right?" she asked.

I almost told her about Mary's invitation to stay, but changed my mind at the last second. Instead I said, "Yes," stumbling a bit on the lie, but Clémence didn't ask.

"We could stay here another night," she said as we turned off the drive and onto the street, "or leave now, if you feel up to it. Are you going back to Ornex?"

"For now. I think I should be with my parents for a while. There are things I need to explain."

"And then?"

I put my hands in my pockets and took a deep breath. Freedom was still so unfamiliar that it felt like an empty space around me, gaping and vast, but alive with possibilities. "I still want to go to university. Not Ingolstadt—not anymore—but somewhere I can learn more about medicine and mechanics, and do research, and work with people who don't think you'd have to be mad to be a Shadow Boy."

"Well, you'll certainly have a leg up on all other applicants. I'd bet none of them can put 'reanimating the dead' on a list of qualifications." I snorted, and she ducked her head with a half smile.

"What about you?" I asked.

"What about me?"

"Where are you going?"

"I don't know," she said, and the words came out in the middle of a frosty sigh. "I don't know if there's any-where I can go."

"Don't say that. You can go wherever you want to."

"And do what? I've got no skills."

"You could find something."

She pushed her nose down into her coat collar so that her voice came out muffled. "There's nowhere I'd fit. When I joined up with the rebellion, it was mostly because I thought I'd found somewhere people could know what I was made of and still want to speak to me. But I wasn't like the other clockworks, and I wasn't like

Oliver either. No one would listen to me, or trust me, not like they did him."

I looked sideways at her. With the sun full on her face, I realized there were freckles across her nose I'd never noticed before. "I don't understand what that has to do with having nowhere to go."

"Because everything about me is wrong," she replied. "I'm not the same as other clockworks, but I'm not wholly human either. I say things I shouldn't. I cuss. I'm contrary. I don't act the way young women should. I can't even love who I'm supposed to." She wrapped her arms around herself and frowned down at the cobblestones. "I've sort of got nothing."

"You've got me."

Her mouth twitched. "And now I'm losing you too."

I remembered the feeling in the days after Oliver died, the impossible loneliness of it, and the way I'd watched him wear solitude for two years after. The same sort of sadness was playing about her face, and before I knew what I was doing, I stopped walking and said, "So come with me."

She stopped too. "What?"

"Come with me. Back to Ornex. You can stay with us until you get things figured out on your own, and after that . . . I don't know where I'm going to end up, but if you want to come along, you could do that too." Her mouth twisted, and I added quickly, "It doesn't have to be forever, but you shouldn't be alone like that. No one should."

She stared down at the ground for a moment, then looked up at me. The sunlight caught her eyes, turned them sea-glass blue, and she smiled, the first true, genuine smile she had given me in perhaps the whole time I'd known her. "That'd be good."

"So you'll come?"

"Yes," she said, and her smile went wider. "I'll come."

"Good," I said. "Because I would have dragged you along if I had to."

She laughed, and it sounded so extraordinary that I laughed too. Ahead of us, the sun was collapsing into the rooftops, turning the sky wine-colored and rosy. Mary's house was long out of sight, and though the street around us was full of people, it felt for a moment like there was no one there but the two of us. Just Clémence and me, and without saying anything to each other, we started walking again at the exact same moment.

Side by side, and sure as clockwork.

AUTHOR'S NOTE

Frankenstein by Mary Shelley is the story of two monstrous young men—the medical student who refuses to believe in mortal limitations, and his creation, whose wild heart proves itself to have tremendous capacity for both love and hate. The creator of this creation myth, Mary Shelley, was herself much like her two lead characters—a bold, ambitious young woman caught up in and trying to make sense of a changing world around her. When I first got the idea of writing a *Frankenstein* reimagining and began my research, I was amazed to discover that Mary's life was not that of a proper Regency woman—it was full of dramatic and shocking stories, even by today's standards. There were secret love affairs and scandals, midnight escapes and haunted castles, heartbreak and grief and misty moors, and through it all, a stalwart young woman struggling to find her footing in her own impossible life. The more I learned about Mary, the more I realized I wanted to write about *her* as much as I wanted to write my reimagining. The plot of my novel finally came together when I realized I could do both.

Mary Godwin Shelley was the daughter of Mary Wollstonecraft, author of one of history's most important feminist texts, *A Vindication of the Rights of Women*, and William Godwin, a prominent English political thinker of the late 1700s. Wollstonecraft died shortly after giving birth to Mary, and Godwin raised his daughter to be "singularly bold, somewhat imperious, and active of mind."[1] He encouraged Mary's curiosity in an age where women were often silenced, and she grew up educated, liberal, and acquainted with a range of important figures, including American Vice President Aaron Burr and Samuel Taylor Coleridge, whose poem "Rime of the Ancient Mariner" is referenced throughout her books.

When she was seventeen, Mary became involved in a forbidden romance with Percy Bysshe Shelley, a notorious and radical poet who already had a wife and several children when he and Mary began to meet in secret at her mother's grave. When William Godwin found out about their relationship and disapproved, the couple fled from England to the European continent, beginning a period of travel as they tried to evade their families' displeasure and Percy's many creditors. By the time they arrived in Switzerland in the summer of 1816, Mary was broke, shunned by her family, and suffering from depression in the wake of her and Percy's daughter's death.

The couple took up residence with Lord Byron, the "mad, bad, and dangerous"[2] celebrity poet in his lakeside villa in Geneva, where he entertained a wild crowd who practiced free love, reveled in substance abuse, and read from a variety of scandalous books that ranged from German ghost stories to scientific texts on the possibility of reanimating dead tissue. They spent most of their summer indoors—due to a volcanic eruption that disrupted weather patterns, 1816 was known as "The Year Without Summer"—and in her 1831 introduction to *Frankenstein*, Mary called it "a wet, ungenial summer . . . incessant rain often confined us for days to the house." It was that confinement, combined with their healthy diet of opium and dark literature, that prompted Lord Byron to issue a challenge to his guests: Which of them could write the best horror story?

Mary's entry in that contest was the resurrection scene from *Frankenstein*. Upon Percy's encouragement, she expanded it into a novel, which was published anonymously in 1818 when Mary was only twenty-one. She claimed the inspiration came to her in a dream—"I saw the pale student . . . kneeling beside the thing he had put together. I saw the hideous phantasm of a man stretched out, and then, on the working of some powerful engine, show signs of life, and stir," she wrote in her introduction.

But that dream was likely a product of the world in which she was living. *Frankenstein* can be read as a science creation myth, a product of Mary's Age of Enlightenment— a period defined by a societal movement away from God and toward scientific scholarship. What happens when we take divinity out of creation, and instead man becomes the vehicle by which life is made? An examination of *Frankenstein* as an Enlightenment-era creation myth was one of my main access points to the story, and the one I found the most fascinating. Months after my curiosity with the novel began, I heard it misidentified as the first steampunk novel. I knew that was incorrect—*Frankenstein* could not be steampunk because it was contemporary for its time, and the definition of steampunk involves creating an altered past—but I started to wonder what that steampunk creation myth might look like. What was the mechanized equivalent of Adam and Eve, and where were the lines drawn between God, men, and monsters when those men were made from metal pieces? With the Industrial Revolution in full swing in 1818, I decided to shift the focus of *Frankenstein* from Enlightenment anxieties to industrial anxieties.

As a writer of historical fantasy, I get the marvelous job of adjusting pieces of history to serve my narrative, and I took some liberties, both with the technological and social landscape of my alternate Europe and with the life of Mary Shelley herself. But the fictional anxieties that plague Alasdair's world are reflections of real anxieties of the time. Though almost none of the steam-and-cog-powered technology in my Geneva existed in 1818 (and some never existed at all) and no one was worried about clockwork cyborg men, they *were* worried about and often fearful of the rapidly industrializing world and the societal shifts occurring because of it. The discrimination and prejudice Oliver, Clémence, and the clockwork men and women face is a reflection of the very real and equally nonsensical cultural prejudices that defined European society at the time. Oliver's failed uprising is fictional, but inspired by the June Rebellion in Paris in 1832 and the age of revolution in which Europe was entrenched.

And then there are facts that I ignored completely, because I am willing to play fast and loose with history in order to tell a better story. Mary Shelley had two children—one living and one dead—when she came to Geneva in 1816, both of which I chose to leave out. She and Percy also left Geneva in September of 1816, but I extended their stay to match the timeline in *Frankenstein*. The university in Ingolstadt was closed in 1800, but I wanted Alasdair to share the same collegiate aspirations of his literary alter ego, Victor Frankenstein. The sections from *Frankenstein* have been altered to reflect my steampunk creation myth rather than Mary's science-based one, and they are meant to read as the novel might have looked had it been written in my alternate hyper-industrialized history.

All stories set in the past are shadows, impressions of the way things were, but still half-imagined. It's what excites me most about both reading and writing historical fantasy—the collision of truth and invention. This book is my invention, and, above all, a work of fiction. I take responsibility for all the truths within it that I stretched, massaged, and fused clockwork to.

1. Quoted in Sunstein, Emily W., *Mary Shelley: Romance and Reality*. (Baltimore: Johns Hopkins University Press, 1989), 58.
2. Lady Caroline Lamb, quoted in Hoobler, Thomas and Dorothy, *The Monsters: Mary Shelley and the Curse of Frankenstein*. (New York: Little, Brown and Company, 2006).

ACKNOWLEDGMENTS

There are many people who made the creation of this, my hideous progeny, possible, and these meager acknowledgments are not enough to express my gratitude to them.

But here goes:

This book would not exist without the keen eye and steady hand of Sharon McBride, who read the first monstrous draft and managed to bring it back to life. Eternal gratitude for your early and continuing dedication to the Brothers Finch.

To Cathie Mercier and the Center for the Study of Children's Literature at Simmons College, who gave me two outstanding years and a creative environment where this project could happen.

To Susan Bloom, her fantastic committee, and the

wonderful people at PEN–New England who put their faith in my weird book about monsters and machinery. Thanks also to the St. Botolph Club Foundation for funding writing time through their Emerging Artists grant.

To the early readers—Anna-Marie McLemore, Clarissa Hadge, Jessica Arnold, Katja Nelson, Kylie Brien, McKelle George, Rebecca Wells, and R. W. Keys.

To the brilliant friends—Mariah Manley (for the airbreaks, the grave robbing, and the author photos), Darcy Evans (for general and unrelenting enthusiasm), Camille DeAngelis (for sitting across the table during revisions), Magna Hahnel (for showing me the Christmas markets), Briana Shipley (for being right about everything), and Hannah Thompson (for talking me out of reading *Frankenstein* in high school).

To my Salt Lake crew, who always have my back— Ebbie Ghaeini and Blooming Studios, Eli Ghaeini, Brian Westover, the Powells (Doug, Steph, Em, and Katie Ann), Jacob Virgin, Josh Goates, Kate Mikell (*Merci pour l'aide avec la traduction française!*), and Megan Graul.

To my outstanding agent, Rebecca Podos, who is both good and clever. My exceptional editor, Laurel Symonds—here's to our shared debuts!—and the entire crew at Katherine Tegen Books, including but not limited to Bethany Reis, Janet Fletcher, Joel Tippie, Amy Ryan, Charles Annis, Ray Colón, Lauren Flower, Alana Whitman, and Ro Romanello, as well as Susan Katz, Kate

Jackson, Katherine Tegen, and the Epic Reads team.

And, most of all, to my incomparable family, who not only tolerate my particular brand of crazy, but embrace it: Maren (because the mom is nice in this one!), Billy (you are my favorite story in the end), and the MT (for all the weeds and wildflowers).

Je vous aime.